ThrillHers

THRILLING TALES IN ISOLATED LOCATIONS

SONJA DEWING   **DEB COLLINS**   **DITA DOW**

SALEEMA ISHQ   **COURTNEY MAE**   **PAT MCGREGOR**

MICHELLE TENNANT NICHOLSON   **AMY RIVERS**

KARA SMITH   **AK WELLER**

Plot Duckies

Foreword

SONJA DEWING

I started the Women's Thriller Writers Association because I had an agent tell me no one would read an adventure fantasy with a main female character. I proved him wrong and now I work with amazing writers creating lead female characters that we can all appreciate. Strong women in isolated locations who aren't going to sit quietly. What an honor it's been to work with these authors.

Get your hot beverage ready and escape into stories that will take you from Costa Rica to Pennsylvania.

And get ready to be thrilled.

Story Descriptions

Are you ready to embark on an electrifying journey through the minds of best-selling and award-winning authors and their resilient, fearless heroines? If you're a fan of gripping thrillers that keep you on the edge of your seat, look no further. The ultimate anthology of thrilling stories featuring strong female characters in isolated locations has arrived.

The Unholy Script - by Dita Dow, Best-Selling Author

Deep in the recesses of Vatican City, Emma must decipher an ancient codex. The text has the power to destroy the world. Can she figure a way out or will deciphering it be the last thing she does?

Dust and Desperation - Amy Rivers, 2021 Indie Author of the Year

Alone at night in the New Mexico desert, Hannah has escaped one nightmare and entered into a new one. Can she survive the elements long enough to find safety? Or will her captors find her first?

Underworld - AK Weller, Best-Selling Author

What scares an underworld assassin? Seffy is sure that someone is squatting in her new house, but so far she's only found a gaping hole in her basement and heard a whisper through a doorway. *"Get out of my house."*

Hidden Waters - Kara Smith, Emerging Author

Sam had braced for a dull summer cut off from normal society. Yet, after her arrival in the secluded Canadian wilderness, she realizes that beneath its tranquil exterior mysteries yearn to be uncovered. The truths she finds is anything but expected.

Lakeside Lodge - Sonja Dewing, Award-Winning Author

Sarah has spent all her savings on buying an old ski lodge. She's determined to make this place into the destination of choice in the Poconos, but she'll have to face down a ghost, an unknown squatter, and a secret she carries from her childhood.

More Flexible Than Water - Pat McGregor, Best-Selling Author

Surrounded by the waters of a catastrophic flood,

Petra must keep her small landholding functional and at the same time fend off threats crawling out of the water. When her life is threatened, can she marshal her resources and overcome one final danger?

Astrid - Courtney Mae, Emerging Author

Astrid's trip was supposed to be relaxing. A trip to visit an abandoned town to inspire her writing. Who knew mistaken identity and kidnapping were on the itinerary....

The Evil Within - Saleema Ishq, Best-Selling Author

After hours of being trapped within the claustrophobic interior of an elevator, someone finally hears Addison's cries for help. To her horror, they respond from inside the elevator, revealing an unsettling truth: Addison is not alone.

The Evil Within is a story of self-advocacy, resilience, and grief that will take you for a thrilling ride.

Dog Days - Michelle Tennant Nicholson, Best Selling Author

Alone in a house that's been the scene of a grizzly death, Michelle must confront the ghosts of the past.

Isla del Coco - Deb Collins, Sonja Dewing, Dita Dow, and Saleema Ishq

A group of people are on an island for a memorial. Turns out their friend was murdered. Who will be next?

The Unholy Script

DITA DOW

I'VE KILLED TWICE

Once for love
Twice to Save the World

Prologue

Dr. Miles Slausson

Near Cairo, Egypt

Our expedition ventured deeper into the scorching desert. We had driven as far as we could before leaving the vehicles and finishing the journey on foot. The sand shifting beneath our feet, each step was a laborious effort as we trudged forward. The unrelenting sun beat down, causing sweat to pour from our bodies as we struggled through the swirling cloud of orange dust.

Despite the harsh conditions, my team and I

remained optimistic as we pressed on in search of an ancient tomb that had remained hidden for centuries.

The towering obelisk of limestone and granite came into view on the horizon, sparkling in the sun. It rose from the desert sands like a colossus, dwarfing us with its immense presence.

The granite surface of the obelisk was etched with a two-thousand-year-old inscription that was still readable, a testament to the skilled builders.

We stood before the ancient monument with an immense sense of awe, our journey complete. I had found the Pillar of Ra.

I looked around at the members of my team, deciding what to task them with first. They were all competent enough—except for my wife, Tasia. The constant prodding of her to double-check her work had become tiresome. She had been one of my top archeology students at the university. She would sit in the front row of the lecture hall, staring at me with those emerald eyes. Her black hair cascaded down her shoulders, flowing around her sculpted breasts. It was a temptation even the most disciplined man couldn't resist.

Every year, two or three students served their purpose to satisfy my needs. None of them resisted, at least not much. Although, there was one who had gone and killed herself. Theresa, something or another. I don't remember names.

How was I supposed to know Theresa had left a diary, professing her love for me? The campus police questioned me about her death, but I could be quite convincing. The police bought my story of a young, love-struck college student who had an unrequited crush on her professor.

Anastasia Chavez proved to be like the others. The only difference: she had gotten pregnant. She hadn't given me any proof of the pregnancy, but I had no reason to doubt her. She wasn't savvy enough to have tricked me into marriage.

It was a complication that could ruin everything. Her pregnancy would result in too much attention on me as her professor and an affair between a student and teacher. In the end, I did what I had to do: I married her.

It was a quick wedding ceremony held in the university chapel. No flowers and no family, only the pastor and his secretary served as witnesses. No fancy dress, no tux.

After the wedding, I convinced Tasia it would be best for us if she ended the pregnancy. Her willingness to let me take her to the clinic had surprised me. Tasia understood that neither of us needed a child to hold us back from living out our dreams. My dream of locating the Pillar of Ra. Tasia's dream of accompanying me on these expeditions. She always had a penchant for adventure in the field—and in the bedroom.

"Hurry, get the tents up," I ordered my team.

"It's magnificent. You did it, darling." Tasia looped her arm over mine.

"I found it. My whole life's work stands before us." I shrugged off her arm.

My entire life had been spent in pursuit of the mysterious Pillar of Ra. For centuries, the fabled obelisk had been lost to antiquity, believed by many to be a mere legend. But I was convinced such a relic actually existed. It was said that the entrance to the tomb of Ra was marked with such a structure, and beyond it laid treasures far beyond comprehension.

I searched the sides of the obelisk, looking for the entrance. Looking for anything resembling a door.

These things were tricky. The builders might have hidden the actual entrance and put in a trap door to deter thieves or vandals.

"Moishe, over here."

"Yes, Dr. Slausson." The young Egyptian scurried over.

"The door. It's here. Get me the tools."

The outline was very faint. An untrained eye would not have seen it.

"Hurry, Moishe."

This expedition had cost a small fortune. The grant from the university covered part of it, but I'd had to finance the rest. Tasia did not know how in debt we were, and now she would never have to know. This discovery would make me rich. I could pay Tasia a nice sum and divorce her. It would be a win-win for both of us.

I pried away the edges of the doorway, careful not to cause too much damage. Thousands of years being sealed up were proving difficult to get through. I was determined. Nothing would keep me out of this tomb. It was mine.

Tasia was standing over me, taking notes. The smell of her floral perfume, which used to turn me on, now made me nauseous.

"Get back, Tasia. You're in the way."

This was my moment. I had waited a lifetime for this.

"I feel the door giving way. Moishe, come here and help me push."

As Moishe and I pushed on the cool granite slab, a loud echo emanated from inside.

"Get up here." I motioned for more hands to help push the giant piece of granite out of the way.

It finally gave way and swung into the tomb, releasing a putrid vapor into the air. Thousands of years sealed up, the air was bound to be stale, but this air had a sickening smell.

I was stunned by the yelling that ensued.

The workers turned in fear and ran to the vehicles we had left a mile away.

Moishe's dark eyes fixated on the inside of the tomb.

"What is it, Moishe? Tell those men to get back here. They can't leave. They won't get paid," I demanded.

"No, Dr. Slausson. This place is under a curse." Moishe turned and raced after the others. The engines revved and sand spun up as they fled.

I saw Tasia standing back, terror on her face.

"Get up here and help me. Cowards are what they are," I yelled at their retreating dust.

Tasia walked towards me. Her eyes fixated on the inscription just inside the doorway.

"Don't pay attention to that. The builders used to put a curse in the doorway to deter robbers."

"I don't know, Miles. Those men were terrified."

"Tasia, ignore it. It's just words. They hold no power. Bring me the rope and the ventilator mask. I'm going in."

I wasn't going to let a bunch of superstitious garbage keep me from my rightful reward.

I sat on the edge of the entrance, my legs dangling into the abyss. There was about a twenty-foot descent, I estimated—the darkness was impenetrable.

"Do you see anything?" Tasia asked.

"No, it's too dark. If I can get to the bottom of the obelisk, there should be another entrance into the tomb itself. Hurry up with the rope and mask. You're too damn slow."

Finally, Tasia arrived with the rope and tossed the mask at me. It arched over my head and tumbled into the abyss. I heard it hit the bottom of the tomb.

"You stupid woman. Why'd you throw that?"

"Sorry," Tasia muttered.

I fastened the rope to a stake I had pounded into the sand and tied the other end around my waist. I turned and faced Tasia as I began my descent into the tomb. A chill went up my spine as the cool air hit my overheated body.

A burning sensation started in my throat. My lungs were on fire. Something was wrong with the air. Not too much further to reach the bottom and put on the ventilator mask. I rappelled faster.

I felt a sharp jolt as the tension in the rope disappeared. I fell farther down than I'd estimated and slammed into the stone bottom. Everything was dark and cold. I couldn't feel my legs.

I couldn't breathe.

"Tasia, Tasia, help me," I gasped.

Only silence met my cries.

Chapter One

Ten Years Later

Washington, D.C.

It was a typical day at the Smithsonian for Dr. Emma Jones. She was in the middle of her daily museum duties of cataloging new artifacts when her phone rang, the sound breaking the monotonous silence like a thunderclap. It was an old friend, Steven Marshall.

"Emma, I need to see you right away." His voice sounded desperate.

"What is this? No, 'Hi Emma, how are you doing? Gosh, I haven't talked to you in five years,'" Emma joked.

"I'm sorry. This is urgent." Steven rambled off his address. "How long will it take you to get here?"

"I don't know, maybe thirty minutes. What is this all about? Steven, are you all right?"

"Thanks. See you then." Steven hung up.

Steven was a historian working for one of the vast numbers of alphabet government agencies. He and Emma had gone to graduate school together, but more than anything, they had been best friends. Eight years had passed since she and Steven graduated. Emma smiled as she remembered the late nights she and Steven spent studying at the all night diner by the university.

He had a particular knack for being able to get Emma to open up about her fears and anxieties, something she usually could not do with other people. Emma had always felt a special bond with Steven, and she knew he was the only person she could trust with her secrets.

Steven received his Ph.D. in history, and Emma got hers in archeology. The Smithsonian had hired Emma as the lead expert in ancient and exotic artifacts. It was her dream job. She had an unlimited budget and access to the most advanced laboratories.

They had not had a falling out. It was just life that got in the way. Emma had left for a year to do her internship in London at the British Museum. Between the time difference and the start of new jobs they had lost touch.

Emma felt an uneasiness grip her in the pit of her stomach. Steven's call had been strangely short and cryptic. She could not imagine what was so important that he could only tell her in person.

Emma replaced her white lab coat with her tan raincoat then stood in front of her office mirror to freshen her lipstick. She pulled the raincoat's hood over her silver-peppered shoulder-length black hair and studied the laugh lines around her piercing green eyes. She wondered if Steven would still recognize her after all these years.

"Max," she uttered to her assistant, "I'm taking the rest of the day off; I need you to hold my calls."

"Got it, Dr. Jones," Max replied.

Emma strode through the museum's ornate double doors and out onto the wet sidewalk. The rain immediately soaked the bottom of her blue slacks and matching pumps.

She glanced around, her eyes drawn to the bright yellow cabs on the busy street, searching for a free one. Raising her arm, she waved until one stopped at the curb. She yanked open the door and hopped in.

Trying to get anywhere in Washington, D.C. on a good weather day was challenging enough. Traffic seemed to creep along extra slowly. The rain beat against the cab's windows, the wipers struggling to keep up.

The address Steven had given Emma was on the northeast side of the city. Her mind raced with suspicion. What was he doing in that obscure area of the city? She glanced out the rain-spotted window as they passed various universities, monasteries, and Catholic shrines —giving the area the nickname "Little Rome" or "Little Vatican."

Emma surveyed the quiet street as she stepped out

of the cab. Her destination, an inconspicuous gray stone building, was protected like a fortress. Guards lined the entrance with automatic rifles slung over their black uniforms, and the security checkpoint held more metal detectors than any airport.

Fighting the urge to turn and run, Emma forced her feet forward and walked into the building. As she waited for the young guard to check her ID, Emma felt a growing sense of urgency and dread.

Emma's thoughts were racing as she recalled the last time she had seen Steven. He had been working for a mysterious government agency, cataloging artifacts and documents for some kind of archive.

She had assumed that was all he was doing, but what if his job entailed more than that? What if he was involved in some kind of dangerous work?

The armed guard took Emma up the elevator and showed her into a nondescript conference room where Steven was waiting. Emma was surprised to find that Steven had hardly changed, despite the years that had passed. His sandy blonde hair was swept back from his forehead and his skin was a deep tan. His broad shoulders and lean, six-foot-three frame were still just as impressive as when they had first met in college, but now he wore a black suit and tie instead of his usual jeans and t-shirt.

He greeted her warmly, but there was a cool reserve in his manner that made Emma wary. He asked her to sit down.

Emma took a deep breath, trying to calm the sudden

knot in her stomach. She scanned the rest of the room. The conference table was long and sleek, made of dark wood that gleamed under the fluorescent lights. A pitcher of ice water sat at the center of the table, surrounded by a cluster of glasses.

To Emma's left sat a woman with long, curly blonde hair. She wore a bright red blazer that contrasted sharply against her black pencil skirt. Emma couldn't help but feel envious of the woman's confidence. She seemed to radiate power and poise.

On the other side of the table sat a young man with a shock of unruly brown hair. He wore a faded t-shirt and jeans, looking more like he had wandered in from the street than a business meeting. Emma couldn't help but wonder what his role was in the meeting, especially as he seemed to be slouched down in his chair, barely paying attention.

At the far end of the table sat a man, who was balding, with a few wisps of graying hair left on the crown of his head. His wire-rimmed glasses perched on the bridge of his nose, and his sharp eyes seemed to follow Emma's every move. He wore a fine brown suit and a burgundy tie, which complemented his olive skin tone perfectly. His dark eyes met hers. She knew him from somewhere, but couldn't remember where.

Without doing any formal introductions, Steven thanked Emma for being so prompt and went right into the purpose of the meeting.

"Dr. Jones," he said, "we believe an ancient manuscript of great importance is now in the hands of an international criminal organization or will be soon."

"What manuscript?" Emma felt intrigued.

"Codex Sanguinis Immortalis."

"The Codex of Immortal Blood?"

"We have information from a reliable source it exists and is about to be handed over to this organization. If true, this would put unlimited power in the hands of very evil people."

Emma's heart pounded in her chest with the thrill of anticipation. She had spent years secretly researching the manuscript to the point of it almost being an obsession. Steven was the only one who knew this. He had endured her endless ramblings without a complaint.

"But why did you call me?" Emma asked.

"Because there is no one with your knowledge of this particular manuscript that would be able to verify its authenticity," Steven said. "Will you please explain to everyone what the Codex is?"

"Sure." Emma looked around the table. "The Codex Sanguinis Immortalis is a mysterious and ancient text, rumored to hold the key to eternal life. According to legend, around 325 CE an alchemist named Armandus discovered a potion that was supposed to give eternal life to anyone that consumed it. He recorded the recipe in the Codex, along with many other secrets of the occult."

"So, this dude found the fountain of youth? Is he still alive?" The young man with unruly hair blurted out, without taking his eyes off his cell phone.

"Well, not exactly." Emma continued. "Armandus thought he found the elixir of life, but instead of giving eternal life to those who consumed it, it enhanced their inner most being."

"Their what?" the young man asked.

"If the person who drank the potion had evil in their heart, it made them even more evil. If someone had kindness in their heart, it made them more kind."

"I don't get it? If it made good people better wouldn't they outnumber the evil people?" The young man finally looked up at Emma. "Aren't most people good?"

"You would think, but that is not what Armandus discovered. He found that the potion enhanced the evil more than it did the good, so he took the book and hid it away in a secret location hoping it would never be found."

"So what happened to Armandus?" the blonde woman asked.

"He was executed because he refused to tell the Roman Emperor, Constantine, of its location. The whereabouts of the Codex remained unknown, until someone reported Adolf Hitler had somehow come into its possession during World War II, but it was never confirmed."

"Thank you for explaining that." Steven stood at the front of the conference table scanning all those sitting around it.

"So, what do you need me to do?" Emma asked, her voice barely a whisper.

"We need you to recover it. You're the only one who

has the knowledge to decipher it and determine if it is real."

"And if I refuse?" Emma challenged, her voice tight and defiant.

"We don't want to consider the consequences of that decision, Dr. Jones," the balding man in the brown suit hissed, his cold eyes narrowing.

"I'm sorry, who are you?" Emma spat out, her body tense. She did not like the veiled threat.

The man did not respond.

Chapter Two

Rome, Italy

The Leonardo da Vinci international airport terminal swarmed with travelers, a chaotic throng of bustling energy that threatened to overwhelm Emma. She battled her way through the crowd toward the escalator. Her flight had arrived an hour late. The rumbling in her stomach reminded her that the dinner she had eaten on the plane was wearing off.

Emma was exhausted. It was late, and she hadn't slept much on the plane. Steven had arranged everything for her, from her plane tickets to her hotel. He even got her out of work. Emma wasn't sure about this organization Steven worked for, but she was too excited with the thought of finally seeing the Codex to ask questions.

Emma grabbed her bag from the baggage carousel, her heart heavy as the memories of her trip to Rome ten years ago engulfed her. She forced them down into the depths of her mind and hardened her focus on the mission ahead—one slight misstep could prove fatal.

The instructions from Steven had been clear: trust no one. She had to locate the manuscript, determine its authenticity, and return it to Steven so it could be secured.

Emma headed outside to find a taxi, her heart fluttering with anticipation. The airport was alive and buzzing with energy, even at this late hour—the honking horns, blinking streetlamps and the smell of exhaust was overwhelming.

A tall figure stepped out of the shadows and approached her. Wearing a black suit, hat, and white gloves made him all the more intimidating.

"Dr. Jones, I presume?" He spoke in a deep baritone voice.

Emma nodded and followed the man, who opened up the trunk of a black Mercedes parked nearby. He loaded her suitcase and opened the back door, motioning for her to enter.

Emma hesitated for a moment.

"Did Steven send you?" she asked cautiously. She could not remember him mentioning a driver, but he might have. The man remained stoic.

Emma's skepticism was still evident in her eyes as she hesitated getting in the car. "How can I be sure?"

He leaned in closer, his eyes narrowing as if assessing her. "You ask a lot of questions, Doctor," he said, his voice low and deliberate. "Now, please, get in the car."

The man's patience was wearing thin, and he slowly moved his hand inside his jacket. A glint of metal shone in the light. Emma felt the pressure of the blade pushed against her. His voice dropped to a dangerous whisper. "Doctor, you don't want to test me."

Fear coursed through Emma as the hairs on her neck stood on end. She had no choice but to comply, her doubts silenced by the cold steel pressing against her.

She nodded, "Okay, okay, I'll get in the car."

Emma climbed in to the backseat, noticing a sheet of Plexiglass between the front and back seats of the car—perhaps to keep her away from the driver? With a sinking feeling in her gut, she reluctantly took her seat and prepared for whatever the night would bring.

As the car sped away from the airport, dark thoughts of the Codex swirled in her mind. Terror at the thought of the powerful relic being in the hands of criminals was quickly eclipsed by the realization that it would be dangerous in anyone's hands. A shiver ran through her body as she wondered what kind of chaos it could unleash.

Emma gripped the seat, heart pounding as she saw her hotel pass by.

"You passed my hotel. Stop!"

She pounded on the Plexiglass separating her from the driver, trying to get his attention. But he kept his gaze straight ahead, ignoring her pleas.

"Where are you taking me?"

The car careened through the crowded, narrow cobblestoned streets. The driver slowed as they approached the walls of Vatican City. A Swiss guard stepped forward. His iconic red, blue, and yellow uniform glistened in the moonlight and his plumed helmet stood tall on his head. He peered into the vehicle and waved them through with a sharp nod.

Emma glimpsed the Egyptian obelisk standing tall in front of St. Peter's Basilica as they pulled into a narrow alleyway. The car stopped abruptly and her door opened. A hooded figure clamped an iron grip on her arm and yanked her from her seat, dragging her inside a building and down an opulent hallway until they reached a heavy, carved wooden door that opened into a cell-like room.

The hooded figure thrust Emma into the room. The door slammed closed with a reverberating thud, followed by the click of a key turning in the lock from the outside.

The musty air smelled of ash and the dim lanterns flickered weakly against the damp stone walls. Emma's eyes roved over the dark wooden writing desk and chair against one wall and a narrow cot against the other. Near the corner, a small wooden door revealed a meager bathroom comprising only a sink and toilet—no shower or bathtub. Emma's heart sank.

She glanced around, scanning for any means of escape or any chance of rescue. She realized she hadn't grabbed her purse, which had her cell phone and passport in it, when they dragged her out of the car.

She had entered an unknown world and was about to find out what secrets lay hidden within.

Chapter Three

Emma ran her hands along the walls of the dim room, feeling for any concealed secrets. She moved her fingers along the surfaces, feeling for any hidden compartments or passageways.

Nothing.

Frustrated, Emma let out a deep sigh and leaned against the wall, closing her eyes for a moment. She thought back to the many archeological expeditions with her ex-husband and how he had taught her to always be vigilant for hidden access points.

When she opened her eyes, she noticed a faint glimmer of light in the far corner of the room.

Curious, Emma moved closer to the corner and saw that there was, in fact, a small door in the wall. She could make out the outline of an ancient symbol etched into the door. As she reached out and touched the symbol, there was a clicking sound.

The door opened to reveal a hidden passageway. Emma let out a deep breath as she took a step into the narrow hallway. She could feel a chill in the air and see a faint light coming from somewhere ahead.

Trembling, she stepped forward, and the door closed behind her. The darkness enveloped her as she walked further through the passageway, her steps echoing off the walls. She was about to turn a corner when she heard a faint whisper.

"Dr. Jones… come this way. There is something you must see."

The words echoed from all around her. She hesitated for a moment before she continued forward.

"Don't stop now, Dr. Jones…" The voice beckoned.

"Who are you? What do you want?" Emma demanded.

The only sound that answered back was haunting laughter.

As she rounded the corner, she saw light coming from an open door in front of her. Taking a deep breath, she stepped into the room.

The walls were lined with bookshelves filled with ancient tomes and scrolls, their bindings cracking with age. In the middle of the room was a large desk with an open book resting on the surface. As she stepped closer, Emma could see that the book was indeed the Codex of Immortal Blood.

"Spectacular, isn't it, Dr. Jones?"

Emma spun around to find a black-clad figure looming over her. The man wore a traditional black cassock, red sash, and white collar, which Emma recognized as indicating a Catholic priest holding the title of Monsignor.

"Who are you?" Emma demanded.

"Monsignor Vittorio Crestini."

Emma reluctantly shook his cold, clammy hand. Monsignor Crestini's slicked-back salt and pepper hair, sharp facial features, and icy blue eyes seemed to strip away all of Emma's defenses.

The Monsignor joined Emma around the glass display case that held the Codex. His hands linked behind his back.

"Yes, it is," Emma answered his initial question as she marveled at the strange symbols and diagrams etched into the parchment. "It's in pristine condition. Where was it found?"

"That isn't important," he replied with a dismissive wave of his hand. "What is important is that this manuscript is here and you are the chosen one to make history by interpreting it." He stepped closer, his breath warm against her skin as he continued. "Everything you need is here: the Vatican's archives and complete privacy while you work. But..." His voice hardened. "I will post a guard outside your door at all times, so don't think about leaving."

"Are you saying I'm a prisoner here?" Emma retorted.

"Prisoner? That's quite a strong word." Monsignor Crestini kept his gaze on the manuscript.

"What else would you call it when I was kidnapped from the airport, dragged out of the car, and shoved in a dark, cold room from which I am not allowed to leave?"

"Dr. Jones, no need to be so melodramatic." The Monsignor tsked. "You had no trouble unlocking the secret passage out of your quarters, did you? Would we have put you in a room with a passage if we wanted to keep you prisoner?"

Emma's heart pounded as she met Crestini's piercing stare. She felt like a trapped animal, with no chance of escape. Her fingernails dug into the palms of her hands as she shifted her weight from one foot to the other.

"What if I alert the Vatican guard or the police?" she challenged, her voice tight with fear as she realized no one knew where she was.

Crestini tilted his head, his fingertips pressed against his temples, and his mouth twisted into a frown.

His eyes burned into her soul, turning her blood cold. His body language spoke of a predator toying with its prey.

"Oh, my dear Dr. Jones, or should I say, Anastasia Slausson?"

Emma gasped in shock, feeling as though the air had been sucked out of the room. "I don't know what you are talking about," she stammered.

"My dear, let's not play games."

"I'm not the one playing games," Emma replied, letting out her breath. "What do you want with me?"

"I knew we could come to an understanding." He chuckled. "You are free to come and go from your quarters as you work. We have provided all the items you will need to perform your analysis and interpretation of the Codex. Food will be brought to you."

"Aren't you worried I may destroy the manuscript?" Emma asked, her voice echoing off the gray stone walls.

"If you do not comply, I can assure you the consequences will be dire," Crestini said, his voice dripping with malice.

He turned and walked out, his black robe billowing around his feet. The light in the room flickered and Emma was alone, enveloped in her thoughts and fear. To survive, she would need to put her knowledge, skills, and will to the test.

She slipped through the dimly lit passageway back to her room. Her suitcase had been tossed onto her cot, its zipper open and contents spilled out. Her reference books were missing, but the few articles of clothing she had brought were still there.

On the desk was a plate of food, its aroma hinting at something savory, and a bottle of cool water invited her to quench her thirst. Despite her trepidation, Emma knew the food was safe; Crestini needed her too much to risk harming her, for now.

She took a deep breath, steadied her nerves, and ate. As she savored the flavors, thoughts of her past came creeping in. She had been so determined to forget the painful memories, but now they suddenly felt so vivid. Tears threatened to well up in her eyes as she remembered the devastating loss that had shattered her world and changed her life forever.

Lost in thought, Emma wondered how anyone would ever find her. How could she get a message to Steven? Could she even trust him? Emma wondered how Crestini could have known she was coming to Rome and for what purpose. She shook off the doubt about her friend.

She pushed away the painful memories, focusing instead on the present and what lay ahead of her.

. . .

Chapter Four

Emma stirred from her fitful sleep, feeling the oppressive weight of her captivity. She slowly slid out of bed, the cot groaning with each movement. She shivered as her feet hit the cold stone floor. Emma looked around the room and thought this wasn't as primitive as other places she had been in the past, but it wasn't the Ritz.

Outside her bedroom door, a heavy key jangled in the lock, and the door creaked open.

A hooded figure appeared. He kept his head low, as if to conceal his identity, and shuffled into the room with a tray in his hands. He set the tray on the desk and scurried out.

Emma wandered over to the desk. The tray held a steaming cup of coffee, a glass of milk, fruit, yogurt, and a huge croissant. The only utensil provided was a spoon; Crestini would not allow her to arm herself with any other tool.

Emma had to admit the food was delicious, or maybe she was just ravenous. After eating, she cleaned up and approached the small door leading to the passageway into the archives. She nervously pressed the symbol and heard the door creak as it opened.

She felt excited about examining the ancient manuscript, but couldn't help but wonder what would happen to her when her usefulness was done. The thought of being expendable caused her stomach to twist with dread.

Emma found the Codex Sanguinis Immortalis where it had been the night before. A long table was set up for her analysis. Emma noticed her reference books neatly stacked on the table. She looked over the tools supplied for her and was impressed. They included a top-of-the-line microscope, a handheld X-ray fluorescence spectroscope, and a laptop installed with the latest technology.

"Do you find everything to your liking, Dr. Jones?" Crestini appeared from behind some shelves.

Emma jumped. "Do you have to sneak around?" She glared at him, waiting until her heart stopped pounding, then replied, "I'm impressed. Looks like the Vatican pulled out all the stops for me. Or is it just you?"

"Dr. Jones, you should not worry about things that do not concern you."

"I find my life concerns me, and the way I've been treated so far has been anything but comforting."

Monsignor Crestini moved closer to Emma. He placed both hands on her shoulders. Emma caught a glimpse of the gold signet ring on his pinky. His eyes glared into hers.

"Dr. Jones, Mrs. Slausson, or should I ask, what name are you going by today? I was hoping we could work without disruption on this little project."

"It is Dr. Jones, Monsignor. And I have nothing to hide. It's not illegal to change your name."

"Everyone has secrets, Dr. Jones. Do you think I would bring you here and entrust you with such a valuable item if I did not have insurance?" Crestini's fingers dug into Emma's shoulders, causing her to wince.

Emma pulled away. "Maybe you don't have reliable information." She crossed her arms over her chest in defiance.

"Oh, my dear, I think we have very reliable information. Don't you think the authorities would like to know the location of your husband's body? Imagine the headlines—prominent Smithsonian scientist is a murderer working under an assumed name."

"I have work to do." Emma turned away and pulled the latex gloves on.

"I thought you'd see it my way." Crestini strode off and slammed the door to the archives shut.

Emma did the only thing she knew would rid the haunting throngs of memories from slipping into her mind: work.

Emma touched the manuscript.

The pages were old, but still flexible and pliable. She ran her fingers over the surface, feeling the grooves made by the ancient reed pen that wrote this text so long ago. Lavish care had been taken in every step of creating this piece of art.

Emma had studied papyri and scrolls and had repaired many of them at the British Museum during her internship. She knew that this text had survived in near pristine condition because someone had meticulously cared for it all this time.

The golden symbols shimmered in the light, almost too bright to look at. She admired the vibrant inks that had barely faded over the hundreds of years. She bent the spine back to read the strange, bold words.

Emma had traveled all over the world examining petroglyphs, hieroglyphs, and languages. These letters matched nothing she had ever seen.

The words seemed to swirl and dance on the page as if they were playing hide and go seek with her eyes.

Emma took samples of the ink and paper, being careful to not damage the text. She placed each sample on a slide and set them beside the microscope.

She scanned a page with ultraviolet light, looking for hidden messages. Emma couldn't help but smile as this reminded her of the invisible ink pen she'd found in a cereal box as a kid. She wrote secret messages to her sister. They'd pretended to be secret agents. Life had been so much fun growing up. Emma longed for that carefree feeling where the biggest decision she had to make every day was if she wanted chocolate milk with her school lunch.

Emma slid one of the paper samples under the microscope and peered into the lens.

Interesting.

The parchment was not plant-based. It was animal skin. That was not out of the ordinary—many cultures used animal hide to write on—but there was something different about this. Emma could not put her finger on it. She removed the slide and held it in her fingers, staring at the skin on the slide. Then she recognized it.

Anthropodermic bibliopegy. Human skin.

She looked at the manuscript and wondered where Crestini had gotten it. Emma had heard of human skin being used to write on, but hearing about it and actually seeing and touching it was very different.

She shuddered as she felt an icy grip pierce the core of her being, realizing the repulsive truth of what she had been handling. Her stomach twisted in waves of revulsion as her hands trembled, and a wave of nausea surged through her body.

The silence broke as the glass slide shattered on the floor. Emma backed away. Her breathing was labored, and her mind raced about what she had just discovered.

The realization dawned on Emma like a crashing wave. She had known the Codex was no ordinary manuscript. But this was something much darker—and infinitely more dangerous.

Chapter Five

Emma looked up as the door clicked open and the hooded figure stepped in. She was still on her knees, shattered glass surrounding her as she attempted to clean it all up with a scrap piece of paper. The figure slowly made its way to the corner, setting down a tray with what Emma presumed to be her lunch.

"Excuse me, do you have a broom?" she asked, looking up at the hooded figure.

Their answer was silent, the long sleeves of the robe covering their hands as they kept their head lowered. No matter how hard Emma tried to make out a face, nothing was visible. She kept her gaze on the hooded figure as they slowly backed out of the room and closed the door behind them. Emma pushed herself up off of the floor.

"Ouch!" Emma yelped as she felt a razor-sharp pain in her finger. She glanced down and saw a small piece of glass protruding from her skin. With trembling hands, she yanked out the shard with a jolt of agony. Her finger pulsed with pain as the crimson liquid seeped to the surface.

Emma grasped her finger and looked over the items on the table, trying to find something to sop up the blood. She watched in shock as her blood dripped onto the manuscript. The blood swirled as the human hide lapped it up. She reached out her other hand to wipe the blood off, but as her skin touched the book, the cut on her finger sealed shut, as if no cut had ever been there. Massaging her finger, she felt no pain, no sting, no opening, and no blood. Emma stared at her finger then at the Codex.

Fascinating, it did have healing qualities. What is this thing?

She snapped a few photos and uploaded them to the computer, taking a seat at the desk. She searched through the Vatican's archives, desperate for any information that might explain the strange document.

She searched the archives for ancient astronomical symbols and references to the Zodiac. She scrutinized religious and mythological texts for similar motifs and used multispectral imaging and infrared reflectography on the Codex to expose hidden symbols and details that helped decipher the mysterious symbols in the manuscript.

Awe and excitement coursed through Emma as she gradually deciphered the ancient symbols. They slowly unraveled before her, revealing the secrets of an ancient and forbidden sect of magic.

But as Emma probed further into the arcane text, an unsettling feeling of dread weighed down on her. What if this document held power well beyond her understanding? Did she have the courage to accept the consequences of unlocking the secrets that this relic held?

Emma saw a pattern in the symbols as she moved them around on the computer screen. They created a chemical structure. She jotted down the elements.

Amazing.

Emma was staring at the formula thought to give eternal life. The precious prize Crestini would do anything for.

Emma heard the lock turn and quickly minimized the screen she was looking at. She scribbled some notes on the yellow legal pad. She knew what she had to do.

"Dr. Jones, I am confident you have good news for me?" Crestini looked at her notes.

"I do. I discovered the chemical formula."

"What is it!" Crestini demanded.

Emma handed him the formula. "Amazing how simple it really is, but do you think the world is ready for this?" Emma asked.

Crestini held the paper up to the light and laughed. "You really think I would share this with the world? This is for me, and you're going to make it."

"I'm not a chemist. I'm a historian and an archeologist. What you're asking for is not possible." Emma was buying time. She didn't want to think about her future or lack of it.

"You're a scientist. Simple, you say. Simple enough for you to put together. I will gather these items and you will create this formula tonight!" Crestini stormed out of the room.

Emma turned back to the laptop. She deleted the files, but she had to think of a way to permanently get rid of them.

The door clicked and Emma turned, expecting to see Crestini, but it was the hooded figure that had brought her lunch. Her lunch! Emma had forgotten all about it.

"I'm sorry, I got busy. Please leave the tray," Emma said.

The hooded figure, head down, picked up the tray and held it out for Emma.

Emma reached out to take the tray and noticed a piece of paper tucked partially under the plate with her sandwich.

"Thank you." Emma tried again to see the person under the hood without success.

Emma stood in silence, holding the tray as she watched the mysterious figure leave. She took the tray to her room and pulled the paper out from under the plate.

Enjoy your new attire. Be dressed and ready before you retire.

Emma looked over at her bed and saw someone had placed her suitcase on it. She opened it and saw, lying neatly folded on top, a nun's habit with a piece of paper on top.

Take nothing with you.

Remember your morning prayer.

For that will be the time to flee the lair.

Doubt crept into Emma's mind as she pieced the puzzling message together. Had Steven come for her, or was it another trap?

Obviously, someone had provided her with the perfect disguise to blend in with the Vatican crowd.

Emma remembered from her visit to Rome years ago that the morning mass was held every day at 9:00 a.m. The bells in the morning were a reminder of time in a place that seemed timeless.

Emma wolfed down the sandwich, then rushed back to the archives. She had limited time to implement her plan.

Chapter Six

Emma was waiting when Crestini walked back into the archives, hands carrying bags of all the ingredients she had asked for. She couldn't help but notice the sinister smile she was used to seeing had melted into one of joy.

"I have everything for you. How long will it take?" Crestini asked.

"At least several hours, then it will have to sit overnight to meld together." Emma chided, "You look happy, Monsignor."

"I am. Wouldn't you be if you knew your death sentence was being lifted?" he asked.

"I'm not sure I understand."

"My dear, I am dying of cancer. I haven't lived a perfect life, but it is one I am not ready to leave yet. Do you understand now?"

Emma's view of the man standing in front of her was melting from fear to sadness. Sadness not because he was dying, but sad that in his desperation he would hurt anyone getting in his way of finding what he needed for himself. He never considered how this could possibly help so many suffering people, hundreds of them, which showed up every day at the gates of the Vatican praying for their miracle.

"I understand." Emma took the items out of the bags and assembled them on the table.

"Thank you," Crestini said, and left.

You can thank me tomorrow.

8:00 a.m.

Emma was dressed in her habit. It impressed her that whoever had picked it out got her size right. She almost didn't recognize the woman staring back at her in the mirror. Was it a crime to impersonate a religious figure, especially when she was full of so many unconfessed sins? Emma pushed the doubt out of her mind, as she had so many times in the past.

She hurried through the passageway one last time. The potion was ready and waiting, and so was she.

8:45 a.m.

Crestini arrived in the archives.

"Dr. Jones? Where are you?" Crestini called.

"I'm back here. I have everything ready."

Every click of Crestini's shoes echoed as he came closer. Emma felt her hand tremble slightly as she set the glass of amber liquid on a small table next to a red cushioned chair. A crucifix hung on the wall behind.

The perfect setting.

"Dr. Jones, why are you wearing that? Where'd you get it? I don't understand." Crestini looked at Emma and scanned the chair and table.

"I asked for the habit. This is such a momentous moment; I feel rather honored to give you the Elixir of Life. Please indulge me and have a seat."

What doubt he may have had seemed to vanish as he eyed the glass. "Do I drink it all now?"

"No, the Codex is clear. I must read a spell first. It is very specific." Emma held the book open wide and stood in front of Crestini.

He folded his hands in prayer. His gold signet ring reflected the golden color of the liquid. Emma spoke the words that she knew were nonsense, and Crestini was none the wiser. He kept his eyes closed and listened intently.

"Now is the time for your renewal. Now is the time

of your repentance. Now is the time, Monsignor, for the rest of your life."

Crestini stood as Emma offered him the glass. Emma watched as he gulped the liquid down, grimacing slightly at the taste.

"How long will it take?" he asked as he sat back down.

"Not long."

Emma took the book and the laptop, and walked to the large incinerator tucked in the corner.

"No! What are you doing?" Crestini leaped out of the chair. His steps stumbled as he tried to reach Emma.

Crestini's eyes bulged and his body quaked in agony as he watched Emma hurl the book and laptop into the inferno. He choked on his own words, desperately trying to call out her name but only managing a few guttural grunts.

His face contorted like a wax figure left too close to the flame. Crestini clawed at the furniture around him, struggling to take one shaky step closer to the roaring hearth before collapsing onto the ground.

"Why?" Crestini choked.

The potion of poison was working quicker than Emma had expected.

Emma watched as his gold signet ring spun across the room.

"Because the world isn't ready for that kind of power."

Emma stepped over the body.

9:00 a.m.

The first bell sounded from St. Peter's Basilica. Emma waited as the lock clicked and her hooded friend entered. Still not showing his face, he motioned for her to follow. They quickly walked up the hallway she had been dragged down only a couple of days ago.

The bells continued to toll as they exited a side door into an alleyway. Hundreds of people were amassed in St. Peter's Square. The sun glistened off the white travertine stone.

Emma and her hooded friend weaved in and out of the crowd, then they turned down a side street. A black car waited. Emma crawled into the back seat and turned to look as her hooded friend finally revealed himself.

"You." Emma's mouth dropped. It was the annoying, balding, bespectacled man from the meeting she'd had with Steven.

"Yes, Dr. Jones."

"But… I don't understand. How… How'd you know where I was?" Emma stammered.

"We knew something was wrong when you didn't check in to your hotel. When the phone locator showed you were headed for Vatican City, it confirmed our information that Crestini had the book."

"You never gave me your name." Emma stared at the man. He seemed so familiar, just as he had the day in the meeting.

"You don't recognize me, Mrs. Slausson?"

"What? Why'd you call me that?"

"Egypt, ten years ago. It was quite hot on that expedition in search of the Pillar of Ra."

"Moishe?"

"Yes, it is I. A little less hair and a little more round."

Emma laughed as Moishe patted his bald head and bulging waistline at the same time.

"I don't understand. Why are you here? Do you work with Steven?"

"Yes."

"You know I killed him," Emma blurted out.

"Crestini? Yes, we know."

"No. Miles. I killed my husband in Egypt that day," Emma confessed.

Moishe's eyebrows rose.

"After you and your men left, Miles was determined to go down into the tomb. When he asked for the ventilator mask, I felt my anger boil to the surface. I just wanted him gone. So, I threw it at him, a little too hard, and watched as it fell into the tomb. He was so angry with me, and he went down after it. The rope came loose, and he disappeared from my sight. I had planned and waited for a moment like that to avenge my sister Theresa's death and all the other girls that fell prey to him.

"I was relieved when I no longer heard his screams for help. But then, when the authorities couldn't find him, guilt flooded through me. Had I done something wrong? Would I ever be able to forgive myself?" Emma wiped away her tears with the sleeve of her robe. "I did nothing to try and save him."

"When did you change your name?" Moishe asked.

Emma took a deep breath before speaking. "It was

about a month after I returned home from the expedition. I found out about the loans that Miles had taken out to cover the expeditions and discovered that we were deep in debt. When I heard about how he'd been stealing artifacts, I felt sick to my stomach. The university got wind of it and stripped all mention of him from their records. I was so embarrassed and humiliated, so I moved far away, changed my name, and started over again with a clean slate."

Moishe nodded in sympathy. "It must have been difficult for you," he said sadly.

Emma sighed. "It was hard, but I knew it was the only way to protect myself." She smiled at Moishe. "But now here I am!"

The car sped through Rome traffic, but Emma was oblivious to anything outside. She saw a slight smile come over Moishe's face.

"Why are you smiling? I just confessed to murder," Emma said.

"Because you didn't kill Dr. Slausson. I did," Moishe confessed.

"You weren't even there. You'd left."

"I had been on many expeditions with him. I watched him abuse my men. I watched him abuse you. He stole many artifacts that were supposed to be turned over to the Egyptian Antiquities Authority. So, when he contacted me about the Pillar of Ra expedition, I planned. Dr. Slausson was blinded by his greed. He was not paying attention as I sent one of my men to find the trapdoor to the tomb and throw a poisonous gas bottle in. He was so focused on opening the tomb."

"That horrible smell when the door opened..." Emma remembered.

"Yes. I had instructed my men to feign panic when they saw the curse written inside the door. Trust me, they didn't need any help to leave your husband to do his dirty work. I watched through binoculars at a distance. I saw him sitting on the edge of the tomb waiting to repel down. Then you tossed the mask, and he failed to catch it. I watched as he hastily tied his rope to the anchor. He was too greedy and anxious. He was sloppy in his tie-off. The rope would not have held.

Emma stared at Moishe in disbelief. "All these years I lived with the fact that I killed him. I accepted I did what needed to be done to avenge my sister. He used her like he used me and all the other girls."

Moishe lightly tapped Emma's arm. "In the end, you didn't kill him and I didn't kill him. Dr. Slausson's greed killed him."

"And, I just killed Crestini." Emma gasped. "I've killed twice! Once for love and twice to save the world."

"Crestini was a dead man walking. All you did was hurry his journey along."

Chapter Seven

The car pulled up at what appeared to be a private airpark. A black helicopter sat on the pad with its propellers whirling.

"Let's get out of these. What do you say?" Moishe pulled his brown robe off to reveal a black polo and khaki pants.

Emma pulled her habit off, uncovering a cream t-shirt and brown pants.

"I don't know how the nuns can wear those things." She pulled her hair out of the band, holding it back, and shook her head.

They ran to the helicopter. Moishe opened the back door and helped Emma climb in before sitting next to her.

"I don't even have my passport," Emma said.

Moishe chuckled, and a familiar laugh came from the front seat.

"I think it's time for a new passport and a new name. Don't you?" Steven turned and smiled at Emma.

"What do you think, Moishe? Did she pass her job interview?" Steven asked.

"She excelled at it," Moishe responded.

"Job interview? I already have a job." Emma looked at Steven and Moishe, confused.

"I think I can make you a better offer. You can't tell me you didn't love the hell out of the excitement. How do you think I charmed Moishe into working for me?" Steven chided.

"How did you come to work for this charming fellow?" Emma smiled at Moishe.

"He was recruiting in Cairo. Steven heard about my assisting the Egyptian Ministry of Antiquities in recovering stolen artifacts. It was shortly after your husband's accident."

"You knew about Miles? You know who I really am?" Emma looked at Steven.

"I heard about a courageous, beautiful woman named Anastasia Chavez, who endured great pain at the hands of a monster. And I know a courageous, beautiful, and incredibly smart Dr. Emma Jones who saved the world from an even greater monster today."

"Speaking of saving the world. Where's the book?" Steven looked at Moishe and Emma.

"She burned the damn thing," Moishe said.

"Burned it? It was ancient! It's been missing for centuries and you burned it?"

"Trust me, the world is not ready for that much power." Emma shrugged. "I'm just doing my job, boss."

About the Author
Dita Dow

Dita Dow is a Best-Selling Author who enjoys crafting stories that sweep you into thrilling adventures. With over three decades of experience in law enforcement, private investigations, and consulting, she possesses a deep understanding of the human psyche, which she skillfully weaves into her narratives.

Her passion lies in all things: mystery, thriller, and the supernatural, where she takes readers on mesmerizing journeys into the unknown.

Beyond her writing, Dita's adventurous spirit

propels her along rugged hiking trails, discovering archaeological wonders, and on globetrotting adventures. She calls New Mexico home, which she shares with her family, a plump feline, a pampered horse, and a tortoise.

To uncover more about Dita and her enthralling storytelling, visit www.ditadow.com. Immerse yourself in her gripping psychological thrillers, including "Cave of Terror" and "The Deceiver's Casket."

Visit her website at: www.ditadow.com

Underworld

AK WELLER

CHAPTER 1

Silent Night

My name is Seffy Nicks. That's as important as it is unfortunate, so please don't forget it.

I arrived in Helena, Montana at 9:14 a.m. on Monday, January sixteenth. It was snowing, and I was happy to be alive.

The flight from Denver International to Helena Regional was not smooth, and the woman sitting next to me had been loudly certain the plane was, to quote her, "One fucking thousand percent going *down*, people." Nevertheless, surviving that airborne journey through a blizzard didn't even make the top five reasons I was happy to be among the living.

I hovered well away from the crowd at the baggage carousel and waited until my steamer trunk was the last piece of luggage. Then I waited again until it made five full circuits on the carousel before I dragged it off. It seemed to have grown heavier in transit—or else my grip had weakened from holding my seatmate's hands for two hours.

This hadn't been an act of compassion. The harder I squeezed, the quieter she was.

I began to appreciate how small Helena was when, a mere half an hour later, I was accepting a Styrofoam cup of too-bitter, black coffee from Staci-with-an-i. She showed me into an empty conference room with a decent view of a sushi restaurant across the street from the title company's office. It took about fifteen minutes to sign the paperwork, and then I was headed to Eighth Avenue with the keys to my new house.

* * *

"The pictures really didn't do you justice," I sighed.

Standing alone on the sidewalk, I gazed up at the house and drank it in for so long my neck started to hurt. It was three stories tall, built on a rise eight feet above street level, and set so close to the sidewalk that it seemed to hover menacingly over me and the shorter houses on Eighth Avenue.

For just under $600,000, the 140-year-old, nine-bedroom, hot mess of a house was mine. It had seven fireplaces, hardwood floors (where there were floors), and a "portal to cannibal hell" in the basement (according to the agent). Soon, I hoped, it would also have working electricity.

Queen Anne style, for what it's worth.

The surrounding neighborhood was quiet but dense. With only three or so feet between some of the historic houses, looking up or down Eighth Avenue gave the impression of one long house stretching from Ewing Street to Warren Street.

I lugged my trunk up the stairs to the front door, let myself inside, picked a solid-looking patch of floor in the front room, and spread my sleeping bag out so near the fireplace you'd think I planned to light a fire. Instead, I crawled inside the sleeping bag, covered my face with a sweater, and fell instantly asleep.

* * *

I woke up at 7:00 p.m. on the dot and drove my rental car through the darkened city to Walmart. I love Walmart. As long as you dress fairly normally, act casual, and don't steal anything too expensive, you're invisible to employees and fellow shoppers alike. In one stop, you can pick up anything a person could reasonably need, and it won't cost you a zillion dollars.

It's also a great way to check out the townies, which I did while roving every aisle, in numerical order, for an hour and a half. The post-dinnertime shoppers were an uninteresting lot, and they paid me little notice in my plaid woolen dress, heavy tights, sturdy brown mules, and quilted coat. The women's clothing section was rife with clues that my standard wardrobe might be coming back into style, but my threads were 100% vintage. They wouldn't fall apart on me after one wash and in fact had survived thousands of trips through the laundry.

The only person who looked twice at me was an employee in the garden section, but I dismissed the intrusion. He was probably about to ask if I needed help loading bundles of plastic-wrapped firewood into my cart, but my "Yes, I see you there" stare seemed to scare him off.

I'm not deliberately off-putting, but I'd long since stopped trying not to be. Without extensive medical and cosmetic intervention, I was stuck with 110 pounds stretched over a 5-foot, 10-inch frame which came equipped with abnormally large hands and feet. Add in limp, blonde hair; glassy, protuberant blue eyes; and a perfectly flat chest, and I wasn't winning any beauty contests in this century. A hundred years ago, when my new house was only 40, I'd have been a real catch.

By the time I paid up, got my supplies home, and then dropped my rental car off at the airport, nighttime had fallen in earnest. The car had been a boon for transporting groceries and other supplies, but I was happy to be rid of it. Rental cars came with records, and neighbors tended to notice a new car suddenly appearing on their quiet street.

I had no phone, which meant no Uber, but I was used to walking. Rather than heading home, I made for the city's walking mall in the hopes of securing a quick and easy meal. It started snowing again, and I considered ducking into one of the bars spilling light and warmth out onto the snow- and ice-covered sidewalks. My quilted coat was warm but not warm enough, and the boots I'd changed into seemed to be made of ice. Though I stalked past every bar in a half-mile radius, none struck my fancy, and I returned home with an empty stomach.

Someone at the power company had dropped the ball, and my electricity still wasn't on. The air inside was only marginally warmer than the subzero outside temperatures. I pulled on a second layer of clothes, found a flashlight, and flipped a coin: heads, top to bottom; tails, bottom to top.

Tails. I'd start my tour in the basement.

The house was so big, and I so unfamiliar with it, it took me a while to find the stairs to the basement. What I'd taken for the pantry door on my first two passes through the kitchen turned out to be the door to the basement. Arctic air rushed around me when I opened the door, but the darkness at the bottom of the wooden staircase was no more dense than in the kitchen.

I descended carefully, panning the flashlight around at a sedate pace to fool myself into believing I wasn't scared. Someone who spends most of her life in darkness shouldn't be afraid of the dark, but there was something about this basement that made me feel like a frightened child.

I'd bought the house based only on a few photos and a terse description from the seller's agent. It sat in the heart of the city where I needed to be, I had to unload some cash, and the façade screamed, "Leave me the hell alone." Deal.

My agent's assertion that the basement "needed some finishing touches" wasn't quite how I'd have described it. He had warned me about the "portal to cannibal hell," but I thought he'd been exaggerating to make the sale to a woman who he believed had more money than sense.

To clarify: I don't believe in hell, and I didn't believe there were or ever had been cannibals cannibaling in the basement; but when my flashlight illuminated the feature in question, the description clicked. There was a gaping, ragged, black hole about chest-height in the southwest corner of the stone foundation. It was just big enough for a good-sized man to squeeze through.

I couldn't bring myself to direct the flashlight into the abyss. The best I could do was ignore its existence and continue perusing the basement, which (aside from the portal) was spacious, rundown, filthy, and uninteresting.

I made quick work of that level and ascended to the ground floor to look through the kitchen, dining room, second kitchen, parlor (where I'd slept), some locked doors for which keys would need to be located, and three medium-sized rooms of indeterminate use. All had been lovingly decorated no later than when World War I was still being called the Great War. I found a similar situation on the second and third floors, except several of the rooms had sinks for some reason. I wondered if the place had been a boarding house. The agent hadn't mentioned that.

I encountered two surprises on the third floor: an open fuse box proudly displaying knob-and-tube wiring, and a wooden ladder leading to an attic. By my count, that gave me five-ish stories—not that a single one of them was remotely livable. The detached garage, which I explored last, was in better shape than the house but still needed lots of TLC. The enormous footprint of the buildings left little room for the shallow yard at the front of the house. The back yard, such as it was, was domed by an oak tree which was probably older than the house.

Back on the ground floor, I found a door I'd overlooked in the second kitchen. I opened it to reveal a study, complete with fireplace, which someone had converted into living quarters by adding a compact kitchenette. From what I could tell at first sight, that someone hadn't received the memo that the house had been sold.

Chapter 2

Eighth & Insomnia

"Hello?"

At the far end of the study, a pair of closed double doors led back to the foyer. I recognized them as the same doors I'd been unable to open from the other side on my first pass through the house. Now I knew why they were locked.

I pushed my way through piles of clothes, dirty dishes, and general refuse on the floor toward the armchair in the center of the tiny living area. It faced away from me and toward an old fashioned, cathode-ray tube television which was on, but muted. Someone liked the sight but not the sound of "Jeopardy" reruns.

The scents of dirty bodies, spoiled food, and stale cigarette smoke nearly knocked me out, distracting me from what should have been rational fear. I was intruding in someone's home (and vice versa), and it fell to me to kick him or her out.

I came around the side of the chair at a wide angle and exhaled my relief. It was empty.

Turning, I scanned the sleeping area, then checked the kitchenette. What I took for a pantry (which I really should stop doing; none of the kitchens had a pantry), was another staircase, this one leading up to the second floor. The upper doorway was nearly invisible behind a cascade of chattel indiscriminately tossed into the stair-well for storage.

No electricity, and now I had a squatter. Fantastic.

"Hold up," I said to myself. "How the hell is the TV on?"

I tried the nearest light switch. Though it gave my finger a respectable static shock, the kitchenette light flickered on. I tried every light in the study. They all worked. It was warmer in this nest than the rest of the house, too.

"What the fuck."

But where was my squatter? A little voice reminded

me there was one place, just one spot in the whole house, which hadn't felt the intrusive beam of my trusty flashlight.

I resolved to swallow my fear and march straight down to the basement and haul out whoever was hiding down there. After all, this was *my* house. I had the paperwork to prove it. And judging by the character of the possessions littering the space around me, the squatter was old, poorly nourished, and rather small. I could take her.

By the time I opened the door to the basement and felt again that rush of freezing air, my resolve had abandoned me. I settled for standing at the top of the staircase and calling, "If anyone is down there, this is the owner of the house. Please come out so I can talk to you. You don't have to leave tonight, okay?"

I told myself that was the wiser course of action, and maybe it was, but I still felt like chicken shit. I retreated to the dirty nest in the study, thinking if someone did creep out of a hiding spot, this is where she (or he) would come. And it was warm.

Since I knew I'd have to sooner or later, I started cleaning. I tuned the TV to a 24-hour news channel and gave it a little volume, just enough that I didn't feel quite so alone. Aside from two trips into the house at large—one for the bathroom and another to bring my trunk into the little apartment so I could keep an eye on it—I stayed in there all night long.

Come morning, all I wanted was to crawl back into my sleeping bag and deny the existence of the day.

Instead, I geared up and walked to the nearest gym, where I signed up for a membership and immediately asked to use their phone.

"Oh no, did you lose your cell phone?" the sales lady, Amanda, asked solicitously.

"I don't have one."

"Oh… well, feel free to use the phone at the front desk. Call it a membership perk."

I nodded, then waited in awkward silence for her to walk away. I called the real estate agent who'd sold me the house and, without preamble, demanded, "Why didn't you tell me someone is living in the house? Better yet, why didn't you tell *them* I'd bought it? And why does the electricity only work in one part of the ground floor?"

"Good morning to you, too, Miss Marsh. Did you find those cookies I left for you? Wife made 'em herself. Someone living in the house, you say?"

I took a slow breath in and out through the nose and said, "Yes, someone is living in the house."

"Well shoot. Hope they didn't give you too much trouble!"

"I didn't actually see them. I found their living area, and the TV and heater were on. And the lights work, but only in those rooms."

"Maybe the sellers left the lights on when they moved out."

"The lights weren't on, I *turned* them on. Are you even listening to me? I have a squatter in my house. You need to fix this. And you need to call the electricity company and send someone to fix the lights in the rest of the house."

The man's unctuous tone sharpened, and he snarled, "Hey lady, haven't you ever heard? Buyer beware. I got another call."

He hung up. I slammed the receiver down, then slammed it down again. Fortunately, no one was around to bear witness to my histrionics. Without checking to see whether I'd broken the phone, I stormed into the women's locker room to shower and think.

Exhaustion, plus the heat of the water, calmed me down enough to consider the situation logically. I couldn't leave the house. It was mine, and I had to make it work. I had to make *Helena* work for as long as it took. Asshole that he was, the agent was right. This might have been his problem before, but the paperwork said the house and its attendant issues were mine now. Calling the police for help was simply out of the question. I had to deal with the squatter, which meant I had to *find* the squatter.

But first, I had to get someone from the electric company out to the house.

* * *

I didn't like the electricity guy one little bit. He showed up within an hour of my call to the electricity company, so prompt it was disconcerting. He was also handsome and nice. I don't like it when good-looking men are nice to me, because I know exactly why they do it. They think they're being altruistic, smiling and almost-flirting and making chit chat with a woman who, by the look of her, probably doesn't get attention from any men, let alone the attractive ones. I shut his attitude down fast, which left him no choice but to see to my wiring and get the fuck out.

He did, at least, get the power working in all the parts of the house which were supposed to have power. This included parts of the basement.

I may not be much to look at, but I'm a quick thinker. Before he could leave, I asked him to check out the basement because I thought I'd heard some vermin in there, maybe chewing on wires or something. I think he saw through my lie, but he consented to follow me down to the basement and right up to the so-called portal. Even with several lights on, it was still too dark to see inside the abyss.

I took a big step backward as he shined his own flashlight into the hole. Whatever I'd been expecting to see, it definitely wasn't a solid wall of hard-packed, brown dirt. The hole was less than a foot deep. The electrician leaned inside and checked right, left, up, and down before turning to me with a shrug.

"No rats. Not much room for anything back there. Want to take a look?"

"Uh… no thanks. I guess the rustling sound I heard came from somewhere else."

He left, and I returned to the study, which I'd decided to call the apartment. Since I'd cleaned it and located the source of its warmth, an electric space heater,

I decided to move in. I locked and blocked every means of ingress I could find, pulled the blackout curtains closed, and went to bed.

* * *

It wasn't even dark when I woke up. I checked my watch—4:15—and then looked around in confusion to see what could have disturbed my sleep. After a few seconds of holding my breath, I heard it. Someone was trying to force their way through the door in the kitchenette.

The need for sleep vanished in an instant, and I leapt to my feet, charging toward the sound. I don't like being woken up on someone else's terms.

Putting my mouth to the doorjamb, I asked with forced calm, "Who's there?"

The doorknob stopped jiggling. I held my breath again and waited.

Again, "Hello? Who's there?"

I counted to 30, then reached for the door lock. As soon as my fingers closed over the lock, I was frozen in place by the whisper that seeped through the door.

"Get out of my house."

Chapter 3

Check, Please

The fear only held me down for a couple seconds

before fury washed over it, switching off self-preservation and caution.

I unlocked the door, yanked it open, and screamed, "This is *my house!*"

I was screaming into an empty hallway.

"Well," I sighed, my arms dropping limply to my sides, "I guess I'm up."

Brave enough to confront a stranger whispering sinister things through a door was one thing, but I wasn't quite up to chasing the whisperer down for round two. I was hungry, and I didn't want to cook any more than I wanted to find and eat those cookies my real estate agent's wife made.

I got dressed and spent some time locking down the apartment again. When I was certain no human could penetrate my defenses, I opened a tiny window in the apartment's kitchenette and slithered my way out.

Yes, I squeezed myself through a window to leave my own house. I got dirt and flecks of lead paint on my pants, I ripped my jacket, and I looked like an idiot; but Little Miss Whisper would have to be a gymnast to get inside the way I got out.

I returned to the walking mall and ducked into a cheery-looking saloon right at five o'clock, as the sun was setting. I wasn't accustomed to eating breakfast so early, but you start your day earlier when you're on a mission.

My mission, as I reminded myself rather sternly, had nothing to do with the possibly crazy old woman perhaps hiding in my basement. She was merely a distraction. Somewhere in Helena lurked the reason I'd moved there, and if I didn't find him by Saint Patrick's Day, I'd be in deep shit.

Speaking of Saint Patrick's Day, one quick glance around the interior of the saloon told me it would be prime real estate on that high drinking holiday. Some of the grizzlier patrons at the bar looked like they had settled in to spend the intervening months right where they were.

I'd been seated in a section clearly earmarked for out-of-towners: a bullpen of high tops right next to the restrooms. Ordinarily I don't care where I'm seated, as long as I'm plied with food and drink, but rubbing elbows with non-natives was a waste of my time.

When my server arrived, I slapped on my very sweetest smile and lied through my teeth, "I'm so sorry to be a pain, but is there any way at all I could move to the other side of the restaurant? It's just that my ex is sitting right over there—" I jerked my head toward a random dude two tables away, oblivious with his mouth around an enormous hamburger "—and I don't think he's noticed me yet. I'm so sorry."

Her answering smile was genuine, which meant I'd succeeded in not pissing her off. She led me to a table amongst the townies, and I slipped her a ten dollar bill to make up for the missed tip. When my new server arrived, he graced me with a knowing smile.

"Awkward over there, huh?" he asked.

"It almost was. Sorry to be a pain."

He made a show of looking around at the tables,

about a third of which were occupied, and joked, "I think we have room for you. So, what can I get you to drink?"

"I would love an ice water." His face fell, then brightened when I added, "And a Glenlivet twelve—fifteen if you have it—neat with three ice cubes on the side. Make it a double."

I saw the battle raging behind his smile. He wanted to card me. I'm 35, but I look about half that, and not in a good way. To save him the trouble of deciding between cutting into his tip and potentially getting in trouble, I whipped out my ID and handed it to him, unsolicited.

"Thanks." He studied the Nevada driver's license identifying me as Susan Abney. I doubt he read the name. He saw the birth year beginning in 19 and passed the license back to me. "I'll be right back with your drink."

While I waited, I studied each of the people around me in turn. Everyone in my section received at least two seconds of scrutiny, except for the people seated directly behind me. It would have been odd to turn in my seat to ogle them, so I saved that for a return trip from the restroom that would have to wait until my fake ex-boyfriend had paid out and left. From the way he was chowing down on that burger, it wouldn't be long.

About half an hour later, when I was working on my second scotch and wondering where my hot wings were, a voice behind me rose to an attention-grabbing volume.

A woman screeched, "I asked for double ranch. Did you not hear me? I know you didn't write it down. See —look—one ranch. Double means two. How am I supposed to eat this salad with barely *any* dressing?"

"I'm so sorry, ma'am," the server tried to say, but the woman was still building up steam.

"It's like this every time we come here! There's always something wrong, and it costs more every time! Why did I wait fifteen minutes for this salad, anyway? There's barely anyone here. Whatever they're paying you people, it's too much."

I couldn't resist any longer. Other customers were openly staring, so I figured it wouldn't hurt to join them. I swiveled my upper body to take a look at the Karen in her natural habitat.

What a specimen she was. I've got no right to critique a physique, but I'm only human. She certainly looked like double the ranch dressing entered her body on a regular basis. Focused on berating the server, she seemed oblivious to the stares she was drawing. Or maybe she was only pretending not to notice. Maybe she got off on it.

One detail about the woman jumped out at me and sparked an idea. Her hair, an improbably uniform, brassy brown, looked a little dry at the roots. Very dry. Kind of like she'd shellacked it with spray-on color to hide something.

A thin, balding man sat with his back to me, across the table from her. He seemed to be engrossed in aligning his silverware with the edge of the table. Laying low. Smart move.

I picked up my half-empty glass of ice water, stood up, walked around the server, and emptied the glass over the woman's head.

As I watched brown dye bleeding down her face, exposing the streak of white at her crown, I smiled innocently and said, "Whoops."

Applause erupted around me, and euphoria faded rapidly into regret. What the hell was I doing, drawing attention to myself? Then I locked eyes with Karen's husband, and I realized the mistake I'd made was much worse than I thought.

Delbert Sherman, there you are.

I skirted the dumbfounded server again, tossed some cash onto my table, and booked it out of the saloon. I didn't stop or slow down until I was back at my gym, where I once again asked to use the phone and waited for Amanda to give me some privacy.

"Marv," came the answer after several rings.

I let out the breath I'd sucked in and checked to make sure no one was in earshot before I spoke. "It's me. I found him."

After a pause, laughter exploded from phone, forcing me to put some distance between my ear and the receiver.

"You've got to be shitting me, Nix! It's been, what, two days?"

"A day and a half," I replied with false modesty. "It's a small town."

"He make you?"

The words "I don't know" were on my lips when I pressed them together, thinking. Had he? Delbert Sherman didn't know what I looked like, because he didn't know I existed. My quarry never did. Marv was asking if Sherman had cottoned on that I was there looking for him. I didn't have any reason to believe he had. I was just some impulsive stranger who'd dumped water on his wife's head. So why was I now picturing him with a spark of recognition in his eyes?

"No," I replied, leaving it at that.

"Great. Look, I can't pay you until next Thursday."

"As in two days from now, or nine days from now?"

"Seffy…"

"Why?"

"Listen, Persephone…" he wheedled. I could almost see him running one fat, be-ringed hand over his greasy hair.

I didn't give him a chance to finish the thought. I demanded, "Excuse me? Do you not recall the part of my contract that adds one-point-five percent to my fee every time you call me that? You're up to five sixty-six and some change."

"All right, take it easy. Thing is, I didn't expect you to work quite so fast. Wait 'til next Thursday and I'll make it an even six hundred thou."

More than I'd paid for the house. I nodded. "That's acceptable. Maybe it'll be done by then."

"Great. Don't blow town the minute you get paid. You understand."

"I plan to stay here until we make a new deal." I held my breath after the pronouncement, wondering if he'd push back on the idea of a new deal.

Our last deal hadn't gone so well. The mark in Vegas, Zachary Polson, had nearly gotten away from me. And there had been witnesses. "No Witnesses" and "No Sign of Foul Play" were my calling cards, and you can't have one without the other. Marv would've killed anyone else for fucking up so badly, but not me. He liked me, so he gave me another chance: Delbert Sherman, who needed to have an accident before a certain trial began on Saint Paddy's Day.

Had I already impressed Marv enough to consider me forgiven?

He neither confirmed nor denied his forgiveness, saying, "Great. Kid, you outdid yourself this time. How're you liking Montana?"

"I miss the desert."

"And the desert misses you. I got to go—take care of yourself."

"You, too."

I hung up, already replaying my side of the conversation in my head. "I found him … contract … new deal … desert." If Amanda were eavesdropping, she was probably riddled with curiosity. I called for her and smiled when she appeared in the doorway of an office just off the reception desk.

"Thanks for letting me use the phone," I said. "You've got some damn fine basketball players in this town, you know that?"

She brightened. "I did know that! What are you, a talent scout?"

"Guilty. One of your guys might be on his way to Phoenix soon. But you didn't hear it from me."

She twisted an imaginary key against her lips. In that moment I realized Amanda was very cute, and there was no ring on her finger. Quelling the urge to ask her out was pretty easy once I remembered how difficult it is to date when you can't tell people anything about yourself.

Chapter 4

Spelunking

What was I saying about the crazy squatter in my house being a distraction? Those words were tasting a lot like crow when I climbed back through my window fifteen minutes later.

Sure, I still had to run down Sherman's address; sort out his schedule, habits, and associates; maybe probe the effectiveness of whatever security system he had in place at home; blah, blah, blah—but that was the easy part. I had plenty of time, and I had to take it slow. An idiot could have tracked down where Sherman lived and worked, but Marv paid the big bucks for someone who could do the finding and the killing without raising so much as an eyebrow.

So, I had to deal with Little Miss Whisper sooner than later.

I shut and locked the window, then went through the

apartment looking for evidence someone had been inside while I was gone. Everything was in order, even the long, blonde hair I'd stretched across the door to the foyer, and the Cheetos crumbs I'd sprinkled on all the window sills except the one I'd climbed through. Waste of a bag of Cheetos, honestly.

Now that night had fallen again, I felt myself raring to tackle another day. All the lights in the house worked, so I switched every single one of them on, even the lights in the basement. This turned all the curtainless windows into so many mirrors throughout the house, putting me in a sort of fishbowl for anyone passing by outside. I didn't care too much about that, but I disliked the feeling of isolation that accompanied it.

I don't mind being alone. That's how I spend 99% of my life. Thing is, being alone hits different when you have the option of mingling with other people. The studied rejection of companionship is what I crave.

The house on Eighth Avenue didn't feel like one of dozens of inhabited structures crammed together on a 150-year-old street in downtown Helena, Montana. It felt like a spaceship drifting silently through a void with no beginning and no end.

And I was sharing it with an exceedingly strange stranger.

While I nuked a package of ramen noodles to make up for the wings I'd never gotten, I allowed my thoughts to drift back to the portal in the basement. Something about the would-be resolution when I'd gazed into the hole with the electrician didn't sit right. It was too comforting, too easy.

The first time I'd gone into the basement, I'd sensed space, depth, volume concealed by darkness. Maybe I'm not a bat, but my ears work pretty damn well, and I knew the sounds I'd made weren't bouncing back to me off a dirt wall ten inches inside the opening.

By the time I'd sucked down my noodles and cleaned up, I was once more resolved. I grabbed a flashlight and returned to the basement, which didn't look so menacing now with its array of naked lightbulbs swinging from the ceiling.

Not much light made it to the far corner where the portal sat, just enough that I could make out the wall of dirt I'd seen before. I got close enough to shine my flashlight directly onto it, then crept even closer so I could lean in like the electrician had. There wasn't much to see.

It took me about ten minutes to gin myself up enough to act on a suspicion I'd formed based on the mirror-like windows in the rest of the house. I didn't want to do it, but I had to. I switched off my flashlight, then turned off all the lights in the basement, then climbed the stairs and shut the door with myself on the wrong side of it.

Pausing at the top of the stairs, I gazed into the tarry blackness below me and listened. Nothing.

I eased down the stairs, keeping to the far edge of each tread to avoid making the wood creak. Totally blind, I clutched the railing until it ended and my soles met concrete. I slowly rotated, seeking any source of light stronger than the feeble moonlight filtering through the grimy windows at ground level, about six feet off the floor.

Then, I saw it. A warm, orange glow beckoning me forward. It was coming from the portal. The light was so faint I had to blink and rub my eyes to make sure I wasn't imagining it. I moved forward heel-to-toe, my hands stretched out in front of me to prevent a face-first impact with a wall or support column.

The faint patch of light became blinding as my eyes adjusted and I moved toward the portal. I stopped a couple feet from it. Where before I'd seen a wall of hard-packed dirt, I now saw a rough, dirty curtain blocking the opening to the portal. The light came from the other side, and it flickered as though from a flame.

Mesmerized, I stood in front of the curtain for a long time. I didn't know what to do next. I was certain, positive, would bet my life that Little Miss Whisper was just on the other side, listening for me as intently as I listened for her. What to do about it?

While I dithered, movement on the other side of the curtain caught my eye. A shadow loomed and grew as it approached the opening, eventually taking shape. I saw a small head with a halo of flyaway hair, narrow shoulders, and skinny arms. The figure, just a silhouette, moved forward until I was sure her nose was touching the curtain.

With courage I didn't feel, I leaned close and whispered, "Get out of my house."

The flame was snuffed out so quickly my words seemed to have made it happen. Darkness collapsed around me, bringing panic so acute I thought I'd die of a heart attack. I took two long steps back, fumbling with my flashlight, as a faint *whoosh* warned me the curtain had been pulled aside.

I found the button, flicked on the flashlight, and pointed it at the portal. The curtain was gone, revealing the hollowness behind. I couldn't see anyone, so I rotated on the spot, shining the flashlight into every single crevice of the basement.

"Hello?" I called.

My search morphed seamlessly into a retreat up the stairs. I broke into a jog and reached the apartment right before my heart exploded, leaning against the door (on the right side of it this time) to catch my breath. All the lights were still on, the heater was cranking out cuddly-warm air, and not a dust mote was out of place. Nevertheless, I made the rounds again, checking and rechecking every means of ingress.

With a normal heart rate came calm, then boredom. I poured myself a glass of scotch and sat down in the armchair in front of the TV, but I didn't turn it on. I checked my watch. Way too late to start running down Sherman. Way too early for bed. I couldn't have slept if my life depended on it.

Reality hit me like a piano from the sky. I had to get her out of the basement, and there I sat in the one other place I knew she wanted to be.

Though it went against every instinct I possessed, I

left the house again and didn't bother with the window. I left the door to the foyer unlocked and exited through the front door, returning to the saloon to while away as much time as I could.

As soon as I walked through the door, I sought Delbert Sherman and his horrible Karen wife, but they were gone. I settled into a seat at the bar, ordered yet another scotch, and tried to watch a basketball game.

That turned out to be a rather unfortunate decision when someone slid into the seat next to me and said, "Hey, don't I know you?"

It was Amanda from the gym. I swallowed a mouthful of scotch with a lot of air and said, "Oh, hi. Amanda, right?"

"Yeah. No, wait, let me get there," she said. She screwed up her face and eventually ventured, "Jessica, right?"

"Julie," I corrected.

"Right. The talent scout." Her gaze drifted to the TV and she asked, "Did you pick out any of those guys?"

I'd been watching the game for twenty minutes and couldn't even remember which teams were playing until I looked back at the TV. Oklahoma City versus Dallas. I shook my head. "Nah, I work for the Suns." God I hoped that was the team from Phoenix.

"Oh, Phoenix, right."

Desperate to steer the conversation away from my poorly-chosen fake job, I asked, "Are you a native Montanan? I've been told that's very important here."

That got us away from basketball, though I was

disappointed to learn after a bit more chit chat that Amanda had a boyfriend. Said boyfriend appeared sometime later, when I was near the bottom of the second scotch of the session. I couldn't remember how many I'd imbibed since waking up that afternoon, but a sociable, fuzzy feeling near my brain stem told me it was enough.

I ordered wings again (actually got them this time) and managed to pass over two hours in the unobjectionable company of Amanda and her boyfriend, Cody.

"Well," I announced during a lull, "I better be off. Nice to meet you, Cody."

As I hunted for the correct paper money to leave on the bar, Amanda said, "Oh, hey, what's your phone number? I'll text you about trivia."

"I don't have a phone, remember?"

"Right. Well, it's on Thursdays. Hope to see you then."

As I tottered home, dreading what I'd find when I got there, I wondered what Amanda and Cody must think of me. Whatever it was, they didn't seem to mind it. Cody had peppered me with get-to-know-you questions and had seemed sincerely interested in my answers (which were bald-faced lies, of course). I wasn't used to having friends, so I resisted the urge to think of them that way. The more time I spent with someone, the more I had to make up about myself, which meant more room in my brain devoted to remembering lies and keeping them straight.

To Amanda and Cody, I was Julie, talent scout for the

Phoenix Suns. To my real estate agent, I was Kathy Marsh, wealthy widow from Los Angeles looking for a fresh start. To anyone who got hold of my current driver's license, I was Susan Abney of Nevada (organ donor, corrective lenses required). To Marv, who signed my checks, I was Persephone Nix, Seffy for short, queen of the underworld, goddess of the night.

Marv knew me best, but even he didn't know the real me. He knew all he needed to know: I could find anyone, no matter how well he or she was hidden; and for an extra fee, I'd do what needed to be done to silence their testimony on the witness stand. Marv really seemed to appreciate that last part.

Chapter 5

Julie & The Blizzard

When I walked into the apartment and saw the detritus of someone else's recent meal, a pile of *my* socks on the floor, and the TV once again tuned to muted game show reruns, I made a deal with myself and my squatter.

I opened the door to the basement, stood in relative safety at the top, and called down, "You just stay out of my way, and I'll stay out of yours, okay?"

Believe it or not, before I shut the door, I heard a very faint, "Fine."

The overwhelming banality of that response, even if I had imagined it, allowed me to fall asleep around 5:00 a.m. and stay asleep for 14 hours. I thought we had a deal, so you can imagine my surprise when I woke up to my usual alarm and found the TV on, tuned once again to "Jeopardy" and thoughtfully muted so as not to wake me.

I exhaled my fury and saw mist between myself and the TV. Sitting up, I tried to look out the window and saw nothing but white. The rectangle of opaque glass glowed with ambient light, but I couldn't see a thing outside. I climbed out of bed and walked to the window. What had been featureless resolved itself into a compressed mass of tiny, white flakes obscuring the entire window.

"Oh, snow," I breathed, again fogging the air. It was so cold in the apartment I couldn't think straight. What had happened to my heater?

Toes screaming in protest as they froze solid, I walked over to the heater and examined it. It was still technically plugged in, but someone had cleanly snipped the cord. How she hadn't electrocuted herself was as much a mystery as why she'd done it in the first place.

I didn't feel a presence in the apartment, but I checked every shadowy corner just to be sure. Maybe she'd given herself a shock and slinked down to the basement to die in the wall like a squirrel. If only.

Thinking I'd go check (I certainly didn't need a corpse moldering away in my basement), I tried to open the door to the foyer, but it wouldn't budge. The handle turned freely, but I couldn't get it open. I set my shoulder to it and rammed it over and over until, with an earsplitting crack, the double doors fell away before me. I stumbled into the foyer and gasped as my bare feet slid over solid ice.

"What the hell is this?" I groaned, surveying the scene with dismay.

The wood floor was an ice rink, a puddle about the size of a VW Beetle spreading from the threshold across the floor. Turning, I saw why the door hadn't wanted to open. The ice extended up the wall, all the way to the top of the door. It had been frozen shut.

The larger house was no warmer than the apartment. I ducked back inside to put on three pairs of socks, then went to the front door. This opened freely onto a Siberian hellscape of fresh, powdery snow that sparkled under a full moon and some pinkish, halogen street-lights. It looked like two or three feet had accumulated while I slept. I couldn't see the cars that were definitely parked on the street when I'd come home this morning, and the raised front porch of my house now appeared level with the front yard. My first blizzard.

No footprints broke the pristine sea of snow between the sidewalk and the house, or anywhere in the shallow front yard. An errant urge to flee from the house caught me off guard. Flee from what? That crazy old bat had iced me into the apartment and probably hoped I'd succumb to hypothermia while I slept, and for what? I thought we had an understanding.

"Still my house," I gritted, closing the front door and locking it.

I had intended to get to work on Delbert Sherman

tonight, but something told me I wouldn't get too far in that snow. With two months until my deadline, the trial, it was tempting to believe I had plenty of time to get the job done; but the last thing I needed was to get rushed, sloppy, and caught—I'd be free and clear with Marv, but he'd never use my services again.

Leaning against the front door, I let out another steamy sigh and asked the empty house, "What's a girl to do?"

Logically, I knew I wouldn't be snowed in too long. This was Montana. These people knew how to deal with snow. By daylight, maybe sooner, the streets would be clear enough that I could go about my business. I only had to wait, and what better way to occupy myself than to kick this crazy lady out of my house once and for all?

I didn't want to admit it, but a part of me wondered if the woman were a figment of my overwrought mind. What if that electrician and I really had seen a solid wall of dirt in that hole, and everything since then was the product of my own weird imagination? Seeing the squatter face-to-face, talking to her one human to another, would cure me of those worries.

Since my attempt to confront her on her turf had failed, I'd have to make her come to me.

I was rifling through my supplies, wondering if I could jury rig some kind of smoke bomb, when someone knocked on the front door. I peeked through the rippling glass in the door and thought I recognized the face of the man on my porch. *Speak of the devil.*

"Hi, sorry to bother you," the friendly electrician

said when I opened the door. "Just wanted to come by and check on you. Lots of folks on this street lost power this evening."

I glanced over his shoulder at the porch light glowing feebly from across the street, and I opened the door a bit wider. "Come inside, have some cookies," I ordered.

"Oh—um—okay," he relented with an unsure smile.

He followed me into the apartment's kitchenette, where I grabbed the untouched plate of homemade cookies the real estate agent had left for me. I peeled back the plastic wrap and offered him the plate. He took one, but he didn't take a bite.

"Your power seems to be working fine," he commented. "Is your heater broken?"

Ignoring that, I said, "I'd really like you to take another look at that spot in the basement. I was down there last night, and that packed dirt we saw turned out to be an old brown curtain. Crazy, huh?"

He dithered, then took the tiniest possible bite of the chocolate chip cookie I'd foisted on him. He made a face.

"No good?" I asked.

"Pretty stale."

"I don't like sweets. The guy who sold me the house left them for me. So, about the basement?"

"Look, ma'am." He took a deep breath, then forged ahead as though against his better judgment. "This house has been empty for a while. Longer than I've been alive, if we're being honest. Whatever's going on down there, I can't say as I'm game to get involved."

The awkward way he spoke forced me to waste a second interpreting his words. Unsure what he meant, I asked, "You're afraid to go down into the basement?"

"Not afraid, just..." He moved the stale cookie toward his mouth again, frowned, and lowered it. "You hear things. Old house. You understand."

"Buddy, I have to *live* here."

"Well then, maybe you ought to call the cops. Or an exterminator? S'long as your electricity's working, I better move on down the block. Thanks—er—for the..."

"Just give it to me," I snapped, extending my palm.

He dropped the cookie into it with a self-deprecating laugh. "Don't worry, these old wives tales are all bunk."

I shadowed him back to the front door and mumbled a mutinous, "Bye" as he exited.

"Have a nice day, Miss Julie."

I carried the barely eaten cookie to the kitchenette and tossed it back on the plate, where it promptly broke in half. Stale, indeed. Still, I wouldn't be getting groceries anytime soon, and I was getting a little peckish. I took a bite out of the untouched half of the cookie and immediately spat it out.

It wasn't just stale, it was overwhelmingly bitter. I rubbed the sleeve of my sweater over my tongue several times, wondering what I'd done to make the real estate agent (or his wife) hate me so much. Bitter cookies? How do you screw up chocolate chip cookies?

They were even more bitter than that cup of coffee Staci-with-an-i had given me at the title office.

I stared at the cookies for a long time, hating them. Bitter coffee was one thing, but not in 35 years on this earth had I tasted a cookie that was even slightly bitter, let alone so bitter I could still taste it in the back of my throat.

"Hold up," I squeaked. *"Julie?"*

As soon as the words left my mouth, all the lights in the apartment went out at the same time.

Chapter 6

It's a Big Problem Here

Alone in the moonlit kitchenette, I picked up an unbroken cookie and studied it. I sniffed it. It smelled like chocolate, big surprise. I touched the tip of my tongue to it and recoiled again.

"What did you do to these cookies, you son of a bitch?"

Either this purported power outage had only just made it to my house, or the electrician cut the power himself. I didn't care which was the case. I was sick of every last bit of this podunk town's shady bullshit. I exchanged the cookie for a wooden rolling pin and left the apartment.

Returning to the top of the basement stairs, I called down, "Guess what, lady? Unless you're a ghost, you're about to have one hell of a bad time."

I started down the stairs, banging the rolling pin

against the wall as I went. The power was out in the basement as well, but a hint of halogen streetlight trickled in through the snow packed against the windows. It was enough for me to make my way around the various obstacles between me and the portal, slapping the rolling pin against my palm as I walked.

"Don't bother coming out, 'cause I'm coming in!" I announced.

I used the rolling pin to push the brown curtain aside, and something shapeless and dark came flying out of the hole toward my face. Though I wasn't quite fast enough to bat it away, the impact was soft. As it crumpled to the ground at my feet, I realized it was a sleeping bag.

"Your buddy Mr. Friendly just cut the power, so it's gonna get even colder down here!" I warned. Picking up the sleeping bag, I headed for the stairs, calling over my shoulder, "You can come upstairs to get this back!"

I dragged the rather smelly sleeping bag into the front room where I'd spent that first night and made a fire. The blaze was just starting to heat up the room when movement in the doorway caught my eye. I sprang to my feet, rolling pin at the ready, and got my first good look at Little Miss Whisper.

She could have been 18 or 80. Like me, she was Caucasian, blonde, and rather homely; but she was about a foot shorter and dressed in ragged, unwashed clothes. She was so thin it made me grimace, even thinner than me; but she was offering me what she probably thought was a disarming smile. I saw a face, teeth, and gums ravaged by years of methamphetamine abuse, and suddenly everything clicked into place.

Meth tasted bitter—and made you paranoid.

Like a pebble skipping across a pond, my mind jumped from one revelation to the next.

The electrician knew the cookies were spiked. That connected him with the real estate agent, and probably to Staci-with-an-i and her bitter coffee.

He called me Julie, which also connected him with Amanda and her nosy boyfriend, Cody.

He'd known about the hidey hole in my basement from day one, which made him an accomplice with Little Miss Whisper here.

What about the servers at the saloon where I'd so fortuitously sat right next to the man whose contract killing had brought me to Helena in the first place? Was "Karen" Sherman's attention-grabbing performance just that?

Holy shit, was anyone in this town *not* in on the charade?

The whole mental exercise only shut me down for a split second, after which I asked, "How do you contact him? Do you have a cell phone?"

One thin hand dove into the grimy front pocket of her jeans, and she pulled out an off-brand smartphone.

"Only he said I could keep the phone, so..." she whined, pressing the treasure to her bony chest.

A flicker of unwelcome pity distracted me. I wasn't even sure yet who 'he' was, only that this sad, methy creature before me had accepted the worst role in the scheme—living in my basement and fucking with me—likely for the least remuneration.

"I'll give it right back," I promised. She tossed me the phone and I caught it, motioning to the fire. "Sit down and warm up. I've got a lot of questions for you."

"Yeah, okay."

The question of who 'he' was couldn't have been simpler to answer. There was exactly one contact in the phone's directory: Sherman.

Delbert Sherman.

I made a call, but not to Delbert.

"Marvin Astor," Marv promptly answered. Impersonal. Good.

"Marv, it's Nix."

"Oh, Nix. Good news. The money's coming tomorrow after all."

"There's something you aren't telling me about Delbert Sherman."

After a two-second pause, he gusted, "Hey, I want the guy pushing daisies. What more do you need to know?"

His sincerity brought me up short. Was I being paranoid? Was that coffee, were those cookies, really spiked with meth? Had any of my other food been tampered with? Then again, if there was no reason to be paranoid, why would there be meth in the first place? I shook my head violently, refusing to confound myself with speculation.

"This doesn't have anything to do with the Vegas job?" I asked.

"You know where we stand on that. You almost screwed the pooch. You begged me for a chance to make it up to me, and I gave it to you."

Undeterred, I tried a different angle. "Who is Delbert Sherman to Zachary Polson?"

"Well, Sherman was Polson's CFO, before he went into the program, of course, but—"

I felt a lurking aneurysm in my brain give an angry twitch. "And you didn't think I might need to *know* that before I went after Sherman?"

"I… did not."

"I'm not getting away clean this time, Marv. Send the money. I'm gonna need it." I hung up, tossed the phone back to Little Miss Whisper, and said, "Call him."

* * *

While we waited for Delbert, Little Miss Whisper— whose name was Beth, not kidding—fessed up. Delbert Sherman had paid her in drugs and cash to hide in my basement and drive me crazy. To what end, Beth had no idea.

Yes, Delbert Sherman was the mastermind behind it all. Not only did he know someone was looking for him, he knew *I* was looking for him. If you think his little plan was stupid, you'd be in agreement with me; but it turned out driving me crazy wasn't his endgame.

At the signal from Beth, Delbert came to my house to personally administer the fatal overdose of the very drug that was supposed to be making me paranoid and unbalanced. Presumably the methamphetamine-laced cookies were intended to help sell the illusion that I'd become a drug addict and subsequently overdosed.

The electrician would tell the cops I was nuts. Even my real estate agent would have to admit I'd seemed a little off from the first phone call, talking about a "portal to cannibal hell" in the basement. Maybe Staci-with-an-I, Amanda and Cody, and the servers at the saloon would also have a chance to remark upon my unfortunate strangeness.

Delbert was, in effect, doing to me exactly what I'd done to his business partner, Polson. I preferred ketamine to drive someone around the bend and eventually overdose, but I guess I'm just a classy kind of girl.

I didn't learn all of this from Beth, of course. She swore up and down she didn't even know about the cookies, because she'd have eaten them. Delbert copped to it once I'd lured him down to the basement, bashed him over the head with my rolling pin, and tied him to one of the concrete support pillars. I didn't even have to torture him. As soon as he knew the tables had turned, he wouldn't shut up. No wonder Marv needed to get rid of him.

As I wielded the syringe of liquid meth over Delbert's arm, searching for a likely entry point, he didn't even have the dignity not to beg for his life.

"Please, Miss Nix—that's your name, right? Persephone Nix? I don't want to die. I have a wife…"

"She seems awful," I argued. "Who told you my name?"

He closed his eyes and didn't answer. I injected the needle, depressed the plunger, and stood back next to Beth as the drug took effect. Beth seemed to be battling some bastard cousin of jealousy while Delbert went under. I was just glad she hadn't attacked me and taken the syringe for herself.

Once he was gone, I turned to her and she to me.

"You gonna kick me out, now?" she mumbled.

"I don't see why. I'm leaving tomorrow, so you do what you want… But I'd stay away until the police are finished with the crime scene. Help yourself to the meth cookies."

* * *

The next morning, I confirmed Marv had transferred the six-figure payment into my account and headed straight to a used car dealership to get a new-to-me set of wheels.

My first stop was the gym to take care of Amanda, but I got lost, which gave me time to think. She seemed so innocent and airheaded, could she really have been in on it? How would Sherman have known I'd even meet her? I couldn't explain why the electrician had called me Julie, and I didn't have time to track *him* down. I decided to let it go.

Las Vegas, Nevada, where Marv lived, was about 14 hours away. That gave me 14 hours to decide how mad I was at him for selling me out to Delbert Sherman. He'd try to deny it, he'd offer the payment as proof he'd never doubted me, but the fact remained that only one other person on earth knew my name, and he knew I liked it that way.

If you enjoyed *Underworld*, please leave a review so I can sell more books and keep writing novels instead of getting a real job.

You can also <u>sign up for my mailing list on my website</u> (https://akweller.com) which means you'll get my newsletters on the rare occasions when I feel like creating one, and you'll be among the first to know when new stories are about to drop. You'll also receive a free copy of *2.15.2020*, the prequel to my debut novel, *Enemy Closer*.

About the Author

AK Weller

AK Weller was born and raised in Texas and currently lives in western Montana, because it's one of the last places in the U.S. where cows outnumber humans. She writes thrillers when she's supposed to be working as a graphic designer, investigator, or technical writer. She loves dogs, dinosaurs, art history, self-defense, and her husband, in that order.

AK Weller writes thrillers with strong female leads. While working as a graphic designer, private investigator, and technical writer, she wrote and published her first novel, *Enemy Closer*, in 2022. She hopes the late Sue

Grafton and Stieg Larsson wouldn't be too mortified to know they're the two authors whose work has influenced her the most. She loves dinosaurs, Krav Maga, and art history; and she hates spiders, Subarus, and carrots. AK lives in Montana with her husband, two dogs, and four cats.

With an amazing new book and more on the way, AK Weller has a great thrilling read. You can find more information and her email sign-up https:// akweller.com

Dust and Desperation

AMY RIVERS

"RUN!"

Tilly's voice hissed from inside the basement.

Hannah turned and sprinted into the desert as fast as her injured body would let her, but after the first few falls, she realized that slow and steady—well, slower—was going to get her a lot farther away. The desert was treacherous under the best of circumstances. Traversing it at night was foolhardy, but with the threat of their abductors catching up with her, Hannah didn't have the luxury of stopping, or even slowing to a crawl, which her aching limbs would have much preferred. Thankfully, fear, anger, and adrenaline were pumping through her veins, fueling each step forward.

Scream all you want. No one will hear you.

The words echoed through her head. In the time they'd been confined to the basement, Hannah never heard any noises outside. No cars, though she figured their kidnappers had to have one nearby. No traffic, which wasn't entirely surprising. There were so many isolated places in New Mexico. Her time upstairs revealed a dilapidated structure that hadn't been lived in for a long time, and as she got her bearings, such that they were, she confirmed what she and Tilly had suspected–they were in the middle of nowhere. The idea of being alone in the desert had terrified Hannah, but after last night, she knew there was nothing she wouldn't do to escape. Dying in the desert was no longer her biggest fear.

With one of her eyes swollen shut, it was hard enough to navigate between bushes and stubby trees that ripped at her clothes and bare skin, but the throbbing in her cheek was a potent reminder of what she was leaving behind. The abduction. The drugging. The beatings. And the final atrocity. It kept her moving away from the house. Away from danger. But also away from Tilly.

After launching Hannah out of the window, Tilly's head disappeared down into the basement room. In her mind, she saw Tilly sink to the floor, exhaustion and exertion finally making her legs give way. She hoped Tilly got to rest before they realized Hannah was gone. She tried to imagine Tilly curled up on the mat in the corner, asleep. Peaceful. She clung to that vision because the alternative was too awful to consider.

Now that dusk had turned to night, she was having a love-hate relationship with the moon. It wasn't full, but it was bright enough to illuminate some of the desert landscape, giving her a fighting chance at not impaling herself on cactus as she fled. Unfortunately, It also created shadows–shadows that concealed snags and barbs, animal burrows, and scarier things she had to push right out of her mind to keep her panic at bay.

She'd only had a moment after climbing out of the basement window to scan her surroundings. The desert butted unchecked against the abandoned house, providing some protection from observation–assuming her captors weren't watching the back of the structure, recapturing her as soon as she stepped foot away. They hadn't been, but the looming threat of being taken back to the basement room was more than enough motivation to keep her putting one step in front of the other.

She hadn't let herself relax even a tiny bit until the lights in the upstairs part of the house were no longer visible behind her. There was no electricity in the house, but a small generator powered lamps the kidnappers used at night. The blackness of the desert crowded around her, taking from her the one landmark that gave her any sense of direction. For a while, she'd been able to see the outline of the mountains in the distance, but as the night grew darker, they became more indistinct, until she wasn't sure if they were there or if she was imagining them.

She listened to the chirping of crickets and the rustle of leaves, the telltale sign of nocturnal wildlife beginning their nightly hunt. Mice, rats, ground squirrels, foxes, raccoons and porcupines. Coyotes. Bobcats. Having grown up in southern New Mexico, she was aware of the kind of scavengers and predators that hunted at night in these deserts. On a normal night, she wouldn't have thought twice about taking a nighttime stroll, but with her muscles threatening to give out and the broken skin all over her body, she felt acutely exposed and vulnerable.

Every move she made brought sharp pains, burning aches, and a million other reminders of the violence she was escaping, fueling her determination when she began to doubt. The scratches and abrasions on her legs and arms were caked with dirt from the falls she'd taken, but the threat of what might happen if she were caught was like a white hot poker prodding her along. She was grateful for the adrenaline but not foolish enough to think it would last her through the night, so she pushed herself hard, hoping to put as much distance between herself and her captors as possible.

She grudgingly ate the meager remains of the food Tilly had given her, barely tasting it. The anger and betrayal she'd felt when she realized Tilly wasn't coming with her was still fresh in her mind and in her heart. If she were capable of allowing herself to think rationally, she knew she might begin to understand Tilly's reasoning. She'd seen how little energy Tilly had in reserve–how much boosting Hannah up the wall and out the window had depleted her. But she didn't feel like being rational.

Instead, her thoughts and emotions churned inside her. Maybe it wasn't fair for her to think this way, but Tilly was an adult. It was her job to be strong. It was

Tilly's responsibility to be the brave one so Hannah could fall apart. The raw and uncontrolled rage she'd felt toward Tilly in that last moment continued to speed her along as she made her way blindly through the desert.

A branch snapped behind her. She jumped, stifling a scream. She twirled around to scan the area but saw nothing. No movement in the shadows. No bobbing lights. The sound of an owl in the distance gave her pause. Her heart thumped loudly in her ears and she gulped air, making the world spin a little. The constant assault of terror on her senses made her feel like her heart was going to explode. She pictured it like a bomb–KABOOM!–and then she'd just drop to the ground and get picked apart by animals…

"Stop it!" she scolded herself, shaking her head like an Etch-a-Sketch to clear her dark thoughts.

"Now. Breathe." The sound of her own voice, quiet as it was, made the night seem a little less lonely. She put her hand over her mouth and tried to slow her breathing, thinking about that paper sack back at the house and all the movies she'd ever seen where a person breathed into one to stop hyperventilating. Then she thought about the comfort of Tilly's arms around her. And about her dad, wondering how scared he must be, not knowing where she was or if he'd ever see her again.

A tear slipped down her cheek and she turned her face toward the sky, marveling for a moment at all the stars she could see. Back home in Las Cruces, the light pollution made it difficult to see the stars like this, but she remembered camping trips with her parents before her mom died, where they'd lay on their backs under the night sky. She was grateful–the bursts of light provided something constant to keep her headed in one direction as long as she remembered to look up. As her fatigue increased, she got distracted, causing her to veer off-course.

She pictured her mother as one of those stars, like in that Disney movie with the lions.

"Mom," she whispered into the darkness. "I don't know if I'm going to make it home." She imagined her mother's face appearing in the sky and then felt foolish. She wasn't a child anymore, and after last night, she wasn't innocent.

The years when her mother was sick were hard, but the year after her death was absolutely bleak. Her dad was physically present, but she could see that being at home weighed heavily on him, pulling his whole frame down into a sort of slump. He started working long hours, and she knew his work at the District Attorney's office was important, but after a while she began to drown in her own grief and loneliness.

She'd finally found a grief support group and made her dad take her. He would have done anything she asked, and she was thankful the work they did in the support group brought him back to her. But she still ached for her mother. "I wish you were here," she murmured, feeling comforted by the sound of her own voice.

Exhaustion pulled at her body like gravity, urging her to sink to the ground, to rest. She trudged forward, but at a much slower pace, unable to make herself move any faster. If the average walking speed was three miles an hour, how far could she get before the sun came up? Of course, her ability to walk at a normal speed had faded early on the journey. Now all she hoped for was to get far enough away that they couldn't find her.

The darkness was a hindrance, but it was also absolutely essential to her survival. A few steps into her escape, she had noticed the clear trail of footsteps she was leaving in her wake. She couldn't afford to try to cover them, and when the sun came up, they would provide a direct path to her–wherever she ended up. Flashlights would also illuminate them, so all she could do was put distance between herself and the house on her hunt for civilization–for someone who could help her. So far, she'd seen no evidence of any houses or roads or other structures that might bring her closer to safety.

Not that that was unusual. She remembered flying over the New Mexico desert once. From the plane, the landscape looked like a field of reddish-brown fabric with green polka dots. She knew the dots were actually bushes and they could be pretty massive. From above, the setting seemed as harmless as a blanket covering the earth.

The reality was much different. Walking among the desert foliage, it was easy to get turned around. Thick bunches of creosote bush provided shelter to burrowing animals and created holes that tripped and trapped her as she walked by. Some of the plants were taller than she was, and without the mountains as a reference, the field before her became endless and desolate. The ground itself was incredibly uneven, bearing the scars of erosion from wind and water. Deep arroyos with unstable edges were dangerous even in the daylight. Breaking a bone out here in the dark might seal her fate. She had to be careful.

She still had one bottle of water in her pocket, but she was nervous about drinking it. She didn't know how long she'd be out in the open. Tilly had been giving her larger portions of the meager food and water they'd been provided, but it wasn't enough to keep her alive for more than a day or two. The injuries she'd sustained kept her feeling a bit dizzy and off-kilter—her face had been a primary target for her captors. But she knew dehydration and exposure would kill her just as surely as Mark or Rick would have.

Rick.

His name made her skin crawl. She shook it away, before her mind could conjure images of the unspeakable violation she'd endured. Nightmares flooded her brain in sleep, and she couldn't afford to invite those images into her waking mind, too. As powerful and unyielding as her fatigue, the fear of falling asleep out here, alone, kept her feet moving over the red dirt and rocky terrain.

As her mind wandered, she had to focus on her feet to make sure she stayed upright, but in doing so she often forgot to check the stars that guided her. More than once, she found herself curving and had to correct her course, hopefully in a direction that would lead her to help.

***

Hannah had no idea where she was, but the familiarity of the desert foliage gave her some comfort. It was unfathomable that only yesterday she and Tilly were driving to Albuquerque. Twenty-four hours, maybe thirty-six, and she couldn't even picture how she'd ever go back to the girl she was before.

Assuming she survived.

Hanging out by the hotel swimming pool or going to the Homecoming dance seemed frivolous now. Had it really only been two days since she'd argued with her dad about staying out late after the dance? She remembered how she'd felt—how unjust and unfair it all seemed—and shame filled her core. She'd been such an idiot.

She and her friends had planned to attend Homecoming as a group, but she'd been hoping Caden Summers would ask her to dance. She'd been nursing a crush on her classmate since middle school, and though he always treated her kindly, she could never tell if he liked her back. The thought of Caden's tan skin and blond hair had once made her swoon, but now it tore at her heart. It didn't matter anymore if Caden liked her. Her days as a normal teenager were over.

Feelings of loss and loneliness overwhelmed her, and she had to force herself to focus on her steps like a meditation.

Left foot.

Right foot.

Left.

Right.

"Ow!" She brought her hand up to her mouth, even though her exclamation had been little more than a whisper. A particularly vicious mesquite thorn had gotten hold of her arm and ripped into her flesh. The night air cooled the area where her skin had broken, but there was nothing she could do. She just hoped it wouldn't bleed much. She slowed her movements, trying to avoid more injury to her already battered body.

Her swift flight had developed into a dreary march. In the deepening darkness, everything looked the same. Chaparral bushes, prickly pear cactus, and mesquite trees were unrecognizable dark blobs that grabbed mercilessly at her limbs when she wandered too close. But she worried about staying out in the open. Being close to the vegetation made her feel less exposed.

It was late spring. The day had been hot, but at night, the temperature dropped rapidly. The sweat that had been forming on her skin was now causing her to shiver as it dried in the cold night air. She rubbed her hands quickly against her arms to create some heat from friction, but the warmth was temporary and her arms were too sore to keep up the motion for long.

When the car broke down yesterday, they'd been near the Valley of Fires, an ancient lava flow outside of Carrizozo. She'd always loved that area growing up–the fields of black rock providing a distinct swath of color against the usual desert hues. On trips to Albuquerque or Santa Fe or Taos, her dad often opted for the back roads, stopping at recreation areas and state parks along the way. When people talked about the New Mexico landscape, it was often in terms of the miles of desert, like the place where she now walked, but in her mind, she conjured visions of all the beautiful, unique spots she'd visited that would have turned those bland descriptions on their heads.

The rolling dunes of White Sands National Monument. Full moon nights and sledding down the hills of powdery gypsum.

The beautiful lush wilderness of Gila National Forest. Hiking and visiting the pueblos.

Camping at the City of Rocks. She loved climbing the boulders, but coming down was a little scarier. Her dad was always nearby to create a foothold or simply catch her when her descent got precarious.

When they'd passed by the Valley of Fires yesterday, she'd almost asked Tilly to stop and take a walk, but she'd hesitated, worried Tilly would see the request as an unnecessary diversion from the serious task at hand– getting to the hotel and checking in for the Advocacy in Action conference both Tilly and Hannah's dad would be attending. The delight at getting to ride up with Tilly was enough to overcome the shock she'd felt at being allowed to join them in the first place–just one more sign that Tilly was a positive force of change in their lives.

Tilly.

For a while now, she had been daydreaming about Tilly as her stepmother. She missed her mother intensely, and Tilly would never be able to replace her, but it felt so nice to have Tilly around. To have someone to go dress shopping with and talk to about boys and friends and life, especially when it felt awkward to talk to her dad.

The anger she felt toward Tilly for staying behind while she escaped was intensified by the tremendous love and devotion she now felt for Tilly.

She wondered what would have happened if they'd made the stop. Would they have walked the loop in the hot sun and laughed about their sunburns when they arrived in Albuquerque? Maybe they'd have taken a few steps and decided it was way too hot, opting for a cool dip in the pool at the hotel.

Instead, a few miles later, the car died, forcing them to the side of the road–the first in a series of disasters. Tilly's discovery that she'd forgotten her phone at the restaurant in Alamogordo. Hannah's realization that her phone was out of juice. And then the SUV.

If they'd been on the freeway, there would have been a steady stream of vehicles rolling by, but out on that highway between Carrizozo and San Antonio, the traffic came in bursts. Tilly had gotten out to flag down a passing car, and Hannah wasn't about to sweat it out inside the car, despite Tilly urging her to stay out of the sun. She shoved her useless cell phone in her pocket and leaned on the car next to Tilly.

When the vehicle rolled up behind them a few minutes later, she breathed a sigh of relief, but it was short-lived. When the two men stepped out, baseball caps low on their foreheads and bandanas tied around their face, she knew they were in trouble.

Tilly seemed to know it, too. Telling Hannah to get back in the car under her breath, Tilly started walking toward the driver, but Hannah could hear the tension in her voice. She quickened her pace, but before she could sit down and close the door, the one of the men grabbed her, stuffing a rag over her mouth while she fought and kicked against him. The sour smell of the rag made her stomach roil and her body started to feel heavy.

She'd grasped for anything she might use as a weapon, but all she found were their pizza leftovers and her school water bottle, both of which she ripped out of the car as she was dragged away. Reaching into her pocket, she pulled out her cell phone and dropped it in the dirt, determined to leave a trace. She saw her abductor step on it as he trudged toward the SUV.

As her vision started to blur, she heard Tilly scream.

***

She woke up lying on a dirty mat in the corner of an empty, musty-smelling room. She could have been unconscious for a few minutes or an hour or a day, and the lost time increased her anxiety.

Unsteadily, she got to her feet, wrinkling her nose at a smell she couldn't identify, and walked over to where Tilly lay a few feet away, facing the wall. As Hannah approached, she saw dried blood caked to Tilly's forehead and chin, and an angry scrape across her cheek where it looked like she'd been dragged over gravel. Tilly's chest moved with breath, but she was deathly still.

Scanning her surroundings, she saw a small window high up on the wall, and a door leading to who knows where. The room had the feel of a basement and she decided it was one. A basement that hadn't been used in a long time—mostly empty, with dusty floors and cobwebs in the corners. She spotted a bucket near the door, gagging as she realized what she'd been smelling. The reek of human waste and vomit hit her like a freight truck, and she pushed herself further against the wall, as if trying to evade the stench.

Her gaze drifted back to Tilly, whose body was so still it was impossible to tell if she was breathing. With her back pressed against the wall, she felt what little courage she had leave her. Her heart pounded. Her ears rang. She started to shake, a hot torrent of tears rolling down her cheeks.

"Hannah?' Tilly's voice was weak and raspy.

"Tilly?" she whispered. She sat down beside where Tilly lay and placed a hand on her arm, relieved to feel the warmth of her skin.

"Are you hurt?" Tilly asked without moving.

"No. Can you sit up?"

"I'm not sure I can even move my head," Tilly groaned. Hannah watched helplessly as Tilly struggled to move. Simply turning over onto her back seemed to take all her energy, and the painful grunts she elicited throughout the process sent a sharp stab to Hannah's belly. Tilly finally shifted her position enough to put one hand on the wall.

"Actually, maybe don't," Hannah said. To her horror, she started to cry again. With hot tears pouring down her cheeks, she realized she had never felt so scared in her whole life. It took a few minutes before she was able to curb the tears and regain her composure.

"Help me sit up," Tilly whispered through gritted teeth. Hannah put her arm beneath Tilly's and helped pull her up into a sitting position with her back against the wall. Tilly panted from the effort, resting her head on Hannah's shoulder where she'd settled beside her. Then Tilly's breathing slowed and Hannah realized she'd passed out again.

Unable to move without letting Tilly fall, she let herself cry again until there were no more tears to give. She leaned her head against the cold wall, calming her breathing. Tilly was badly hurt. Would they be able to fight or run if the opportunity presented itself? Looking at Tilly, she wondered what would happen to her if Tilly died.

***

A scuffling sound stopped Hannah in her tracks,

bringing her mind back to the present. She crouched down and listened hard. She'd been so lost in thought, the sound had startled her, but she hadn't been paying enough attention to even know which direction it had come from.

Suddenly, a loud screech sounded only a few feet away from Hannah's right arm. She heard the whoosh of large wings and the cries of some small animal being snatched up by an owl. As the bird rose over the nearby bushes, she saw the briefest outline of its body.

Falling back into a sitting position, she pulled her knees up to her chest and buried her face against her legs. It took longer this time for her to calm her breathing and slow her heart rate. A feeling of utter despair seemed to hold her body in a state of suspended animation. She couldn't move. She couldn't even think about what to do next, and she was so tired. She closed her eyes, wondering if she'd ever had a chance of actually getting away.

Tilly's voice urging her to run played in her mind like a broken record until she put her hands over her ears in exasperation. She wanted to obey. While her initial reaction to finding herself in that basement had been to curl up and wait for someone to save her, their first encounter with the men who'd abducted them had made it perfectly clear they might not make it long. Still clutching her legs, she let her mind wander back to that moment.

***

The door knob rattled, and the door swung open. The two men who had abducted them walked slowly into the room. Their baseball caps were still pulled low over their foreheads, and they wore bandanas over their faces, making it impossible to see any of their features, even the color of their eyes. But they wore the same clothes they'd had on, which made her think not much time had passed. Light poured through the small window, casting shadows that made the men seem even more sinister.

While the taller man watched, the shorter one walked up to Hannah and grabbed her arm, yanking her to her feet. She fought against him, screaming, as he tried to wrap his arms around her jerking body.

"Stop! Leave her alone." It surprised Hannah to hear Tilly's voice. She felt Tilly's hand on her arm, and then Tilly was pulling herself up to stand, using Hannah as leverage. The pressure on her arm was excruciating, but her attacker stumbled, loosening his grip a bit.

Hannah turned her attention to the man holding her, raking her fingers down his arm, feeling both thrilled and repulsed as she felt his skin break.

"Fuck!" he yelled, dropping her to the floor. She looked up in time to see him kick Tilly in the ribs, bringing her back to her knees.

"Stop it!" Hannah screamed, preparing herself to lunge again as the short man kicked at Tilly's prone form. But the taller man got his arms around her. The added height gave him the leverage to keep her subdued.

"Come on." The taller man barked orders. The short one got in one last kick, then turned as the tall man dragged Hannah out the door and up the stairs. She heard the click of the lock behind her and hoped Tilly was okay. The brutality of the beating had quieted Hannah momentarily, but when they emerged at the top of the stairs, she began kicking and clawing again. The tall man held tight.

"Bitches," the shorter man cursed.

The air smelled musty here too, but fresher than it had in the basement. She took a few deep breaths.

"Put her in the room," a new male voice, deep and authoritative, ordered from somewhere out of her line of sight.

The tall man carried her into a small room, shoving her hard through the doorway so she couldn't get her balance before he'd locked the door. She pounded on the door, screaming and pounding until the skin on her fists was raw and red, and her voice cracked. When she stopped yelling, she could hear the men talking. She pressed her ear against the door, trying to hear. Then she lowered herself to the floor and tried peering under the door.

Nothing to see, and whatever conversation was taking place was low and muffled.

She looked around the room. The windows had been boarded over on the outside. There was a mattress on the floor, with a paper bag nearby. She sat down on the mattress, ignoring the smell of sweat and other disgusting bodily odors that seemed to emanate from it.

Picking up the bag, she peered inside. A bottle of water, an apple–old, but still edible–and a meager sandwich were tucked inside.

The sight of the food made her stomach growl. "Probably poisoned," she muttered, opting for the unopened bottle of water instead.

She drank slowly as she inventoried the rest of the room. A closet, doors and rod removed. The paint on the wall was cracked and peeling. A hole in the ceiling tiles with surrounding water damage. That was it. Nothing she could use as a weapon.

Gaps in the boards on the window let light in. As the hours passed, the light changed and began to dim. She finally succumbed to hunger, eating the apple first and then the sandwich, which turned to bologna-flavored glue in her mouth. She washed it down with the last of her water, and then scooted into the corner, resting her head against the wall. No way was she going to lie down on that mattress.

She heard doors opening and shutting, and then more voices. All male. Moving back to the door, she listened closely, hoping to pick up any clues about their captors, even if she wasn't sure she'd be able to use it.

You never knew what might be important–it was something her dad always said. Her stomach twisted, and she pushed thoughts of her dad away. There was no room for happy thoughts in her brain right now, not if she was going to survive this.

At one point, the volume of the conversation increased. She recognized one of the voices as the man who'd kicked Tilly. He was arguing loudly with someone else. She smirked. His pals didn't seem to like him either.

When the house quieted down again, she resumed her position in the corner. She'd almost drifted off when she heard footsteps coming nearer, putting her on high-alert. The door swung open, and the short man appeared in the doorway, this time with his face bare. She pushed her back into the wall, ready to resist being moved, but after a few minutes with him standing in the doorway, staring at her, her hackles rose.

The house was silent behind him. Was he alone? Was she alone with him? He stepped forward, and she could hear his ragged breathing. He paused and looked over his shoulder, then closed the door quietly. That covert action made her tremble with fear.

***

Hannah hoisted herself back to standing. She couldn't sit with the memory of Rick touching her. She had to move.

She started out again, though her legs protested at every step, bringing tears to her eyes. She shouldn't have stopped walking. Shouldn't have given in to her despair. All she'd done was waste time and her aching muscles made sure she knew just how stupid a move it had been. She wouldn't make that mistake again.

For the first time, she realized she hadn't seen anything moving in the sky. The stars shone brightly, but she hadn't noticed the blinking lights of airplanes overhead. Was it significant? She couldn't be sure. The road they'd been driving along when they were attacked ran parallel to the northern end of White Sands Missile Range, a vast tract of land that provided space for routine weapons testing and was known as the infamous site of the first atomic bomb test.

Was it restricted air space? Could she have wandered into the missile range by mistake?

They'd also been close to a huge wildlife reserve, the Bosque Del Apache. The state of New Mexico was covered by national forests and other restricted lands, which limited the traffic in those areas, especially at night.

These thoughts amplified her feeling of isolation. If she was a hundred miles from the nearest house or road, how long would it take for someone to find her? She couldn't walk that far. Not without water. And would Tilly still be alive by then, even if Hannah lived to tell her story?

God, she just wanted to lie down and sleep. To forget this had happened to her. She wondered if death would come peacefully.

As if her mind wanted to punish her for those thoughts, images of what she'd endured in that house filled her mind, reengaging her need for justice. Or revenge.

***

At sixteen, and having a dad who worked violent crime cases, Hannah wasn't naive. She'd had boyfriends. She knew about sex, though she was still a virgin. And she knew about rape, maybe more than any girl should know. But until last night, her knowledge had all been anecdotal. She wished it had stayed that way.

She pushed past some branches as tears streamed down her face. Despite her best efforts, memories of what happened with Rick flooded her mind in terrifying detail. After raping her, he'd beaten her until she passed out and then left her on the mattress. He didn't even bother closing the door. She'd faded in and out of consciousness, and at one point, she'd overheard a blow-up fight between several of the men. It seemed Rick's actions were not condoned, not that anyone had been willing or able to stop him, nor did they seem particularly worried about her wellbeing.

That's when she'd heard their names: Mark and Rick. The men who'd delivered her into this hell. Rick, the shorter one. The man who'd kicked Tilly, and stolen something from Hannah she could never get back.

She was so wrapped up in her thoughts that she didn't see the dark patch ahead of her until the ground underneath her gave way and she fell.

***

The arroyo wasn't terribly deep. She slid down to the

bottom, grasping at weeds and loose clumps of dirt as if they might break her fall. She landed hard, a sharp pain shooting up her spine. Frustrated and angry, she pulled out the bottle of water, which had thankfully stayed tucked in her pocket, twisting the lid and gulping the liquid until she began to cough. Time passed, but for a moment, her more petulant, defiant side was on full display. When she finally relaxed, she felt stupid, but also relieved no one had been around to witness her childishness.

Wearily, she pulled herself up to standing. She'd played in plenty of arroyos in her life, and she was glad she could see over the side of this one. She wasn't sure she'd be able to escape from a deeper trench. Her muscles complained as she found a foothold and hoisted herself up, scratching and clawing at whatever she could reach until her belly slid over the edge and she could take a breath.

Carefully, she crawled away from the edge until the ground felt stable enough to stand on. She retrieved the plastic bottle from her pocket and finished off the rest of the water, using a little of it to rinse some of the dirt away from her eyes. She looked around, trying to decide on the best course forward—one that would keep her heading the same direction she'd been going but keep her well away from the arroyo. She'd need to go a little slower—her body felt ragged and heavy, but she couldn't stop, so she'd have to be more careful.

She took several steps and began to count, distracting her mind from the fatigue she was feeling.

The bushes scraped her arms and the palms of her

hands. The pain felt good. It kept her awake when her eyes began to droop. The burning in her legs and core was less pleasant. It made her want to lay down and sleep. She clung to the empty water bottle like it was gold, crunching the flimsy plastic in her hand as she walked.

Mark and Rick. Rick and Mark. She repeated their names like a mantra to keep them fresh in her mind.

Suddenly, she was flying through the air. She landed face first in the dirt, her foot tangled up in a root. She rolled over and stared up into the sky. Laying down felt good. The starry sky was so beautiful, it hurt her heart. So much splendor in a world that could be so mercilessly ugly. She wanted to stay in that position, but a coyote howled not too far away, so she struggled to her feet.

Could a coyote kill her?

Coyotes were scavengers, or they hunted small prey. She remembered learning something about it in her biology class, and she knew they were skittish. A coyote might not attack her normally, but she felt so tired and done in, she wondered if it would matter that she wasn't dead yet. Would she be able to fight them off? Could she even muster enough energy to scare a coyote away?

Looking up to the sky, she tried to find a constellation that might help her stay on course. When she was little, her dad would take her out at night to look at the stars. She could easily identify Orion, Ursa Major (the Big Dipper) and its counterpart, Ursa Minor (the Little Dipper), Cassiopeia. On a clear night, she could spot more, though she couldn't always remember their names.

Those nighttime star-gazing dates had become rare as her father's career got busier. Between her school schedule and her father's work, it seemed like they barely saw each other. Then Mom got sick and the whole world changed.

Stumbling forward, she thought about her mother. She wanted to cry, but her body was depleted of what little water she'd been able to consume. She clenched the water bottle tightly, feeling it collapse in her grip. The sound seemed to echo loudly in the quiet night.

She froze, listening for signs she'd given herself away, but all she was met with were more sounds of the desert. The wind blowing. The howling. Scurrying feet. And the beating of her own heart as it slowed a bit from the thumping palpitations that pounded in her ears. She staggered forward, but it was becoming harder to keep her mind focused on anything at all. Her spatial aware-ness had narrowed to the most immediate bubble of space around her, making it impossible to anticipate obstacles. As a result, she stumbled along, paying less and less attention to the world around her.

It hadn't rained lately, leaving the red earth soft and pliant under her feet. Her shoes sank into the dirt with each step, but she somehow managed to keep herself mostly upright, though the effort was taking its toll, both physically and emotionally. All she could do was take one more step. Then another. And if she stopped, she knew it would all be over.

Step.

Step.

Her legs felt like noodles, wobbling and shaking with every movement—her knees threatening to buckle. Her strength was nearly gone, and she felt that at any moment her muscles would give out and she would end up on the ground, unable to pull herself up again. A line appeared ahead of her, stretching across the earth like jungle vines. She laughed at the absurd image. In the jungle, vines hung down from trees vertically. Or at least, that's the picture she'd always had in her mind. She wondered if it was real.

When the horizontal vines ahead turned out to be barbed wire, she gasped, a dry breath of excitement that gave her one last burst of energy. A sign of civilization. Something touched and maintained by human beings. If she made it across, she'd be in a new place. A new piece of the desert. Even if it didn't matter, it felt like a victory and she was much too spent to care one way or another. She eased herself through the loose fencing, barely noticing the barbs that dug into her flesh and tore at her clothing. The effort left her breathless. Black spots floated in her eyes, obscuring her vision.

On the other side of the fence, she let her body sag to the ground. Her vision was blurry, as though a film coated her eyes. She blinked, but the surrounding land-scape remained indistinct. Then again, she could see a little further out than she had before. Was the sun finally starting to come up? She was too tired to lift her head, to look for a sign that sunrise was imminent. Hand over hand, she pulled herself a few more feet until her fingers landed on something hard. It looked black, like the Valley of Fires.

With the last of her strength, she rolled to her side, pulling her legs in and making herself as small as she could. She blinked a few more times, but her brain couldn't interpret the input her eyes were sending. The desert had parted. She could see more bushes in the distance, but something kept them from growing here, like someone had cut a line right through the middle. That meant something, didn't it?

In the distance, pinpricks of light grew larger. They reminded her of something from her childhood. A small strand of lights her mother had pinned to her wall. Two little fairy lights floating toward her. But that wasn't right, was it? No. This was something else. Something better, though she couldn't remember what. She smiled thinly; her cracked lips resisting the movement. Her hearing began to fade, dull white noise taking the place of the desert sounds, and she laid her head down on the hard ground like it was a pillow.

She'd made it as far as she could. Whatever happened next was out of her hands.

Read more about Tilly and her sister Kate in Complicit. https://www.amyrivers.com/

About the Author

Amy Rivers

Amy Rivers is an award-winning novelist, as well as the Director of Northern Colorado Writers.

She was named 2021 Indie Author of the Year by the Indie Author Project. Her psychological suspense novels incorporate important social issues with a focus on the complexities of human behavior.

Her most recent novel, STUMBLE & FALL, is the second book in the A Legacy of Silence series.

Amy was raised in New Mexico and now lives in Colorado with her husband and children More on her https://www.amyrivers.com/

Hidden Waters

KARA SMITH

THE TRIP TO KITSAULT, British Columbia was not Sam's idea, and she didn't go willingly. Her mom had said going to the middle of nowhere for the summer would help her "find herself." Sam knew exactly where she was: in the middle of nowhere in the Canadian wilderness.

The drive through British Columbia in a musty Toyota RAV4 that smelled of old people and stale coffee. Sam's Mom had borrowed it from the neighbor knowing that their own broken down junker wouldn't survive the trip. The long haul from their home in Seattle to Kitsault was 20 hours and nearly 1,000 miles of nothing of interest to a teenage girl.

Sam stared out the window, daydreaming of the caramel macchiato she had savored at Starbucks earlier that morning. It was her last taste of civilization before departing Prince George, the only stop on this arduous road trip. However, it wasn't all bleak.

Besides the obvious natural beauty, the highlights of the drive consisted of seeing one moose, three bears, and a lot of deer—which were more populous in these parts than pigeons in New York City. Sam found herself appreciating the views and enjoyed soaking in the beauty of nature, but she didn't give her mom the satisfaction of knowing that. If anything, it was better than going to summer school, which was the other option her mom had suggested.

Sam had spent a few weeks preparing for the trip. Recognizing that she might not have full control over the situation, she decided to gather as much information as possible about what lay ahead. Her natural curiosity was easily satisfied by turning to that pesky technology that adults loathed so much. Her research helped her to not be completely in the dark upon her arrival in Kitsault. This approach helped her satiate her continuous natural curiosity she had all her life.

Pulling up to Kitsault's harbor, she saw it was desolate, as she'd expected, with just one seemingly abandoned building and a boat ramp. But what she didn't expect was the color of the water. No Google search had prepared her for this. Black as night and eerily still for a summer evening. The water was the kind of dark that one looks into and away quickly—in fear of either getting lost in the unknown underneath or falling victim to some watery predator that might suddenly propel out of the darkness and drag one in.

The water was this dark because the sun was hidden by the sky above, which was colored a gloomy grey, a Pacific Northwest staple. The weather was a reflection of Sam's sentiments of her impending isolation. She was taking up residency in a real ghost town; she'd officially be the third resident of Anyox for the summer. The other two residents were her Uncle John and Aunt Mira.

They ran a copper slag reclaim operation in the skeletal remains of the town. The slag was left over from the copper mining that took place over 100 years ago when Anyox was a bustling town of 3,000 Canadian miners and their families. The reclamation process consisted of loading the fine black sand that had washed down from the abandoned mines to the edge of the water onto flat freighter ships to be reused, mostly for industrial purposes. One man's hazardous waste was another man's treasure.

Sam's uncle and aunt were waiting at the harbor, in an alcove near the water. John was her father's older brother who she had only met once at a family gathering years ago. He seemed nice enough, an ex-pat, Afghan war veteran who looked exactly as one would expect. He was tall and muscular, with an air of sad guilt hanging over him, and a thick red beard shaped around his cut muscular jaw. His blue eyes had seen more than many could imagine, which could be why John now preferred nature to people—except for his wife of course. Mira was one of those women who was everything her husband wasn't. Soft features were framed by her light brown hair, with wisps of grey being the only sign that she was in her early 40s. Mira had a kind smile and welcoming demeanor. A certifiable genius, she had been a physicist in her past life and also had a double PhD in Biology. She waved enthusiastically as the RAV4 pulled up. Sam could see the small floating dock where their black Kodiak raft was tied up, overflowing with supplies.

Sam took her time climbing out of the RAV4, cracking her back and stretching her gangly teen limbs. She felt grungy and stiff after the long ride. It was cold by the water, so she buttoned up her red flannel before fixing her shoulder-length, wavy, light brown hair into a make-shift messy bun. Her blue eyes and strong jaw resembled her uncle's; no matter how hard she tried to hide it, she looked very much like her father. Seeing her uncle reminded her of this. *Probably why Mom is glad to get rid of me for the summer*, Sam thought to herself.

"Hi Sue!" John greeted Sam's mom with a big bear hug. "I hope your drive up here wasn't too tedious." His voice was soft and gravelly and, although he was talking at a normal speed, the deep cadence in the way he spoke seemed to slow down time.

"Oh, you know. Twenty hours in a car with a disgruntled 15-year-old, it was just peachy," she said, laying the sarcasm on extra thick.

"Don't talk about me like I'm not here," Sam cut in, removing her earbuds and giving her aunt and uncle a hug.

"Well, you acted like I wasn't here for the last six hours, so we'll call it even, honey." Sue grabbed Sam's pack out of the back of the car, as if anxious to get rid of her.

"Mira, call me if you have any trouble with her. If she goes into shock due to a lack of Wi-Fi, just throw her some beef jerky and back away slowly." Shooting a sarcastic smile Sam's way, Sue handed over a pack of papers with powers of attorney and such to Sam's temporary guardians before turning to Sam.

"I'll be back here to pick you up the last Saturday in August. Please listen to John and Mira and follow their directions precisely. The BC wilderness is no joke, and I don't want you getting eaten by a grizzly," she said, pulling Sam in close to kiss her on the forehead and give her a tight hug.

Despite Sam's full-fledged objections to being there, she hugged her mom deeply, taking in her smell and warmth, knowing she wouldn't see her for nearly two months.

"Love you, Sam."

"Love you, Mom."

Just as quickly as they had arrived, their goodbyes were over and Sam's mom got in the vehicle and drove away.

John grabbed Sam's pack and strapped it down into the Kodiak, covering it with a tarp. Meanwhile, Mira handed Sam water waders with attached boots and a thick waterproof jacket to put over her base layers.

"Put these on, Sam. The ride over there should be mostly smooth, but we don't want to get you all wet and miserable on the first day of your trip."

John and Mira had sent Sam a packing list two weeks ahead of her trip with directions on what to wear and what to bring, including moisture-wicking under-garments and wool socks. Even though it was summer-time, Sam needed the necessities for a temperate rainforest. After donning the waterproof layers, Sam looked down at the dark waters and saw her reflection. She was dressed like a deep-sea fisherman going into battle with the North Atlantic. *If only Mike Rowe were here to narrate my journey*, she thought.

"Grab a seat, and we will get going," John instructed.

Sam took a seat in the mid-section of the raft while Mira helped John push off from the dock. John sat in the back and piloted the dual outboard motors, moving them out of the channel. Mira took a seat next to Sam and put a reassuring arm around her shoulder. As they propelled through the dark glassy water, Sam looked back at the boat dock, watching it get smaller behind them until it disappeared from sight completely—along with the safety of civilization.

It took over an hour and a half by water to get to Anyox requiring they wind their way through the Observatory Inlet around Larcom Island and into Granby Bay. Mira pointed out bald eagles and narrated the journey. The mountains cradled the water. From the edge of the water they reached up, sprawling into what seemed to be endless alpine rainforest scraping the belly of the grey sky and blocking the shy Pacific North West sun hidden above.

Pulling into Anyox after their tour through the inlet,

Sam could see two old smokestacks and a few dilapidated structures. There were huge piles of black slag sand stretching out away from the shore, making the water even darker as the leftover mining sludge from over a century saturating the ecosystem with heavy metals. John pulled the dinghy alongside the large dock to the south of the slag piles, and they unloaded the supplies into a small trailer attached to a robust ATV.

As Sam helped unload, she felt a wave of vertigo hit her. She held onto the trailer, attempting to stop the spinning sensation. She could hear the blood pulsing in her ears, and then a warm hand grabbed her shoulder.

"You okay?" Mira asked.

"I'm dizzy," Sam replied. But as quickly as the feeling had come, it stopped. "Or I was."

It seemed darker outside than just moments before. But it was hard to tell with the cloud cover looming overhead.

"Sea legs," Mira said. "If you aren't used to being on the water, you can feel woozy when you get back onto land. Don't worry, it's normal," Mira assured her.

Sam took a deep breath and grabbed her pack. She climbed into the back seat of the ATV, shaking off the weird dizzy feeling.

They traveled along the shore, heading north beside the black sand slag banks. Passing a large metal shed with an open garage door, she saw a large backhoe, a loader, and another four-seater ATV next to two off-road quads. Just past the shed were large piles of black sand, built up in a circular shape on an area the size of a football field that jutted out into the bay from the shoreside. It looked like an alien landscape compared to the surrounding wilderness.

Looking over his shoulder, John noticed Sam staring at the slag. "A barge comes every two weeks, and I have six hours to pile as much on there as possible before it departs. But at this pace, it's going to take another 20 years to clean all of the slag out of here."

This made no sense to Sam. *Why are they even here performing this hopeless task?* she thought to herself while the ATV crossed a bridge over fast-moving white water rushing down from the mountains. The water smelled fresh and the mist felt cool on her face. The road then inclined up around a steep corner into the woods, and the ATV climbed up the switchback dirt road through the trees. The trees along the road were smaller than the surrounding forest—much younger than the others. A few minutes past the bridge, the trees cleared into an opening along the side of a hill. Foundations of cement and steel structures polka-dotted the landscape in between bushes and rubble piles. They were now in the town of Anyox.

Situated at the end of a clearing, where the hill rose up, stood a container home. As they pulled closer, Sam could see that it consisted of two containers joined to make one large structure, with a third container stacked perpendicularly on top, creating a perfect T shape. The top container had a slanted roof covered in solar panels. The foundational structure of this home was no longer the shipping containers once used for commerce; they had been repurposed and transformed into a beautiful, cozy cabin in the woods with large windows and a deck. The container cabin was painted green to match its surroundings, and it had wood trim to round off the rough edges, softening the boxes into a home.

John pulled around and parked the ATV under the overhang of the top container that projected out, creating a car park for the ATV to protect it from the elements. The inside of the cabin was even more amazing than the exterior. Entering through the back door to the side of the overhang led into a small mudroom where they took off their wet clothes and jackets sticky with salt spray and dust. They hung them up in the built-in cubby spots next to the stackable washer and dryer. Adjacent to the mudroom, conveniently situated, was a small powder room to rinse off and get cleaned up before entering the main home.

Just off the mudroom was a small yet capable kitchen that opened up into an open floor plan, starting with a dining room with a table big enough for the three of them centered on the main floor. Sitting at it, one could look out through the large sliding glass windows that spanned the length of the container wall, opening up to the deck Sam had seen when driving up. On the other side of the table was the living room, complete with two cozy couches, one backed by a half bookshelf stocked with dozens of classics. House plants, driftwood, and netting combined to create a bohemian-southwest-ocean vibe that was reflected throughout the home. Behind the couch that faced the window was an open door, through which Sam could see an office. Up against the wall opposite of the dining table was a black wrought-iron, spiral staircase leading up to the top level.

The only object that did not fit in was a large, black, antique wood-burning stove situated in the corner, where John had already parked himself in front of to start a fire to warm the home for the evening. John took a torch lighter out of his cargo pants pocket while he added wood to the stove. The kindling cracked and creaked as it caught on fire, spreading the smell of smokey burning pine through the home.

"Please stay out of my office back there. There is nothing in there you need to bother with," John said, noticing Sam looking at the open door curiously. Sam nodded in understanding.

Mira grabbed Sam's bag from her shoulder. "Come on, let's show you your room." And she headed towards the spiral staircase.

Sam had never been on a spiral staircase before. It moved a little with each step, and every movement reverberated back into her hand on the outside rail. At the top, it opened up to half the size of the bottom floor, since there was only one container up there, not two.

"To your right is the full bathroom, and just past that is your uncle's and my room if you ever need us. To your left is your room." Mira invited Sam into her room with a welcoming gesture.

Entering the room, Sam found herself at the tail end of the container. The entire wall was one giant window looking out over the woods with a view of the inlet to the left. It was the kind of room one would see in Airbnb advertisements, not in real life. There was a twin bed, a small desk, and a dresser for her things, all decorated in bohemian-modern decor.

Mira handed her a remote and instructed her on how to operate the blackout shades. "You will need this. It stays light until about 10 o'clock right now, and the sun starts to creep up around 4:45. Go ahead and get yourself situated, there are towels in the top drawer of the dresser. I will get cooking, and we can go over some ground rules over supper."

Mira left Sam to herself and her thoughts. The container home was nicer than any place she had ever lived. *Maybe this summer isn't going to be too bad after all,* she thought to herself.

When the trio sat down to dinner, the sun was still up but was low and dimmed behind the grey clouds. Mira had prepared venison with wild rice and oyster mushrooms, accompanied by baby greens she grew in the garden box on the deck and sprinkled with pine nuts she had harvested nearby. John poured Mira a glass of red huckleberry wine before serving himself and sitting down.

"There are only two ground rules," he said, pulling out a little red Garmin inReach Mini 2 radio and setting it in front of Sam. "Rule one. You don't ever leave this structure without this radio. It works anywhere in the world and is connected to satellites. The only way it won't work is if you are underwater or underground."

She picked up the little radio, examining it as he continued. "Rule two. You don't go underwater or underground."

"And how would I accomplish that?" she asked half-seriously, laughing slightly at the idea that she would end up under water.

"Don't go into the mines," he said sternly. "There are miles and miles of abandoned tunnels with drop-off shoots and shafts that go down thousands of feet. Some of them are filled with water, and some of them aren't. But they are dangerous, and you need to stay away from them. Do you understand?"

"Yes," she said, swallowing a bite of deer along with any hopes of real adventure. "So where can I go?" she asked.

"Mira will get you situated on one of the quads tomorrow down at the shed and give you a tour of the full property. I will only need your help when barges come in, so you can help Mira with chores around the cabin. You can spend most of your time however you wish. Despite what your mother might have hoped, I am not going to run a child labor camp around here this summer," John said as he sipped his wine. He turned to Mira with a nod, signaling it was her turn to speak.

"I agree with what John said—always carry your radio, and don't go into the mines. Also, I don't suggest crossing the dam. If you fall in either direction, you won't make it." She looked at John for his approval on this addition, and he nodded in agreement.

"You also always have to have bear spray on you,"

she continued. "We haven't had any trouble with griz-zlies, since this land still seems to deter them because of the toxins and such. But you can never be too careful. I'll get you a can out of the mudroom in the morning."

"What do you mean 'toxins'?" Sam asked.

John looked up from his meal. "Granby Consolidated Mining, Smelting and Power Company didn't really care too much about the environment when they started mining copper in the early 1900s. To separate the copper from the rock they pulled from the ground, they would crush the rock, put it into a smelter, then use chemicals and heat to separate the copper from the ore. This caused acid rain from the sulfuric gas that was created in the process. It covered this entire town, killing everything around. Along with two different forest fires that have wiped out this area in the last century, nothing really ever grows back the same, and some animals tend to still stay away."

Sam looked down at her baby greens and pushed them around her plate, wondering if they were safe to eat.

"You're fine, honey," Mira reassured her, laughing. "I brought that dirt in from the Home Hardware Store in Prince Rupert." She picked up one of the pine nuts and studied it closely. "You would have to eat about a pound of these tonight and every night for six months to get sick. Animals stay away because of multiple reasons, not just the food." Turning to John, she asked, "Since when did teens get so health conscious?" He shrugged in reply.

"Since the three generations before us poisoned the earth," Sam replied.

"Fair enough," Mira agreed and redirected the conversation. "I can't wait to show you around tomorrow, there is some cool stuff to explore out there." Sam nodded with a half-smile.

After dinner, Sam took a long hot shower. During dessert, John had explained that the cabin was completely off the grid. Photovoltaic solar panels collected energy even when cloudy for power and stored it in a home lithium battery. The gutters on the roof caught and stored water in an underground tank, and the wastewater was connected to a septic system. The only source of energy that had to be brought to Anyox was fuel for the vehicles stored in the shed.

Climbing into bed, Sam thought back on her day. This wasn't at all what she had thought it was going to be like. John and Mira were both very different from what Sam had imagined, although they seemed to have their secrets. Why were they here? Given their backgrounds, Sam wondered why they weren't working in some far-off country, saving lives or pursuing other humanitarian endeavors. She shut the shade to her ginormous wall window and laid down on what seemed to be brand-new sheets, softer than she had ever felt before. Hopefully, her curiosity about her new guardians wouldn't become all-consuming so she could just enjoy being a kid and explore this summer—just not underwater or underground.

***

Sam woke up to a loud, vibrating sound permeating through her entire body, as if a phone were vibrating in her brain. The vibration was both unsettling and comforting at the same time. For a brief moment, she felt weightless, as if driving over a rolling bump on a country road. The moment she opened her eyes, it stopped. *It must have just been a dream,* she thought to herself.

It was almost pitch-black in her bedroom, except for a light halo glowing from the edges of the blackout window shade. She reached for the remote and pushed the up arrow. The shade rose slowly, letting bright light spill in and revealing a beautiful day with blue sky breaking through the perpetual marine layer.

Sam could smell bacon being cooked downstairs. She threw on a sweater, pulling it over her messy hair, and worked her way down the spiral staircase as quickly as gravitational forces would allow her. Mira was sitting at the dining table, reading *The Elegant Universe: Superstrings, Hidden Dimensions, and the Quest for the Ultimate Theory* by Brian Greene.

"Some light reading you're doing this morning?" Sam asked while taking a seat at the table.

"I actually pulled this out for you," Mira said. "It's never too early in life to start conceptualizing multiple dimensions. I reread this every year, and even 24 years later, it's still a page-turner."

Taking the book from Mira's outstretched arm, Sam said, "Thanks, I think. I don't know if you're trying to expand my mind or torture me. It's too early." She reached for a piece of bacon.

"Once you're done eating, I'll radio John so he can come get us and take us down to the shed so I can give you the grand tour," Mira said before reaching for the coffee carafe to warm up her cup. "Do you want some? Are you allowed to have coffee?" She poured Sam a cup without waiting for an answer, pushing the tray with cream and sugar towards her. "Just don't tell your mom that I was trying to corrupt you with quantum physics and caffeine on the first full day in our care."

"Your secrets are safe with me," Sam smiled, taking a sip. Mira was growing on her.

When Sam arrived at the shed, John immediately went into full military mode and insisted that she perform a Preventive Maintenance Checks and Services, or PMCS, list on her quad. Mira found it amusing, having gone through the same ordeal herself the first time she took out a vehicle in her husband's care. John even had the paper checklists in a small blue binder—he was deadly serious. Thirty minutes later, after checking the air, oil, filter, blinker fluid (which Sam learned was a joke as it didn't exist), and a dozen other items, she started up her quad and followed Mira away from the slag piles to explore the rest of the Anyox property.

There was much to see, including abandoned buildings that had been burnt to the ground during the fire in 1942. Sam had seen pictures during her online research, but nothing prepared her to see it in person. All the wooden structures were gone, but the steel and cement foundations, along with some fascinating artifacts, remained. One such artifact was the steel buckets they used to hang outside buildings in case of fires. To prevent theft, the buckets were made with pointed bottoms, rendering them mostly useless for anything else. Another interesting item was the light bulbs that had "Stolen" etched into the side of the glass—so that if people took them for personal use, it would be known. Apparently, theft was a significant issue in a remote location with over 3,000 people.

Sam and Mira explored the Power House and the graveyard where many people were buried through the years—children and adults lost in mining accidents or victims of the Spanish flu. This town had seen more loss than Sam could comprehend.

They visited the foundations of some of the Smelter Stacks, the heart of the old mining town. Everything was dead and abandoned, yet also alive and flourishing. A soft velvet of moss and plants thriving in the summer light touched almost everything. The piercing blue sky guided the sun into the open crevices of all the ruins, soaking the foliage in light and creating a sense of serene, fairy-tale beauty amidst the sadness of a past world.

Sam and Mira arrived at their last destination of the day in the mid-afternoon: the dam. It was about three miles up a dirt road past the cabin, deeper into the mountains, with remnants of snowfields from the previous harsh winter polka-dotting the hills above. They parked their quads and began walking towards the dam.

"You sure I can walk on that?" Sam asked Mira.

Mira turned around, smiled at Sam, then continued walking confidently out onto the dam. "I wouldn't lead you anywhere I wouldn't go," she reassured Sam. Mira's adventurous spirit both intrigued and inspired Sam to follow her.

They made their way toward the middle of the dam. Sam couldn't help observing the significant drop of 130 feet to the left and a similarly precarious view to the right, overlooking the dark waters held back by the sturdy cement structure. Despite a hole blasted in its base, the reservoir remained resilient. The dam, constructed in 1912, had once been the tallest in Canada.

Sam gazed at the deep blue, freezing waters nourished by the melting snowfields, finding little solace in the sight. "Didn't you tell me to stay off the dam last night?" Sam asked Mira.

"Yes, but I needed to give you a taste of the forbidden so you aren't likely to pursue something more dangerous," Mira responded.

Sam continued to look down. The small stream trickling out of the hole in the dam below didn't provide much reassurance to her safety. To alleviate her anxiety, Sam decided to concentrate on Mira's footsteps, mirroring every step she took, hoping to minimize the possibility of the dam crumbling beneath them. This place possessed a distinct energy, unlike any other they had explored that day.

After what seemed like an eternity to Sam, they reached the center and settled down, facing downstream towards the inlet. Mira retrieved some seltzer water from her backpack and handed Sam a can.

To feed her curiosity from the evening before, Sam turned to Mira and asked, "What is so special about this place that you and John decided to come up here?"

"You are now sitting where less than 25 people have sat in the last 25 years," Mira said, raising her can for a cheers. "This might not mean much to you now, but when you are older, going to places where people rarely go and being the person who isn't part of the crowd is something to strive for. That's one of the reasons why your uncle and I took this job."

Sam looked at Mira staring off into the openness, trying to convince herself that Mira really wanted to be there—but there was something in Mira's voice that didn't sound quite sure.

Sam didn't believe her.

They sat there, staring out over the forest top sloping downwards towards the water, when Sam was hit with another wave of dizziness. It felt like the world had flipped upside down. This time, it felt like her head had been put in a vise, and there was a pressure like she had never felt before. Sam reached over to grab Mira to steady herself. She took a glimpse at Mira's face, and her eyes were closed with her face grimacing in pain. Then, just like the day before, as soon as the nausea had started, it passed.

Sam let go of Mira's arm and stood up, taking a deep breath. She looked behind her at the reservoir, and she could swear she saw the faintest texture rippling across the water—like the vibration experiment her science teacher had conducted with a pan of water on a speaker to demonstrate what sound waves looked like. Staring in awe at the slight motion over the surface of the entire reservoir, she caught her breath before turning to check to see if Mira was okay, but Mira had already gotten up and was headed back to the quads.

"Mira!" Sam called after her, but Mira kept walking. Sam followed her as quickly as she could. She didn't want to be left on the dam all alone. When she caught up to Mira, who still didn't turn around, she asked, "Did you feel that?"

"What?" Mira replied nonchalantly.

"The seasickness hit me again, but I hadn't been on the ocean. Your eyes were closed too, did you feel it?" Sam asked with concern, thinking maybe she was going crazy.

"You're probably just dehydrated. We've been all over the place today, and you've hardly drunk any water. Let's get you back to the cabin," Mira deflected.

"Your eyes were closed. You felt that, I know you did," Sam said assertively.

"Sam, you're tired. Let's get you back," Mira responded as if Sam hadn't said a word.

"I'm not crazy! I even saw the water move!" Sam

raised her voice, hoping that getting louder would get her point across. She was not only scared but angry that she wasn't being taken seriously.

"No, you didn't," Mira said sternly and turned around, grabbing Sam's forearm and squeezing it to the point of pain while looking her directly in the eyes. With a soft whisper, she said, "You didn't see anything."

Sam felt as if she took a punch in the gut. Mira was not making an observation, but giving her a command.

They went back to the quads without saying another word to each other. Sam was angry and scared all at the same time. She knew now that her dizzy spell the day before wasn't seasickness, and Mira was hiding something and definitely didn't want to be in Anyox herself.

On the way back to the cabin, Sam realized it was much later than she had thought. The sun was slowly disappearing behind the trees, and the coolness of the evening started to creep its way along the dark shadows of the towering pines overhead. Even though they'd had a bluebird day, the dampness of the forest chilled her skin as they cruised down the service road. They had been exploring all day, yet it seemed impossible that they could have been out on the dam for that long. They rode in silence, and Sam took in the different view of the forest as her mind pondered what could be happening.

Not more than half a mile down from the dam, Sam saw a turnoff to a road she hadn't noticed on the drive up because of its angled position away from the road. A metal gate blocked the road and a steep grade up the hillside. She slowed down to take a look at the gate. It was in decent shape and seemed no more than a year old; it was locked with a large, brand-new gold padlock. The apparent newness was nothing like anything else in the ghost town she had seen earlier in the day.

Mira slowed her quad to look back when she realized Sam wasn't directly behind her any longer. To avoid raising Mira's suspicions, Sam hit the gas to catch up and followed her back to the cabin. They parked their quads under the overhang of the cabin, and Sam handed Mira her key.

"Don't say anything to John about the dam," she directed and walked into the mudroom without giving Sam time to ask any more questions.

After dinner, Sam lay in bed staring at the ceiling, questioning whether she should tell her uncle or not, until the exhaustion of the long day took over, and she drifted off to sleep.

***

Sam woke up to a gray glow coming from the window. She had forgotten to shut the window shade when going to bed, and the sun was rising behind the cloud bank. The sunny bluebird sky of the day before must have been a fluke. In Seattle, she would sometimes get beautiful summer days, but they never lasted long. The Pacific Northwest was just the way it was, but at least the weather reflected her mood.

She was deeply conflicted. There was something strange going on in Anyox, and now she was invested.

Sam got dressed and went downstairs. Placed on the table was a note.

Ship coming in unannounced, feel free to get yourself some cereal and come down to the shed when you are ready. - John and Mira.

It was just past 5:30, and the house was eerily quiet. Sam walked around, taking in the silence and looking more closely at the first floor of the cabin. Her eyes were immediately drawn to the office door. She knew she shouldn't go in, but she also knew that there might be an answer to what may be going on. Sam walked over and grabbed the handle to the office door and, only contemplating for a second whether she should abide by her uncle's wishes of not entering, she turned the door handle.

Locked.

Disappointed, she retreated to the kitchen to retrieve a bowl of cereal. Sitting there eating the granola mix with dehydrated blueberries, she stared intently at the office door. Why would her uncle not want her in there? Didn't John know when you tell a teenager not to do something that they will make it a point to disobey those orders? Sam got up, stepped into the kitchen, and rummaged through the drawers. The drawer she needed was three drawers down. The coveted junk drawer. She pushed aside a lighter, rubber bands, a twirly straw, and some hand sanitizer until she saw what she was looking for in the back corner: a heavy-duty paper clip. Exactly what she needed to pick the lock.

She'd learned this on the internet one weekend when she locked herself out of the bathroom. She hadn't thought she would actually be able to do it, but it turned out she was pretty good at breaking and entering. She had wondered if it would turn out to be a valuable life skill.

Sam straightened the paper clip into the proper lock-picking position and went to work twirling and manipulating the clip in the lock. It took no more than a minute for the lock to give in and click. She opened the door cautiously.

This wasn't a normal home office. There was a desk in the corner with a laptop that was connected through the desk, with the cables leading into the wall behind the desk where two three-foot-wide, cone-shaped screens were mounted at eye level. The setup looked like something out of a sci-fi movie. John's military memorabilia counteracted the modern office furniture and lined the wall directly adjacent to the door. Sam saw pictures of groups of men in full tactical gear standing side by side with men dressed in triple robes and head-dresses native to some Middle Eastern country. There was a photo of John hugging a Gatling gun attached to an A10 Warthog with a shark's face painted on the nose. And most interesting to Sam, there was a shadow box with all his military medals and ribbons—so many to look at and admire, none of which she remotely understood. Sam looked at them intently, wondering what they might represent.

Sam decided to get to work and learn more about

her aunt and uncle when she realized this office was hardly an office at all. There wasn't even one sheet of paper or even a post it note. There weren't even any drawers to go through. *So much for snooping.*

Giving up hope of finding any answers, Sam turned to leave. Taking up the entire wall next to the office door was a massive map of Anyox. It showed the entire full area in detailed satellite imagery. On top was a pane of glass, making the map a massive dry-erase board. The map itself was even more detailed than Google Earth. The detail in the imagery was so precise that Sam could see Mira next to her garden boxes. In the bottom right corner of the map, there was a government insignia for the National Geospatial-Intelligence Agency with the words wrapping a logo of the Earth. She wondered why the government would give her uncle this map for just moving toxic sand around. In the bottom right corner was a scale bar starting at six miles and going down to a detailed five feet.

Sam found the main road and traced her finger along the dirt road that lead to the dam. She followed the split in the road she had seen yesterday and traced along with her finger. It dead-ended at what looked like an entrance to a mine. Surrounding the entrance, the area had been completely clear-cut of all trees. She carefully measured the five-foot mark in the scale key with her fingers and estimated the clearing to be 50 feet in every direction around the entrance. She stared at the map intently then stepped back, immediately noticing two other clear-cut areas on the map—together, they created a perfectly symmetrical triangle.

In awe of her discovery, Sam's thoughts were interrupted when she heard a quad coming up the drive. Before stepping out of the office, she realized one of the furniture pieces didn't match any of the others. A grey metal container sitting flush against the wall. It resembled a waist-height dresser without doors or drawers, with only an embossed line cut along the border of the top. Intrigued, Sam wanted to investigate further, but the approaching quad urged her to act quickly. She slipped out of the office, locked the door from the inside, and closed it behind her before rushing back to the table.

Sitting down in front of her now mushy granola, her heart raced with anticipation as the quad entered the clearing. Unsure of who was riding it or who would be entering through the door, Sam noticed that her hands trembled while holding her spoon and opted to put the spoon back into the cereal. Snooping in her uncle's office left her with more questions than answers, eroding her trust in those responsible for her well-being.

John entered the kitchen through the mudroom door. Sam kept her gaze fixed on her mushy bowl, not looking up.

"Hey Sam, I didn't expect you to be up yet," he remarked in his gravelly voice, opening the fridge and grabbing a water.

Sam swirled her granola, hoping he wouldn't notice

its aged state. "Yeah, I'll get dressed and come help," she replied.

"Don't worry about it, we're all done. You can do your own thing today. Just remember to take the GPS radio," John said, walking past her toward the office door, retrieving the key from his pocket, and entering without another word.

Sam held her breath, hoping her actions hadn't left any evidence. She swiftly cleared the table before going upstairs to prepare for her outing. The urge to explore the mine was irresistible. While packing a small bag, she followed John's instructions and grabbed the GPS walkie-talkie, tossing it in. Sam understood that some rules made sense while others didn't, and if she were going underground, the GPS wouldn't work and she wouldn't get caught. *In and out, 30 minutes tops*, she thought to herself.

***

The padlock on the red gate was easier for Sam to pick than the door to her uncle's office. Despite the steep climb up to the mine, she had no issues maneuvering the quad taking her only a few minutes to get to her destination. The clearing that she had seen on the satellite map was still in place. Sam stood at the edge of the mine, looking down the steep sloping shaft into the cold darkness. She could feel the chilled air drafting up, smelling of earth and hard metals. Her heart was beating thousands of miles per minute. She was about to do exactly what she had been told not to do.

The steep path down was recently packed and in better shape than any "abandoned mine" should have been. In fact, it wasn't even dangerous. Walking farther down the tunnel path, the temperature became cooler and cooler. Just as the light was getting nearly too dim to see, a metal walkway appeared with guard rails on either side for stability. Right at the start of this metal walkway was a large electrical handle in the down position. Sam pushed it up with little effort, and the tunnel in front of her lit up in a crescendo of lights placed along the handrail's outer edge, illuminating the walkway so brightly it may as well have been daylight.

She followed the path, which was perfectly straight with a steady downgrade. The earth muted sound so well she could hear her own heartbeat. She walked for more than 20 minutes, maybe equaling what felt like at least one mile, when she came upon a solid metallic wall. Sam looked behind her, contemplating if she should just go back, when a wave of dizziness hit her again. The pressure she felt in her head almost became unbearable, then it released, and she felt her entire body vibrate. It felt soothing, and she felt weightless, like when she had woken up from her dream the morning before. Then the vibration subsided.

Instinctively, Sam shook it off and focused on what was in front of her. She touched the metal. It was freezing cold, almost too cold to touch, and she recoiled as the freezing metal burned her fingertips. While examining her fingers for damage, the metal dissolved into a door-like opening. Sam stepped into a massive room the size of a school gym. White, cold light illuminated directly from the walls. The metal wall re-solidified behind her, leaving her with no exit.

Perfectly-placed metal containers, similar to the one in her uncle's office, were meticulously lined along the floor. The only wall that didn't glow was the one opposite to where Sam had entered; it was completely dark. But the other three walls were lined with futuristic lab inserts from ceiling to floor. There was a ladder in the corner that slid along rails to reach the higher inserts, like in an old college library. Sam examined the labels more closely and saw that the scientific names of animals were marked on each insert. Although she knew she should keep her hands to herself, she touched the outside of one of the inserts. It was as cold as the door, and she recoiled her hand.

"Shit, I need to stop touching things," she said out loud.

The insert slowly responded, ejecting itself from the wall and sliding out smoothly. A cold, smoke-like substance flowed out of the container, like dry ice. Sam blew away the fingers of cold smoke that were hugging whatever was below. She watched the smoke sulk to the floor, revealing frozen test tube-like objects that were marked with male and female biology symbols. The walls were lined with hundreds of thousands of these inserts. Perplexed, she walked down the line to examine further. There was no way John and Mira didn't know this existed. *Why are they hiding it?* Sam thought to herself.

She examined the names of the animals and recognized one that she had learned during the biology dissection lab in school earlier that year: *Felis catus*, a domesticated cat. She noticed that this particular row consisted of all kinds of cats, including *Panthera leo*, *Lynx rufus*, and *Puma concolor*. Looking closer, Sam tried to identify other species down the line.

Suddenly, the white light of the room around her transitioned into a warm yellow. When she turned around, she saw that the dark wall behind her was no longer there; it had been replaced by some sort of vertical tunnel. She could see shadows being cast along the pitted dirt on the other side. The massive shaft was being illuminated by the warm yellow light from below, and she could tell it was getting brighter.

Sam walked slowly past the metal boxes for roughly 45 feet and reached the edge of the shaft. As she carefully leaned forward to look down, she was blown backward by a punch of air. A wave of dizziness hit her simultaneously, but it passed quickly. She pushed herself up to her feet and watched as a massive ball of brightly glowing light filled the space. Seeming to be observing her, the perfectly symmetrical orb, about the size of a VW Beetle, hovered in front of her, nearly blinding her with its warm light. She shaded her eyes, and in response, the ball dimmed its light, revealing a metallic surface identical to the metallic material that made up the lab room. Her entire body began to vibrate. Sam took several steps back, not knowing what it would do next, when she heard her name being called through the buzzing sensation filling her head.

"Sam! Sam! SAM!" the voice called out.

She turned around and saw her uncle standing in the room, in the spot where she had entered. She rushed towards him and he urged her to move faster. The orb behind her reverted back to its original brightness and continued to illuminate brighter. Sam could feel the light blazing into her back. John stretched out his hand, grabbed her arm, and pulled her out of the room. The door materialized back into its wall form microseconds after she rushed through. John picked her up and held onto her tightly, stepping onto a board floating above the ground.

"Hold onto me and don't let go," he instructed as he leaned forward.

They took off at an incredible pace. All she could hear was the wind whipping by her head, which had stopped buzzing the moment they moved away from the metal wall. They reached the end of the metal walkway in less than a minute. John stopped the hover-board and put her down, picking up the board and carefully setting it behind one of the handrails before shutting off the large power switch. The tunnel below disappeared into darkness. He turned toward the exit of the mine tunnel, and she followed him up the steeply graded part of the shaft.

"You have a hoverboard?" Sam asked timidly, trying to keep up.

"You aren't really in the position to be asking me questions, Sam," John responded sternly as he stopped and turned to face her. "You were explicitly instructed to stay out of the mines," he barked in a militaristic cadence and immediately pivoted back to his mission of getting out of the tunnel. They exited into the clearing, and John turned to Sam as she emerged.

"How did you know I was here?" she asked.

"I have a GPS monitor on that Garmin radio, and when it goes quiet for more than ten minutes, I get alerted to where it last pinged."

He pulled his phone out of his back pocket and showed her the screen. She looked down at it, avoiding eye contact.

"You have no clue what kind of mess you just created for yourself. Do you?" he asked. She shook her head no. "Let's get you back to the house, we have to have a talk," he said, climbing into his side-by-side. "Let's go, I'll follow you." He motioned to her quad.

She jumped on and headed down the hill towards the house as directed. *Did that really just happen? Did I just see extraterrestrial life?* Sam asked herself.

***

Sam sat at the kitchen table while her uncle and aunt argued outside on the deck. She wondered why they were arguing outside, since she could hear them clearly.

"She isn't ready," John said.

"They connected with her the moment she set foot on Anyox soil, and you should have seen her at the dam yesterday," Mira explained.

"We already knew that was going to happen. There's no reason to rush things. And why did you take her to the dam? She hasn't even been here for three days."

"We have to tell her, John. We have to get this moving. We can't miss out on this opportunity."

John stood there staring at Mira for what seemed like an eternity before walking off the deck. Sam continued to sit quietly, not sure of what to make of the situation. Obviously, they knew what was going on.

Mira came back into the cabin and sat down next to Sam at the table. "Remember the book I gave you yesterday?" Mira asked softly.

"Yes, what does that have to do with the fact that you have extraterrestrials in the basement?" Sam asked.

"It has everything to do with it. But to spare your head from exploding, let me give you the CliffsNotes version, specifically on string theory. The idea is that everything that creates existence is interconnected by strings, not just particles such as atoms and photons. Do you remember when they taught you X, Y, and Z in geometry?" Mira asked.

"Yes, it's how you can measure a sphere in three dimensions."

"Precisely! It's how you measure what is seen in three dimensions: up, down, left, and right. It's proven and accepted." Mira headed to the kitchen, grabbed a dry-erase marker from the drawer, and using the window glass as a whiteboard, she drew her descriptions with precise accuracy. "Shifting back to the concept of string theory, or more like the superstring theory, there are seven other dimensions, ten in total. The fourth is time, although we measure this regularly, it has yet to be proven. The other six theoretical dimensions, which I'm not going to try to explain right now, make up ten dimensions. If this could be understood, then the mystery of how and why the universe exists and how to control it would be answered."

Sam stood up and looked at Mira's drawings. "Even gravity?" she asked.

"Even gravity," Mira confirmed.

John came back in through the mudroom door, holding a metal binder in his hand. He spoke from behind them, "Sam, are you getting it?"

Sam turned around and responded, "Did the aliens figure out the superstring theory?"

"They aren't aliens, Sam. They are us from another dimension. We don't know how they were able to figure out string theory, but they have been detected and part of our world ever since we detonated the first nuclear weapon in 1945," John said.

"Why are they storing animal DNA in the mine?" Sam asked.

"They have plant and humanoid DNA in the other two vaults," John responded.

"Are you referring to the other two marked locations on the map, forming a triangle?" Sam inquired.

"You went into my office?" John asked.

"Yes. But are you going to be more mad about that or focus on the real issue here?" Sam asked. Remaining composed and calm, she repeated her question. "Why are they stockpiling the DNA?"

John and Mira exchanged glances. John walked over and set down the metal binder on the kitchen table. On the outside, the binder was labeled "Samantha Ludlow," Sam's full name. John opened the binder. At first, it looked completely empty, then a three-dimensional holographic image of Sam as a baby in the hospital appeared. Her exhausted mother held her while her father embraced them, with doctors and nurses passing by in the background. John motioned with his finger along the bottom of the binder, and the hologram accelerated, revealing Sam as a toddler in a black dress and hat, holding her mother's hand in front of a coffin draped with an American flag. John accelerated again, taking them to Sam in the RAV4 driving through the Canadian wilderness. With one final swipe, the hologram showed her standing in the DNA vault, staring at the glowing orb in the tunnel just an hour earlier.

"How did they see all of that?" Sam asked.

"The dizzy spells you have been having, the vibrations, the pressure, it was them downloading your memories, even the ones you can't remember. They do this with anyone they trust, and it's also how they communicate."

"What do they do with those they don't trust?" Sam asked.

"They simply leave them alone, never revealing themselves," John answered.

"But why stockpile the DNA?" Sam asked yet again.

"We don't know," John explained. "They have been working on this particular project for many years. This is Project Anyox, and they have had a few others throughout their time on Earth, but this one is different."

"Why?" Sam asked.

"Because it involves you. They have chosen you," Mira said.

"What? Why did you bring me here? Does my mom know?" Sam asked in a slight panic. "Chosen me for what?"

"They have asked to take you back to their dimension and they need to do it soon," John said.

"Does my mother know you are about to traffic me to an alien race?"

"Yes, your mom knows. She and your dad were the caretakers here in 2005-2008, just before you were born. We think that's why they have chosen you," Mira said softly, trying to calm Sam in her distress.

"Are you saying you knew this was going to happen?" Sam wailed.

Sam stood up. It was too much information to take in. She rushed up to her bedroom and lay down on her bed, trying to process the news. She lay there for over an hour, feeling exhausted from everything that was taking place, when Mira knocked on her door.

"Sam, we need you to go," she pleaded from the other side of the door.

Mira cracked the door and continued to speak. "In the 78 years they have been interacting with us, you are the very first person they have ever wanted to take back. You have to go and learn from them and help us understand how they do what they do. Our entire existence could depend on it."

"Will I come back?" Sam asked nervously.

"Everything they have communicated has always been honest and kind. We don't have any reason to believe that they wouldn't bring you back someday," Mira assured her.

Sam turned around and looked her aunt in the eyes. "Will this get me out of having to go to school next year?"

Mira laughed at her niece. "I would suppose so," she said, giving Sam a tight hug.

"Let's get you a good meal, and then we will show you why we forbade you from going underwater."

***

After her meal, Sam called her mom and said good-bye. Then John, Mira, and Sam got into the ATV and headed up the road to the dam. The sun was just starting to set. Instead of going up to the top of the dam, they took a lower road to the bottom where the water from the hole was released into the stream below. The dam looked very different from this view.

John parked the ATV near a wooden door in the canyon's side wall. The three of them entered the door, and John switched on the lights, revealing the walls of the hallway and floor constructed of smooth, cold cement. They took a left and then another left, walking 100 feet into the base of the dam. John stopped and touched the cement surface, and a doorway opened into a cool, white glowing room. It wasn't much different from the DNA lab, just smaller and with nothing on the walls. There was only one metal container instead of many.

The far side wall was completely dark. John took out his flashlight and pointed it toward the darkness. Sam saw a large rainbow trout caught in the light; it scurried away in the opposite direction. Like in the DNA lab, the wall wasn't a real wall. Mira went to the metal box and touched the top. It opened, revealing a small, 1-inch-diameter, round metal disk. Mira picked it up and, grabbing Sam's hand, placed the disc on her wrist. Mira then laid her own hand on top of the disk.

"I want you to think and say 'space suit'," she directed.

Sam did as she was told, and a sleek white and grey space suit materialized around her body. Sam was amazed as she examined her new outfit.

"What happens now?" Sam asked apprehensively.

"Give it a minute, they will show up, and then it will be time for you to go," Mira responded.

John walked over and gave his niece a long hug. "I'm sorry we didn't get to spend more time together.

When you come back, this world will be a different place."

"It already is," Sam commented.

Mira looked at her niece with admiration. "You are going to change the direction of mankind, and I'll be waiting here for you when you get back."

The white light of the room transitioned into a warm yellow, and the orb emerged from the depths of the lake. The light wasn't blinding this time. It felt inviting and filled Sam with curiosity rather than fear. She took one last look at her uncle and aunt before approaching the orb. She saw that it was miraculously breaking the plane of the room without letting one drop of water in. Appearing from within the orb, a human hand stretched out. Sam reached out and took the hand's welcoming embrace. The orb grew brighter and brighter as Sam dissolved into the structure. John and Mira watched the orb pull back, ascend, and disappear into the hidden water without out a trace.

Sam's journey was just beginning, and the human race would soon have her to thank for its survival.

About the Author
Kara Smith

Kara Smith is a career intelligence analyst and Air Force OIF/OEF Veteran. After separating from the military she continued her work in counter-terrorism first at the NSA and later working at the FBI.

Kara has dedicated herself to the pursuit of hunting

criminals worldwide. Her expertise in intelligence began serving in the United States Air Force deploying to both Iraq and Afghanistan. This is where she honed her expertise in various fields, including SIGINT and All Source Analysis. Throughout her career, she has served esteemed organizations such as the National Air and Space Intelligence Center (NASIC), National Security Agency (NSA), Air Force Office of Special Investigation (AFOSI), Federal Bureau of Investigation (FBI), and other law enforcement entities from coast to coast. Find out more about her consulting here: https://karasmith consulting.com/

When she isn't busy being a workaholic she is a single mother, an outdoor adventure addict, a movie buff, and an animal lover. You can find her shiny new author website here: https://karasmithbooks.com/

Lakeside Lodge

SONJA DEWING

THE TIRES CRUNCHED on the old gravel road. Even though the previous owner had never upgraded it, it didn't matter to Sarah. As she came around the curve of the trees, the charming stone facade of Lakeside Lodge appeared. She parked and stepped out of the car, and it hit her, all of this was hers.

Three lodge buildings, a restaurant, and acres that included a lake. She took a deep breath. The place smelled of pine trees being warmed in the late spring sunshine.

Many of the windows stared out at her with empty space. Even though she knew she was alone here, she'd have to shut all those curtains so she wouldn't feel so exposed when she was outside. But it would give her a chance to see each space for herself and think about how she would upgrade this place and make it spectacular.

She'd start with the main lodge first. She unlocked the double doors and threw them open.

"Damn it." The previous owner hadn't even taken down the Christmas decorations. A giant fake Christmas tree reached up to the high ceiling. The pictures that had been on the sales page must have been promo pics from before the last holiday season.

Although, it did bring back sweet memories. She remembered when she was ten, coming with her family in late January, and the holiday decorations were still up. It had rankled her mother.

"Henry, I can't believe this. Are you sure you want to stay here? It doesn't seem as if they keep things up if they're going to leave holiday decorations up this long?"

Her dad had talked Mom into staying, and Sarah had loved it. The sparkles and the feeling of home away from home. She was sure that was why she came here every year. She preferred to come in the summer, though, when there were few people around, the ski season was over, and she could quietly lounge by the pool or the lake.

Her phone unexpectedly dinged. There were a few isolated places where one could get cell service; this must be one of those spots. She glanced at it: a text message from her ex-boyfriend.

When you're ready to come back, I'm here for you. - Josh.

. . .

She deleted the message and smiled. She was quite happy where she was. He would be waiting a long, long time before she'd ever return.

She moved toward the front desk. For the last few years, even though she had never thought she'd ever own this place, she had imagined redesigning the front desk area. As an interior designer, she did that a lot. She imagined finding old barn wood and placing it on the back wall in clean lines and a handmade wood sign. But wait, Lakeside Lodge was the name it had always had, but she could change it to whatever she wanted.

Maybe "Sarah's Secret" or "Sarah's Hideout," But those seemed too specific to her.

She jumped at the sound of someone sneezing. Her heartbeat shuddered as a shadow moved at the open front doors.

A man was standing in the doorway. He was wearing baggy jeans and a zip-up grey sweatshirt with the hoodie up.

She wanted to kick herself. She knew from experience that she should never go anywhere without something to protect herself. She wrapped her hands around her keys, slowly pushing them in between her fingers.

"Who are you?" She asked, an edge in her voice.

"Sorry. Didn't mean to scare yah. I'm Doug; I was the caretakeh here. I came over to drop off my phone numbeh in case anyone was actually going to buy the place. Didn't realize you were here until I walked up the road."

Did he? Or had he been watching for a car to come up the driveway?

He set a piece of paper on the table by the door. Sensing her unease perhaps?

As he stepped away from the bright sun, she could see more details.

He had dark brown hair, maybe in his thirties. "You seem to be a bit young to be a caretaker." She said.

He laughed. "I worked as a pahk rangeh in Massachusetts right out of college. I like being outside a lot. And I like how quiet it can get around here."

The tension in her shoulders relaxed just a little, but then she realized how very secluded she was out here and maintained her distance from the stranger. She leaned against the counter but pulled her hand away as the wood on the edge was rough.

"What kind of work do you do exactly?"

"Old Sam was a cheapskate, so he never let me do much. If somethin' was falling apart, he'd hire me to fix it. But, I can fix and build almost anythin', and I've done my share of carpentry." He stepped back out into the sun. "Just call me if yah need anything. Just.. well, be careful at night. I've heard of ghosts roamin' the hallways." Then he walked away.

Sarah followed him out onto the porch and watched him turn right and walk into the woods, and then disappear. Maybe she should open the lodge soon so that there were people around, but she'd have to hire staff and she wanted to make this place shine before people came back. It was important to her that this place had the look of new management and a new lease on life.

Sarah went back to her car to check on the cat. Kalie was curled up on the front seat. Sarah had left the windows open just enough to let the cool, morning mountain air in.

She grabbed her pepper spray from the glove box and put it in her back pocket, just in case.

As she walked up the stairs to the top floor she thought about what he had said about ghosts roaming. She had been here every year of her life and knew more hiding places and hidden corners than anyone. She had definitely had some weird ghostly experiences here, but none that were bad enough to keep her away from this beautiful location. Besides, humans scared her more than ghosts.

A single knock made her turn around. It was coming from the outside wall of the lodge. That side was facing the sun. Probably just one of those noises an old place makes when it heated up.

She selected a music app on her phone and turned up the volume.

Right now Sarah needed to open up the room that would be hers. At the top of the stairs, on the fourth floor, was the room she had seen as a kid.

In the last couple of years, she had stayed in the newest building, never being able to get a reservation for the room at the top of the stairs. As she reached the top, she found a wood wall was now blocking entry to the fourth floor.

There was no door. There was no elevator and other than the emergency exit through a window, there were no other stairs. She wondered when it had been closed off.

The broker had said that some rooms had not been used in years because the owner had neither the money nor the time to update or maintain the whole complex. It was a shame he had chosen this floor, her favorite.

Sarah dashed downstairs to get the tools out of her car. As she opened the trunk, an ice cube tray fell out. She hadn't even realized she had packed it. Seeing it filled her with anger again. It was a symbol of her empty career and her empty relationship. The final straw.

It had been just two days ago. She had gotten home from a long day at work to find the garbage in a bag on the front porch because Josh was too lazy to take it all the way to the trash can. Then walking in to see he had cooked himself a hotpocket, part of it still on a plate on the counter. All she wanted was a cold drink and to put up her feet.

To pull that ice cube tray out of the freezer and find it empty. Empty! Was just the last straw.

She had decided right then that she was done with Josh, gone to her computer to reserve time at her favorite spot in the Pocono mountains in Pennsylvania, and then saw it was for sale. Why not? She thought.

Now, she wondered if maybe she had been too hasty, but here she was. She was going to make this place hers.

She threw the tray back into the trunk and grabbed the tools.

Upstairs she inspected the wood panels. They had been screwed together, so using her electric screwdriver she removed each one until finally the pieces fell slightly open. She kicked one of the pieces out of the way and a cloud of dust filled the air and filtered through the sunlight. She swore she heard a gasp as the wood fell, but it had to be the wood falling against the floor.

Sarah put on a mask and a pair of protection glasses, eager to see the room. Straight ahead she opened the dark wood door.

Surfaces had been covered with sheets. The furniture was there— all of it from the 70s and she'd replace it all. It was the gable she loved. The slope of the roof coming down at the end of the wide room, leaving a perfect spot for a window seat where she could sit and relax and look out over the green property. And there was the balcony that extended out from the roof that only this room had access to. Her own bit of heaven would be this room.

There was also the old hiding cubby in the wall. She opened it up. It was too small for her to fit into anymore. Maybe she'd open it up and display the treasure she had found there so long ago. But that was a project for another time.

It was getting warmer outside so she went downstairs and nabbed the cat, who looked around as if suddenly realizing they were somewhere new. Sarah put her in the janitor's closet with food and a litter box.

Then, with her protection gear still on, Sarah pulled down her room's curtains, uncovered the furniture, dusted and vacuumed, and stripped the bed of the old sheets. By the time she was done it was lunch time and she realized she hadn't ever stopped for groceries.

First, she cleaned the floor of the layer of dust from her door to the stairs, then made her way back to the car. She had passed through a small town on the way with a Stop and Shop. She'd run there for whatever she could find.

Twenty minutes later she reached the store. While she sat in the parking lot, she took advantage of the cell phone service and made some calls to the internet and phone companies.

Walking into the store, she realized she'd made a grave error. She had no idea what kind of cooking facilities were on her property. Sure, there was a restaurant, but was the stove gas? Was it hooked up? Was there an employee break room in the main lodge with cooking facilities?

She spotted an aisle of camping equipment and picked out a camp stove and some camp pots and pans. She choose soup and cheese and crackers and plenty of cat food.

The blonde woman behind the counter shook her head. "Oh hun, you going camping? The weather isn't supposed to be so good."

"No. I just don't know what I have to cook with. I bought the Lakeside Lodge and I forgot to even see if there's a microwave."

The woman smiled. "Oh, well welcome. My name's Laura. Old Sam didn't come in here often, he normally ordered all his food through some big shipping company."

Sarah realized she had a lot to learn about running the lodge. For a moment she felt overwhelmed.

Laura patted her arm. "I'm sure you'll get it all figured out." Then continued to scan Sarah's items. "And I see you have a cat. Have you seen this?" Laura pulled out what looked like a small dog harness. "My husband, in his infinite wisdom, bought these ridiculous harnesses for cats. As if anyone around here walks their cats. But we're giving them away for free now. I'll add it to your bag."

Sarah smiled at the idea of walking her cat. But then again, maybe. She had always been more of a dog person. Kalie had been her friend's cat until Charles had suddenly decided to travel to India and couldn't take the cat with him.

Back at the lodge, Sarah set the groceries on the front counter and let Kalie out of the janitor's closet. Kalie gave a look of displeasure.

"Look Kalie, I didn't want you wandering around without me here."

Sarah shivered, it was cold in this rambling building. She ran up the stairs to her room to grab a sweatshirt. Kalie wasn't following, so she went back down and picked her up. "Come on, you can see our new room."

Sarah jogged up the stairs and as she reached the top flight Kalie was making a sound she had never heard before. It was a high keening, almost like a tornado warning siren. Sarah looked down to see Kalie's eyes were glued to the top of the stairs and when Sarah reached the top, Kalie went wild in her hands. Sarah let her go and Kalie galloped down the stairs.

"Kalie!" Sarah watched the cat go all the way down and then sit on the bottom of the stairs. "What the heck."

Maybe Kalie was just wound up being in a new place. Uninvited, Sarah remembered watching Kalie stare intently at a corner of the apartment and her mother musing if cats could see ghosts. Sarah shook that thought away and grabbed her sweatshirt. She wasn't going to let that spook her, and if she came across any ghost again, she'd figure that out later.

Standing in the room, she remembered why she had hidden in that cubby at ten years old. Late at night, she had snuck out of the room to see the Christmas tree. Then the stairs had beckoned for a little adventure, to wander around. On the top floor, a voice from nowhere had whispered and had sent her running into the only room that wasn't locked.

She had looked for a place to hide, still hearing the word "gold" whispered in the hallway. She had fallen sideways into the wall and the wall panel had popped open to reveal a space just her size. She had crawled inside, grabbing a rock off of the floor in her way and putting it in her lap. Closing the panel, it had gotten dark, but she couldn't hear the whisper anymore.

Sarah took a deep breath and smiled. That had been

a long time ago, and she had been sure it was some adult playing a prank on a nosy kid.

She had sunk a lot of money into this place. And, even though she still had her treasure, she wasn't sure what to do with it. She had taken it from this house all those years ago. Did she own it now because she owned the house?

In any case, she wasn't going to let anything stop her now. Besides, it was just the cat being weird.

At the bottom of the stairs, Sarah shook her head at Kalie. "The sooner we get this place in shape, the sooner we can fill this place with people and sound."

Sarah set out the camp stove on the front counter and cooked her soup. She'd figure out the cooking situation later, she was too hungry to wait.

The sound of something like wood breaking upstairs echoed through the lobby. A shiver went through her as she looked up at the top floor.

Ghosts don't break things, right? She had her pepper spray in her hand as she walked up the stairs.

"Hello?" Sarah called.

She walked from one end of the top floor to the other, disturbing the dust on the floor. No one else was up here. Sarah approached one of the windows covered with a board that was broken. It had to be the window with the emergency exit ladder outside, she was sure of it.

The board appeared to have been broken from the outside. Sarah dashed down the stairs and then ran around the building. She stopped when she thought she saw a dark shape running into the woods. Was that her imagination?

Had someone been trying to break in?

Over at the back of the house, she found the emergency exit. The metal ladder that was only supposed to extend when someone was standing on it was touching the ground. Another thing to get fixed.

She climbed up the ladder to the top window. From there, it was obvious that someone had been pushing on the wood to try and get in. This was no ghost.

At the bottom of the ladder, she tried pushing the extension up, but it was rusted in place. She brushed off the bottom of her pants from the cobwebs she had collected from the ladder.

Back inside the lodge, she went to the boarded window and hammered nails into the board, hoping it would hold if the person came back.

She stalked back downstairs and ate her meal while keeping her eye on the stairs.

***

She set the cat harness on the counter and considered it. It would be nice to get some fresh air and maybe the exercise would unwind her and the cat's stress.

She took Kalie outside and spent a few minutes figuring out how the harness went on. Kalie took one step, wobbled, and then fell over. Sarah rolled her eyes. As if putting on a harness had made it impossible for the cat to walk.

"You ridiculous cat." Sarah looked over the land and the buildings. She was going to need a lot of help getting all of this looking good. Luckily, she did have enough money to sink into fixing up the place.

Kalie was walking again. This time she made it five steps before falling over into the grass. Then ten. Then twenty. Sarah let her lead the way. They went across the open grass to the wooded area.

Up ahead was a dilapidated two-story house. The windows were broken and she could see through some of the wood planks in the house.

"Oh!" Maybe she could find some old wood that would work behind the counter at the lodge.

She picked up Kalie and walked softly toward the house. She didn't want to disturb the quiet and peace that she felt here. The front door was lying in the front yard, stripped of its hinges and doorknob.

Through the door, she could see a wall of dark wood. The wood would be perfect for the back wall of the lodge, but first, she'd have to tear it down, carefully. She stepped inside the first room.

Old furniture sat with a layer of dust, one plastic chair lying on its side. A lamp still sat upright on an old table. More shocking than the old furniture that had been abandoned and had once been beautiful was the carpet of half-smoked cigarettes. These weren't that old.

They had definitely been smoked by the same person. Each one had been smoked halfway through, then crushed. From the looks of it, someone had crushed them against the white wall next to her that was covered in small dark circles.

Then she smelled cigarette smoke. Not the lingering scent of the pile of old cigarette butts, but fresh cigarette smoke. She stepped quietly forward and looked through the breaks in the walls. Instead of sunlight on the other side, she saw a man. She couldn't see his face. There was a jacket and a touch of grey hair. It wasn't the caretaker. A black jacket with pockets, and the flaps of the pockets were sticking up. He was just standing there. Did he know she was there?

She gripped the cat closer and wrapped her hand around the pepper spray in her pocket.

Sarah stepped back quietly. As she turned at the door, the floor creaked loudly. She would be exposed anyway, so she said, "Who are you? Why are you on my property?"

There was silence. She moved back to where she could partially see him. "Who are you?"

He tossed his cigarette to the floor and turned to walk out. She exited the house and stood outside as he came out the front door. His scruffy, grey beard was a contrast to his clean black jacket. She noticed he had cobwebs on his pant leg.

His face was emotionless as he spoke. "I didn't know anyone owned the place yet. I'll get out of your way."

He walked away, toward the road.

Sarah watched him go, and then she headed back to the lodge.

"Shit." What had she gotten herself into? From the

dust on his pant leg, she was sure he had been on the ladder earlier. She went inside and locked the front door, then went through every room on the bottom floor to make sure the windows were closed and locked. She also took the opportunity to shut the curtains. On her locking spree, she found the owner's room.

He had left most of his furniture, including a lamp that looked like a woman's leg in stockings wearing a red high heel. The lampshade was the perfect match. Red with long frilly tassels. And there was a kitchenette. It had a built-in microwave, a two-burner stove, and a toaster oven. She'd move her cooking things here and in the future, turn this into the breakroom for all the workers.

She also found the old library. She had fond memories of sitting in here and reading Dancing Shoes for the first time. It was also where she had found another of the hidden doors. She tucked a tall, thin hard bound book under her arm titled, *Lakeside Lodge*.

***

Sarah spent hours cleaning up her bathroom of cobwebs and dust. Luckily, the plumbing seemed to work okay. She cleaned up for dinner and headed to the lobby. She was hungry but she wasn't looking forward to more soup.

A knock at the front door made her heart skip a beat, but when she saw Laura from the store, her shoulders relaxed a bit. The tantalizing scent coming from the casserole dish in Laura's hand made Sarah's stomach rejoice.

"Hun, this is a welcome gift. My ham and noodle casserole will warm you up and keep you going."

"Oh!" Sarah gladly took the still-warm dish. "I don't have anything ready for visitors, but we can find some space if you want to join me for dinner."

"Love to." Laura followed her in.

Sarah took her to the owner's room where at least there was a cleanish couch.

Laura pulled out a bottle of wine from her bag and a couple of wine glasses. "I don't know if you drink, but I hate to drink alone."

"Laura, you are awesome! I will definitely join you in a drink."

Within moments of opening the casserole dish, Kalie strolled in. There were cobwebs clinging to her whiskers and dust in her fur. Laura swooped her up into her lap and wiped off the debris. "Oh, your cat. So sweet."

Sarah nodded and then took a big bite of the casserole.

"Laura, you are a lifesaver."

Laura smiled. "My mom used to make this casserole whenever we had family visiting. It was always everyone's favorite meal. I'm glad you enjoy it."

"Laura, is there anything you can tell me about this place?"

Laura nodded. "My grandad was a coal miner out here. He used to tell stories about the people who stayed here at the lodge. The rich folks who owned the mines, or travelers thinking they could make it rich somehow."

"What about a ghost?"

"Oh yeah." Laura looked around the room as if one was going to appear. "There've been lots of rumors about ghosts."

A wind whipped at the building and made a mournful sound, seeming to agree with Laura.

Laura continued, "Most of the speculation is it's a miner from the 1900s. George Deme was a local, caught in the house trying to steal something. The owner at the time, a woman, shot him where he stood. Rumors were that he's always looking for something to steal."

"Great, well, I guess I'll see if he's looking for anything tonight. And, do you know a local named Doug?"

"Doug Hanson, sure. He's a good egg. When our porch was starting to fall in, he came over and fixed it like new." Laura laughed. "You could definitely use him around here."

Sarah laughed too. Laura was certainly right about that.

***

As the sun set, Sarah emptied her car.

Then she found the one location in the house that had cell service and gave Doug a call. He'd be over in the morning to get to work.

She double-checked the windows, made sure Kalie knew where her bed was, and made her way upstairs.

She took a hot shower and put on her softest PJs.

As she sat on her bed, Sarah paged through the Lakeside Lodge book. It was the history of the place dating all the way back to 1903. But, it had been famous for a local find. The hand-drawn picture was exact.

Sarah gasped. It was her treasure! The gold nugget had been found in the local creek by the owner, Madelyn Grange. The nugget had been worth a fortune. There was a rush of gold diggers, but the rare find was just that. Only a handful of nuggets, much smaller than the original, were ever found. The book went on to say that it was soon reported missing.

Missing, Sarah wondered. Had Madelyn hidden it away in the cubby only for it to be found by a ten-year-old almost a hundred years later?

Sarah dug into her luggage and pulled out the nugget. All this time she had really just joked to herself that it was a treasure. She had always wondered if it was fake, some kind of prank, but it was heavy and it was a dead ringer for the picture in the book.

She put the nugget back in its original hiding place and closed the door. The wall paneling made it look like just another piece of the wall. But what was she going to do with this crazy nugget?

She turned off the lights and crawled into bed.

***

Sarah opened her eyes to the dark room.

"Gold."

The words were a whisper, right outside her door. She threw back the covers and walked to the door. Her heart was pounding.

"Gold."

It was the same damn voice she had heard as a kid.

She turned on the lights and opened the door. The dust outside the room was hovering in the shape of an old man. His face was a scruff of beard and hair, he was dressed in dark clothes and a black hat, but he looked almost like the man she had seen earlier, the scruffy guy from the abandoned house.

The dusty old man was looking up and down the hallway.

It had to be a trick of the light or a mirror. She reached out and her hand went through the dust and through the image.

The ghost turned toward her and she jumped back into her room, sure that it couldn't follow her into the light, but it did. The dust and image stepped into her room and she swore she could hear a footfall on the wood floor.

"Gold." It whispered again.

She grabbed the book and threw it at it and the ghost disappeared.

"Fuck." Sarah sat on the bed to let her heart slow down.

She grabbed her pillow and then went downstairs. She nabbed Kalie who was sleeping on the front desk, and went out to the car to sleep.

***

She woke as the sun was rising and was glad to see a truck coming up the drive. She opened the door of the car and breathed deeply of the morning air, cool and clean.

Doug approached the car, his hands holding two cups of coffee.

"Sleepin in yah car because of ghost, maybe?" he asked.

She gladly took one of the cups. "A ghost. Or just a trick."

"Nah. I've heard about the ghost."

Sarah unfolded herself out of the car and sipped at the coffee. "How does one get rid of a ghost exactly?"

He shook his head. "Don't ask me. I'm just a handyman."

"Do you know who George Deme was?"

He nodded. "Sure. That's supposed to be the ghost."

"Any relation to anyone around here?"

"Well, yeah. The whole Deme family lives around here. Bunch of useless good-for-nothin's. Always gettin into trouble like their great grandpa."

Kalie jumped out of the car and rubbed herself on Doug's legs. He bent down to pet her and looked up at Sarah. "Are you okay?"

She nodded and smiled. "Now that I have coffee and I'm not alone out here, yes. Thank you."

He stood back up and pushed his hat farther back on his head. "You're welcome."

She could see his blue eyes now, full of friendly energy. It was a good start to the morning.

"Watcha want me to work on first?"

Right, she thought, business. "I'd like to get started in the lobby. Clean it up, and get a new front desk. Something that fits the look of the place but isn't rough or a piece of junk."

He nodded and his smile lit up her morning. "Finally, I get to fix some thins around here. Thanks for the chance to do this."

Sarah smiled. The rest of the gloom was wiped away.

She unlocked the front door for Doug and glanced up at the landing. All was quiet.

***

While Sarah cleaned the first floor, Doug took away the old front desk and started building a new one. By the time she had made half of the rooms presentable, he had built a ten foot wide counter out of a dark, gleaming wood.

"Wow!" Sarah said as she approached. "It's gorgeous, but isn't it a little big?"

"I imagine that when you open this place up, people are going to come streaming in to see it. So, you'll need a big desk."

Sarah could see the future in his words; the place looking fresh and new, and a line of people checking in. "Doug, you're right. It's perfect."

Her stomach growled in hunger and they both laughed.

"Common." He nodded to the front door. "I'll share my dinner with you at the best spot on the property."

"Really?" she said as she followed him. "I'm getting spoiled. Laura was here last night with a casserole."

He led her to the lake where he had set out two chairs, both facing the lake, and a small table. "I thought you should know about this spot."

He set out two beers, a container of cold fried chicken, some apples, and cheddar cheese. Then he started a fire at a fire ring in front of them.

"Sorry, it's nothin' fancy."

"Doug, this is great. Just what I needed."

The view of the lake was indeed beautiful and it reminded her even more why she had wanted this place. The clouds were building so the sunset was hidden, but the reflection of the clouds in the glass-like lake was mesmerizing.

She said, "I've been here quite a few times. This is

actually my favorite spot. I could see putting hammocks and picnic tables out here."

As the embers of the fire died, Doug packed up. She almost wished he'd asked if he could stay and she considered asking him to hang around, but she also didn't know if he had anyone waiting for him at home.

She waved at him as he got in his truck, with the promise to be back tomorrow.

Inside, she sat with Kalie in the lobby while she considered her next move.

From the clouds, she could tell it was going to be a stormy night. Should she sleep in the car again? Everyone knew storms were a precursor to even more ghostly activity, right?

But, she'd have to figure out this ghost. She couldn't have it ruin her time here, and besides, it couldn't actually hurt her. It was just dust. She kissed Kalie goodnight and did her evening shower.

In her room, she looked at the book again. There was nothing in there about the miner or his death. But then, maybe this book was supposed to be an advertisement for the lodge. A way to peak travelers' interest to come and check it out.

As she drifted to sleep, she wondered if she should change the name to Ghost Lodge.

***

The storm woke her. The wind was whistling against the window and the rain was falling softly on the roof.

Then there was the whisper. "Gold."

She got up, turned on the light, and opened the door to the apparition.

'There's no gold here." She told it, but it ignored her. "Look, this is my place now. Get out of here!"

It looked left, then right, then turned toward her. She was determined not to let it scare her.

Then his doppelgänger walked through the dust and stepped into her room. The real, live Deme relative.

He stood in the doorway, his arms crossed.

"Oh, there's gold around here. George was looking for it when some fucking woman killed him. Our family would be rich if it weren't for her."

Sarah's pepper spray was across the room, but she had her keys in her robe pocket. She slipped her hand into her pocket and took another step back.

"Get out of my house."

He shook his head. "Nah. The funny thing is, George's ghost is never so clear as when he senses money. In all the times I've been searching in this place, I've never seen him look so real. Must mean there's money here."

He stepped closer.

She pulled her fist out of her pocket and stepped forward. As she jabbed her keys in his eye, he punched out with his fist.

He knocked her back and grabbed his eye. "You bitch!"

She snapped up the pepper spray and ran out past him out of the room and through the dust of George's image. She shivered and ran down the stairs. She could hear the real man coming down the stairs behind her.

She ran outside into the rain and turned at the door, spraying him in the face as he came toward her. He went down on his knees.

"God damn it!" He screamed as the spray enveloped him and touched his injured eye.

"Sarah!" The yell came from the woods. She could see someone was running toward her. She readied her pepper spray.

In the dim light from the front porch bulb, she could just make out that it was Doug.

"Where were you?" she asked him.

He nodded to the forest as he glanced at Deme, still holding onto his face. "I was sleeping in the forest, keeping an eye out for you. Is this your ghost?"

She shook her head, "Not exactly."

"I'll keep an eye on him while you call the police. I think there's good cell service in the middle of the lobby."

She went back into the lobby, shivering in the cold and her now wet PJs. The phone was answered right away. The sheriff would be at her place shortly.

***

Sarah looked at herself in the mirror. It had been a long couple of months, but tonight was the night. All her friends and family were downstairs in the lobby, ready to celebrate the soon-to-be grand opening of the lodge.

The whole place felt lighter.

As she walked down the steps, she could see the party was starting.

Her staff was passing around champagne and food, Doug turned on music, and Kalie was trying her best to get up on the cake table.

With Luke Deme in jail for breaking in, the property in tip-top shape, and Doug spending more and more time around the lodge, Sarah knew that she was in the right place.

***

The next morning, Sarah stretched as the sunlight lit up her room. Then she realized George hadn't made a peep last night. That was the first night she hadn't heard him wandering the halls. Maybe George's ghost didn't like laughter. She'd make it a habit to laugh more often.

After breakfast, she asked Doug to make her a new sign for the road. She named the place in honor of the original owner and for any ghosts that might still be around.

She proudly hung the new sign that announced the place would now be Madelyn Grange's Ghost Lodge.

If you enjoyed *Lakeside Lodge*, please leave a review.

About the Author
Sonja Dewing

Sonja Dewing is an award-winning author for her adventure/thrillers, loves travel, drinking too much coffee, and lives with her giant puppy, Bo. An agent told her no one would ever read an adventure book with a main female character. She proved him wrong.

Her most recent novel, *Relics of the Gods,* is the fourth and final book in the Idol Maker series.

You can sign up for her email and receive two free short stories http://eepurl.com/cAzV5v

Find her books at sonjadewing.com.

More Flexible Than Water

PAT MCGREGOR

PETRA SEVILLE-CONGO

(TheRock-2043@expedition1.gov)

Thurs March 10 2085 7:23 pm

To: Maria.Consuela2046@selene-city.lun

My dear Maria–

We are covered by water. It rained for several days, inches per hour. The river came out of its banks, and now all around us is a flat, shiny surface as far as the eye can see. I can hear the church bells at St. Croix ringing the hours; they echo strangely, bouncing off the liquid, and are the only signs of life these past four days.

By "us" I mean me and the cats. They are very twitchy in this circumscribed situation. Since the house is at the top of a rise, we stick out of the water like a knee out of a bathtub. The cats went outside and explored the dry area around the house yesterday for a while. I figured it was reasonably safe because I could see any predators coming.

The feed shed is mercifully above water, so I have food for the chickens. I keep them on the back porch at night and let them out in the morning – they circle the dry area, scratching and clucking, and I put grain out for them twice a day. The garden shed was swept away when the waters came rushing in.

Let me tell you about the water. The levee burst at the highway crossing, and the force of the water carried away the dike for almost a mile in each direction. I was watching from upstairs with my binoculars when it happened. The surge leaped forth like a dog with the back gate open – full bore, no hesitation. At first the water was silent. Then the roar hit me. All that water let loose in a rush, churning up the dirt into a milky-brown surge heading right for us. It looked shallow at first, but then it swept one of those autoharvesters clean away. The water rose so swiftly that I worried that the house would be engulfed, but no. It stopped about forty feet from the porch and stayed there, with little wavelets lapping up for a while but gradually resolving into this mirrored sea. No other houses or even roofs are visible from here, even with binoculars – I assume everything on low ground was carried away.

Luckily, we are self-sufficient – the propane tank and generator are above the water level, so I have cooking fuel and electricity. The composting toilets I installed last year are working fine, too. I don't know if the water supply is contaminated, so I am drinking and cooking from the five-hundred-gallon emergency supply stored in the house.

Once the rain stopped, our satellite link came back up, which is why I feel confident I can send this message. Just wanted to let you know that we are all fine, if confined by the water, and safely snug as bugs in rugs.

Love, Petra

***

Petra Seville-Congo
(TheRock-2043@expedition1.gov)
Fri March 11 2085 9:34 am
To: Maria.Consuela2046@selene-city.lun
Maria –

Haven't heard back, but I'm just going to write and send to you as the mood strikes, like lag time between astronauts and ground control. I am going to assume you got my letter and are just too busy with the girls to write back, but I do hope to hear from you soon. Just drop a note to let me know I'm not talking to myself. The cats are lovely but they are not good conversationalists.

We had deer on our island when I got up this morning – two does and two fawns apparently swam across from who knows where and took refuge with us. They cropped peaceably on the radishes and carrot tops – I didn't have the heart to shoo them away since they must have been swimming for hours, and the little ones looked droopy and tired. They are still here, down by the water's edge where the forsythia bush is, the fawns tucked up under the bushes and the moms sitting on the upslope side, surveying the house. Probably think that's where the danger will come from. I fed the chickens on the back side of the house today to try to keep them from wandering around and bothering the deer. Who knows how long that will last!

Oops! That's the oven going off – I made muffins for breakfast and they're ready to come out now. More later.

Friday afternoon

The deer are gone. After I had breakfast and tidied up, I cleaned the bathroom and vacuumed in my bedroom, and the next time I glanced out front they were nowhere to be seen. I checked the back, too, but no sign of them. I guess they swam off. Hope we didn't somehow scare them. I have no idea where they'll go – I can't see dry land in any direction. I can hear the bells of St. Croix, so I assume the church is above water. At least the steeple and belfry must be!

You're probably wondering where Andre is in all of this. Clearly, he's not here. We had another big row last Sunday, and Monday he packed a suitcase and headed for the spaceport. He said he was going to sign on for a long tour, long enough to give him time to think. I told him to go, but not to be surprised if I changed the locks and entry codes while he was gone. I'm tired of him using this house as a hostel instead of a home, and if he's gone for good, I don't care. Honestly, I'm done. He was good to have around for cuddles and sex, but recently his temper has gotten the better of him and even cuddles were far and few between.

The locksmith was due to be out here today, such is my luck. I guess I'll get the locks and codes changed when the water recedes. I was actually worried someone got in the house today, even – this afternoon I was up changing the closets from winter to summer clothes, and when I came down the back door was open, as was the basement door. The cats were sitting on the top step, watching the basement, but didn't seem to have gone down. There was a big puddle on the floor. Maybe it was Andre, sneaking back to get something he forgot but too cowardly to confront me. I'll keep all the doors locked from now on.

Weather folks say it could be two weeks before the water recedes. The upstream dams are all still releasing water, and it's still raining to the north. The fact that it's still raining is kinda weird. This is not the usual monsoon season for us; usually this time of year is when the rains end, not ramp up.

I've got enough fresh food to last a couple of weeks, but not much more than that. I wonder how we'll get food if the waters haven't receded by the time I run out of coffee!

Love,

P

***

Petra Seville-Congo (TheRock-2043@expedition1.gov) Sun March 13 2085 1:08 pm

To: Maria.Consuela2046@selene-city.lun

Holy Hannah, Maria. We have snakes!

Hundreds of them. They crawled up out of the water in a huge crowd, as if they had been swimming together in a bunch. Within an hour they carpeted the front yard and festooned the front porch like something from a horror flick. I put the chickens in the coop and haven't been out to check to see if they survived – there are still big snakes on the front porch, and I am too nervous to go out the back and see what's going on. The cats are prowling and chirping at the baseboards. I hope there aren't snakes in the walls, or the basement! The plasticrete was supposedly without holes or joints so as to be waterproof, and there aren't any wires or pipes coming into the basement. I confess I'm a coward about snakes – no way am I going down to look. They make my skin crawl, literally. Even writing about it, my hand is shaking.

Something big swam by the house early this morning, maybe chasing the snakes. It wasn't a shark – though I know they can survive in fresh water – but it was about three meters long and the tail stuck out above the surface. I'm not as familiar with the fauna here as I should be – that was Andre's job – but I snapped a few pictures and sent them off to the wildlife people to see if they could help. A tail's not much to go on, I fear, but maybe they'll have tail-identifiers there.

I know they brought snakes to keep the vermin

down when the colonists first arrived, but I hadn't realized there were so many types. I expect to see corn snakes or king snakes from time to time in the garden – they hunt down vermin but are not venomous – but I swear I saw at least two rattlesnakes in the front walkway. I wonder what predator is above a rattlesnake in the ladder of life? Sure isn't humans!

I've got to go – the cats are howling at the basement door and I must at least shout down there and chase the monsters away.

Creeped-out,

P

***

Petra Seville-Congo (TheRock-2043@expedition1.gov) Tue March 15 2085 6:14 pm

To: Maria.Consuela2046@selene-city.lun

Maria, dear heart!

It was so good to get your email yesterday! I didn't want to be right about the girls – chicken pox sounds dreadful. I thought that was one of the diseases we got rid of ages ago – maybe their vaccinations wore off? Anyway, ugh. Hugs and air kisses to all of you.

The snakes are mostly gone – they left in a big bunch Monday morning. I lost four chickens out of the twelve to snakebite – no eating those ones. All the eggs are gone. The rest of the chickens are skittish as hell, fluttering and jumping at every crackling branch or waving bush. I found a corn snake under the feed shed this morning and made sure the metal bins were closed tightly. There may be bugs or rats under the shed, and Mr. Snake is welcome to them! Never have seen rats on the property, but the floodwaters could have chased them up.

Hovercraft came by this morning, and we shouted back and forth for a while. They're checking on those of us who didn't evacuate and making sure we're fine. I put in that order for coffee. They can come by any time: it's good to see real humans. They're supposed to come back with food and carboys of water tomorrow. Some variety will be nice. I've been living off the walk-in freezer – lots of pasta and ground bison imported when it was cheap. When it started raining I transferred several pounds of meat from the basement freezer up into the everyday freezer, and I have a couple of days left before I have to down and get more . . . and face the possible snake infestation.

Thanks for including the news links about the flood – it's interesting to see what it looks like from the outside. I'm surprised so many people died – we certainly had plenty of warning. I got an email from the priest at St. Croix yesterday – they have 123 people holed up, sheltering at the church. That big recreation hall is proving its weight in gold. Just plasticrete, but big and waterproof. I hope everybody there is warm enough – we've had some unseasonably cold nights the last few days (uh, you know what I mean), and I've gotten out the winter comforters to put on the bed. Turned on the light in the chicken coop to keep it warm at night, too. You know it's cold when the cats crawl beneath the covers to snuggle in with you.

Heard from Andre yesterday. He's been offered a position as expeditionary biologist on a five-year mission exploring new planets and cataloging what's good for colonizing. So he won't be back for a long time. So it couldn't have been him sneaking in the house a few days ago. More than ever I need to get the lock codes changed!

I know you think I should stick with him. Can't stick with him if he's gone for five years out in space, now, can I? We'll see what he's like when he comes back. Unlikely I'll meet someone else in the meantime – our ratio is still stubbornly 4:1 women to men. They supposedly recruit more men, but lord knows where they go – not here, for sure, as there's nobody new in this township the last two years. We're farmers, though, and that's not a sexy profession. Newcomers probably go to one of the bigger settlements.

Speaking of farming, I'm glad this came in the spring, before I had the crops in. We'll be late planting, but with luck the water will have brought a new layer of nutrients for the soil, just like the old Nile stories. So glad I shipped all of last year's harvest out in the fall, rather than storing it on my property. It would all be gone now if I had. The big barn washed away in the first surge; thank goodness I had the equipment over at the mechanic's for spring tune-ups. If they washed away from the mechanic's, her insurance will have to pay for it.

We did have one big mystery today. I got up to feed the chickens early, and when I went out on the back porch there were big muddy footprints in front of every window, as if someone had stood there and looked in. There was mud on the handle of the screen door, too. Luckily, I had locked all the doors with security bars before I went to bed. There were footprints pointing down the stairs but no trail beyond that in the endless mud. I checked the feed shed, too

We've had prowlers before and scared them off with a few blasts from the shotgun, but this one must have swum in overnight. I hate to think that one of those poor folks washed away from their home might have swum all this way for help and left. That they could have swum on, exhausted, and drowned. But I didn't hear anyone knock or call out, and I'm not that heavy a sleeper. Maybe they knew about the shotgun and decided not to surprise me.

That's it for today – I need to go swap in a new fuel cell for the generator and bed the chickens down for the night. Thanks for writing. I hope the chicken pox calms down soon – send me pictures of the girls all spotty!

Love,

Petra

***

Petra Seville-Congo

    (TheRock-2043@expedition1.gov)

    Wed March 17 2085 11:01 pm

    To: Maria.Consuela2046@selene-city.lun

    Maria –

Catastrophe struck – luckily not here, but terrible anyway. Apparently, the soil under the church in St. Croix was all sand, not substrate, and washed away from under the rec hall, carrying away sixty people when it went in the middle of the night. You'd think church builders would have known their scripture better.

I heard about it from the hovercraft folk when they came back this morning. They brought twelve carboys of water, bacon, some sort of emergency rations in case the power goes out, pasta, cheese, dried milk, QuikMix, and lord love'em, a pound of medium-roast coffee beans. Thank goodness I still have a coffee grinder. Andre didn't take that with him! He must have raided the emergency rations before he went, though – I'm down to the last dozen power bars already. I asked the hovercraft folks to bring some next time if they could scare up a case.

There's oddly little news despite all the devastation around us – lists of folks who made it to emergency shelters (where they sit playing board games until the water recedes and they can see the extent of the damage) and lists of folks thought to have been swept away. Most urgent is the twice-a-day weather report – more rain is predicted, and the water could hang around longer than originally thought. We've never seen anything like this in my nine years on the planet!

I'm more than ever convinced there's something in the basement. The cats keep sniffing at the basement door as if they sense something down there and patrol the baseboards in the living room as if something were behind them. I hope the snakes didn't nest in the basement – how would I ever get them out? Yeesh. I asked the hovercraft crew to go down and take a look, and they all tromped down the stairs in a great mass, kidding about scaredy women. Well, shoot to that. I can be scared of snakes if I want to. They didn't find anything – if it was snakes the noise would have scared them away – which relieves me but not the cats. They're still prowling the baseboards and sniffing at the basement door.

Still Creeped Out,
Petra

***

Petra Seville-Congo
  (TheRock-2043@expedition1.gov)
  Thurs March 18 2085 1:56 pm
  To: Maria.Consuela2046@selene-city.lun
  Ma-REE-ah!
  Can't get that old song out of my head. "Just met a girl named Maria!" Missing about half the words in my head, but the tune is lovely. I'll have to look it up on the

'net, maybe watch the movie tonight. What are you planning to do with yourself?

How are the girls? I was reading up on chicken pox and it sounds like managing it is terrible! How do you keep them from scratching? Will they have scars? Do you have medicine? Tell me all!

Yes, Friday the cat is guarding the basement door as I type – he settled himself there this morning after I fed the cats, and he's been there since. The other three are patrolling the house. I got up the guts to open the door and shout, "Who's there?" very loudly last night, but no one answered and I slammed the door shut again just as quickly. I've locked the door and put a doorstop wedge underneath it. I didn't see anything in the puddle of light at the bottom of the stairs – you'd think if it were snakes, they'd be crawling around on the plasticrete and be visible, wouldn't they?

Heard from Andre again. Can't think why he keeps writing. He's going to Jupiter for training for six weeks. He asked me to ship him his big duffle full of ship suits and book chips. I answered back that I wasn't going anywhere until this water recedes. He'll have to wait. Probably cost me a fortune to ship it so he gets it while he's still at Jupiter Station. I'll have one of our security patrol people search it before I send it – who knows what else he has stuffed in there?

Heard some more about the St. Croix disaster – the local newsletter thing came out this morning. The water table rose under the rec hall, and it just floated off its foundation and down toward the deeper water. About seventy people got out before it sank; most of the women and children. Ten men were trying to get more people out when it capsized and filled with water. The pictures were gruesome. I will have to watch that movie or something else cheerful before bed to keep from seeing those pictures in my sleep all night long!

The wildlife people got back to me about the big thing in the water. Remember I sent the picture to them? They say it's a big amphibian that migrated here this spring from the south and competes with the native bear-like things for food. Sounds like we'll be seeing more of them. It eats fish in the water (yes, maybe snakes too) and smaller animals on land. Something tried to get into the chicken coop last night – the whole coop was shoved around on the porch, some of the wood had scratch marks on it, and some of the chicken wire on the front was deformed as if something had pressed on it. Big round footprints in the muddy yard leading to and from the water. A scary thought – what if one of those things got into the basement? I'll put up a security camera on the porch to keep an eye on things – probably should have done that ages ago – and see what I see.

Creeping Along,
Me

***

Petra Seville-Congo
(TheRock-2043@expedition1.gov)

Sun March 21 2085 7:23 pm

To: Maria.Consuela2046@selene-city.lun

Hello Maria!

You wrote! Hooray! I know you write when you can, but to messages two days in a row is luxury. Either the girls are better or you're sedating them to get more time for yourself. Just a joke. Or maybe not – it would keep them from scratching! I can't believe you have to put socks on their hands when they sleep. The little ones must be miserable. Give them love from their Auntie Petra.

The water is starting to recede! I put a stick at the high-water mark, and today it is a foot back from the highest point. It's leaving tarry black mud behind – I hope it's good for the soil. Smells bad, of course. They say the water in floods is full of poo and bacteria and all sorts of nasty things. Makes me feel sorry for the animals trapped by it – they don't have clean water to drink or safe places to den up.

Speaking of animals, the deer are back under the forsythia bush. Three fawns now, and two does, so I wonder if the other one was lost before or is a foundling. My carrots and radishes are gone, and they ate all the hostas at the foundation of the house. I offered them grain; they nuzzled and lipped at it, but most of it was still there an hour later. Who wants old grain when you can have fresh hostas!? If they had anything else to eat, I'd do something about it. But luckily hostas are always going begging down at the hydroponics center and I can replace these easily. If they stay long, I'm going to be giving them hay from the feed shed. I've got sweet timothy, perhaps they'll like that.

The cellar is still a mystery. Now I have two cats guarding the door and the other two spread out behind them like a rear guard. They're certainly alert to something!

Yes, if Andre were here, I'd send him down. I know it's sexist of me, but I'm the one who's scared of the cellar. Since he's not here I'll have to find someone else – maybe someone with a big scary dog – to check it out for me.

I'm feeling a little tired – I think I'll take a nap. Have a great afternoon, love you bunches!

Petra

***

Petra Seville-Congo

(TheRock-2043@expedition1.gov)

Mon March 22 2085 3:18 pm

To: Maria.Consuela2046@selene-city.lun

Dearheart –

You'll never guess. Never. The mystery of the basement is solved!

Yesterday I went to take a nap, right? Well, the cats wouldn't let me settle. They kept pawing at me and mewing and generally making nuisances of themselves. So I went back downstairs to make a big cup of coffee.

The door to the basement was standing open, and

tarry footprints led into it from the back door of the house. I had my hand on the transmitter to call the Security Patrol for help when an unholy ruckus broke out downstairs: banging and shouting and crashes and general mayhem. I was terrified –what could it be? I crept down two or three stairs and peeked in below the floor joists.

There were three struggling people. One was huge, wet and muddy and covered with tarry nastiness, and holding a machete and trying to cut the other two. The other two wore prison jumpsuits and were wrestling with the muddy one, trying to get the big knife. Someone was already cut – there was blood on the floor – and the muddy one appeared to have the advantage for sheer size.

The two in jumpsuits were women, and I decided to help. I lifted a spade off the hook on the wall and crept down the stairs. When I had a clear shot, I waded into the fight yelling and swung for his knee, though he moved and I got his thigh instead. He whirled at me, and I got a slice across my face from the machete – shallow, don't worry, the medics say it might leave just a tiny scar at worst – and the two women used the distraction to jump him. He was slimy with mud and worse, so getting hold of him was hard. They finally pinned him, and I whacked him one over the head with the spade. He went down like a felled tree.

I swung that spade at the others like a sword and demanded to know what they were doing there. The tall one – her jumpsuit said "Clemmons" -- told me that the prison was evacuated by boat the day of the flood, and this muddy guy and another woman had started a fight and knifed the guards. Clemmons and Azari jumped out of the boat to avoid being killed by Machete Guy. They said they hadn't intended to escape – they were convicted of falsifying the breeding strains of their seed crop and willing to do their time, but they didn't want to be cut up by a giant with a machete!

They made it to my island and figured it had been evacuated too, but then I came out to feed the chickens and surprised them. They snuck inside and took refuge in the cellar, dried out, and settled in to hide, eating my emergency rations – mostly energy bars and bottled water. When I sent the hovercraft crew down to check, they hid in the walk-in freezer, back in the back behind the big boxes of seeds. Lucky we had one of those escape buttons so they could let themselves out! Clemmons said that they were hiding rather than explaining things to me because they were afraid of the big man,

Machete Guy tracked them down and assumed they were hiding in my house. He told them when he found them in the basement that he wanted no witnesses to the killing of the guards. He had already killed the other woman on the boat.

I had them tie Machete Guy up – he was still out – and I went upstairs and called the SP. They told me someone would be there within an hour. So I made three cups of coffee, put creamer and sweetener on a tray, and took the drinks down to the basement. While I didn't necessarily want them up in my living room, we'd vanquished a marauder together and it seemed only reasonable – and the basement was cold!

So that's how the SP found us, drinking coffee in the basement and occasionally tapping Machete Guy on the head with the spade.

So, my dear, all is well. I'm OK – I've got some stitches in my face but the scar should be small, I've proved to myself that I don't need Andre to protect me from bad guys in the basement, and I've made two new friends! Clemmons and Azari are working on coffee plants that will grow in our native soil, and I'm going to sponsor their experiments when they get out of jail!

Love,

Petra

About the Author

Pat McGregor

Pat, like many other retired grandmothers, is active on Facebook and has two cats. During her 35-year IT career she worked on the project that built the modern Internet backbone, and helped physically build some of the first modern routers used on that backbone.

Pat likes to write speculative fiction. Most times it is paranormal romance with a dash of urban romance thrown in.

You can find her current published witchy romances.

Astrid

COURTNEY MAE

WAKING up with a start is never fun, it always takes me a bit to realize where I am when I first wake up. I feel the sweat running down the back of my neck. I hear creaking coming from above me. This causes my heart to race even more than it did from startling awake. I hate not being able to see where I am or who is with me because of the blindfold that was placed on me.

Once I get my bearings, I realize I am still captive in the basement of the run-down cabin. I swear that there is a river flowing through this basement with how close the sound of water is. I notice that I am still tied to the chair with a blindfold. I don't hear anyone in the room with me, just the creaking from above. The only reason that I know that it was a man that brought me here was because I got one kick to the man's side the day he brought me here. After that, he has made sure to stay further away from me.

By now someone will have noticed that I am missing. I was supposed to start classes on the Monday after this trip. My best friend Stella will have by now noticed that my phone is off which is something that I promised her I would not do so that someone would always be able to locate me.

I start to muse to myself that it is a good thing I only brought a blank notebook and not my computer. I really should have researched this town more. It is a "ghost" town in the middle of nowhere. The closest town is over 40 minutes away.

I am still trying to figure out how I got here. The last thing I remember was walking down the road of an abandoned town near the university. I was here to get some inspiration for the book I am writing. The run-down town with no residents seemed like it would be the perfect place to find inspiration for my novel.

No one comes out here. It feels like it has been days without the sun. I am not sure how many have passed at this point. I am working on rubbing the restraints together so that I can get them off and escape this hell-hole. I have tried to squeeze my hand out but that has just made the sting worse. It feels like my skin has been rubbed raw from all of my attempts at trying to get out. I feel flakes coming off as I twist my wrists. It is most likely the dried blood from my last attempt to get out but it could also be dried dirt.

I wake up with a start. I thought I heard something in the distance. I start to work on the ropes binding my hands again and I feel something starting to loosen. I stop when I hear someone coming down the stairs. I don't call out as I can tell it is him. I have learned to decipher if it is him or something else upstairs. He has a very specific walk, almost as if he is limping. It sounds like he takes one step at a time. I have heard a few animals running around the house. I am pretty sure there was one down here last night. It is eerie not being able to see through the blindfold. I never know if an animal is in the room with me unless it is loud enough for me to hear it. I tried to talk to him when he first brought me here, but he did not answer me. I decide to try again. I hear him splash through the puddle near my chair, alerting me to him being right behind me. That is how I can tell he is in the room with me that telltale splash of water. Every time I hear it my heart starts to race and I start to breathe faster. I work on trying to get my breathing slower but not being able to see him makes my heart race and panic start to set in.

"What's your name?" I try to ask him. I am interrupted by a phone ringing.

"I ask the questions, and I will be right back to ask them" He responds.

I hear him walk back upstairs through the puddle. I am still frozen in fear when, unfortunately, he comes back to the basement. I hear the cadence of his walk down the stairs. If I did not know it was him coming it would almost be soothing the thump thump thump of the steps sound like a bass drum. The splash of water at the bottom that alerts me he is back in the room with me.

I start to panic about if it is going to be the same questions as the day he brought me here. Asking about people I don't know and some flash drive. He kept ranting that he needed to find them under his breath when he left. I wish I knew everything he was saying as he left so that I could be more prepared for what is to come.

"Elle, why don't you just tell me where the flash drive is so that this can all be over?" he asks me in an eerily calm voice. It makes me tense up even more.

"I have no idea what you are talking about. My name is not Elle." I whisper.

"I know for a fact it is you Elle, no one else I have ever met has your unique eye coloring." his voice rises making me flinch.

I do not know how to respond to that. It catches me off guard. It is rare to have heterochromia or in other words have two different eye colors. I do not know anyone else with it.

"Just tell me where the Flash Drive is!" I feel his warm breath as he screams in my face.

"I don't know what you are talking about!" I say with tears running down my face.

"If you do not give me the information that I want about where the flash drive is I am going to kill you just like I did Ashton! I refuse to let that evidence of my crimes be handed over to anyone," he growls at me.

I stay quiet not knowing how to respond to that. I do not want to die, but I have no idea where what he is looking for is located. He is starting to become more unhinged since he is not getting the response that he wants from me. I must have taken too long to respond to him because the next thing I know I feel the chair falling to the side as he kicks it in anger. My head bounces off the floor making me see stars even blind-folded. There is a ringing in my ears from how I hit my head. Once I can finally focus on what is going on I notice that the blindfold is starting to come off so I use the ground to try to get it down so I can see who my captor is. It finally comes down. I try to look around as much as I can but with the position of the chair, it is not easy. I see that he is pacing and pulling his hair across the room. I take note of everything that I can about him. He is younger than I expected. He can't be older than thirty. He is of average height and I notice when he walks into the light of the lantern he set up that he has the palest blue eyes that I have ever seen with blonde hair that comes down into his face. Those eyes will haunt my nightmares.

"I will be back later and you will tell me what I want to know. I need to get more supplies. I thought you would have told me what I wanted to know by now " He says glaring down at me and kicking the chair.

He leaves me on the floor and stomps through the puddle and up the stairs. I hear a vehicle start and drive off in the distance. I am still panicking when I realize that I need to start trying to escape. I start working harder on getting my hands free. I keep reminding myself that I need to get out of here before he comes back. He is escalating his anger and it is only a matter of time before he decides that knocking me over is not enough to get what he wants. What if this is a test to see if I can escape and he is still here?

As I am recounting all he said I feel the rope break. My hands feel like they are being stabbed as the blood flow starts to return. I untie my hands as quickly as I can with how numb they feel and try to stand up. I am weak from the little water and food he provided. It was not much and that was when he first brought me here. I start to make my way to the stairs and fall my legs feel like jelly. I decide to slowly crawl my way to the staircase. I notice that there is a floorboard that looks different, almost like it has been pried up from the ground. If I was walking or crawling I would not have noticed. How did I notice, I fell face-first into it trying to get myself over the giant puddle that has always alerted me to his arrival. I look up trying to see where this puddle came from and notice that there is a stream of water coming from the wall. Either there is a pipe leaking or water is coming in from the outside. Which would not surprise me since this place is so run down.

I think I see a baggie when I focus back on the floorboard that I just smacked my head on. There should not be baggies in this place unless someone put it there deliberately. No one has lived here in a really long time, probably hundreds of years. I know I should be saving myself but what if this is why he kidnapped me? I dig the baggie out carefully from the pried-up space and see it is a flash drive. This has to be the blackmail that he is so worried about. I shove it in my pocket and start to make my way up the stairs. My heart is racing with every creak that they make when I step on one. I finally make it to the top of them and my heart is racing. I do not know if he really drove away or if he could be lurking around any corner.

I slowly push the door that is already falling to the side. I freeze and hold my breath when it makes a loud creak. When I do not hear anything I continue to the hall that looks like it leads to the only way out of the cabin. I slide along the wall using it to support me. I feel like my heart is going to beat out of my chest by the time I finally make it to the door. I slowly open it waiting for someone to jump out and attack me. When that does not happen I slowly step out.

The first thing that I notice when I get outside is that it is close to nighttime. It's not so dark you can not see in front of you but it is dark enough to where light would be helpful. When looking around trying to figure out my next move I notice that in the distance there is a car or something headed this way that has lights on it. I take off to the treeline as fast as I can in case it is him coming back. As the light gets closer I can see it is a vehicle. As the vehicle gets closer I duck down into the grass. It is overgrown so it covers me. I am so close to the trees. If I can make it there I can find somewhere to hide for the night. I slowly crawl through the grass and only pause when I hear the vehicle door open. I don't want him to hear me. Once the door slams I have to stop myself from crying out in fear. I don't want him to know I am gone before he even gets inside the cabin so I bite down on my lip to stop the sounds. I can taste the metallic taste of blood from biting my lip.

Once the coast is clear I move as fast as I can to the trees by low crawling. I use one to pull myself up and continue to use them to make my way through. I have no idea where I am going. I just know I need to try to get as far away from him as I can. Especially now that I have his flash drive. I pat my pocket to make sure that I did not lose it when I was crawling in the grass. I feel it still in my pocket.

I startle when I hear yelling. I realize that he knows I am gone and I need to figure out what my next move is. I see that there is a group of fallen trees up ahead. If I make it to them maybe I can find a way to hide in them so that he does not find me. I know it is a long shot but I need to try.

My breathing starts to become ragged as I am trying to go faster. I hear the yelling and it sounds like it is closing in on the treeline. I make it to a fallen tree and climb into the center. I see once I am in the mound that there is a small nook that I can crawl into and hide. I shove myself in it and try to calm my breathing. I know if I don't I will give my position away to him. I hear him stomping around in the distance near where the trees meet the overgrown grass. After what feels like an eternity I hear footsteps right next to the fallen trees I am hiding in. My heart is racing.

"Where are you, Elle? I know you have to be close!" he screams. I cover my mouth so that I don't let the sound escape. Tears are falling down my face. I want this nightmare to be over. I hear him kick something. It sounds like he is about to try to move the trees by the way they are shaking. It makes my heart pound even more. He is going to find me, this is the end.

His phone rings. He curses rambling about horrible timing. He finally answers walking off back to where the cabin is based on how his voice becomes distant. I don't plan to move from here until there is daylight. I don't want to make a mistake in the dark. I try to stay awake but before I know it I am drifting off into a fitful sleep.

I wake up with a start when I hear something near where I am hiding. I bite my lip just in time for no sound to come out. I have no clue what made the shuffling sound. I wish I had my phone so that I could call for help. I hope it is just an animal and that dawn will be here soon. I try to settle back in for some rest as I know that I need to preserve my strength. I have to make my way back to that town. That is going to be miles and miles of walking. I won't be able to walk on the road either. I will be navigating this rough terrain in the forest.

As soon as the light comes I need to check my injuries. Something is wrong with my arm. Every time I move it away from my body it shoots pain up to my shoulder. I am worried that it may be broken. I also need to check my leg it is extremely wet and my jeans are stained crimson. I knew I should have worn darker jeans out into the middle of nowhere. Who wears light jeans out to see a ghost town? On that line of thinking, who goes to a ghost town alone for inspiration for a book? I am really losing my mind. I make a promise to myself that if I get out of this I will make better choices. I need to make better choices, take a self-defense class, learn to cook, graduate, and publish my novel. The very one that might just lead to my demise.

I snap out of it when I notice that the sky is starting to brighten. I will need to carefully see if the coast is clear and make my way out of this mess. Just as I am about to move I hear something in the distance and freeze.

"Come out Elle! I know you are close! It is only a matter of time before I catch you again. When I catch you this time there will be no way for you to escape. The closest town is 20 miles away" he yells.

I really hate that he is calling me that. I want to know where the real Elle is. What happened to her? Is she in these woods too? I notice that his voice is getting farther away. I hear the vehicle he is in start up and peel out. He must be heading into wherever he goes every day. I should start making my way out of here. I slowly crawl to the opening and peek out. I don't see or hear anything so I make my way out of the fallen trees. The bark scratches my skin even more than it already is.

I start to slowly walk to the treeline hiding behind trees just in case I was wrong and he did not leave. Every sound is making me jump and look over my shoulder to see if it is him. As the day goes on I know I need to find water or I am not going to make it. I start heading away from the road, back deeper into the woods. I hear something that almost sounds like water and head that way. I see that it is a stream in the distance. I make my way to the stream. It is probably not safe to drink and I might catch something but at this point, I don't care. I cup my hands and gulp as much as I can. It is not the best tasting but it could be worse.

I am not a camper or a survival guru so this could be my demise. Escape a kidnapping killer and end up dead from drinking water from a random stream. That would be just my luck. At least I think I am still sane. I am not hearing people respond to the questions that I am saying in my head. There is hope for me yet. I splash some water on my face and drink some more. Standing up I look around. There is nothing in sight. The stream is not that far from the treeline and road like I thought it was, so I decide to follow it in the direction I was headed. Hopefully, I do not get lost in the process of following this stream. Being so directionally challenged is not working for me right now.

After what feels like hours I decide to take another break and drink from the stream. I need to rest. I probably only made it a few miles if that with my excruciatingly slow pace. I give myself some time to regain as much strength as I can and then decide I need to get a move on again while the sun is still out. I take one last drink and continue heading on the path along the stream.

When the sun starts to set I know it is time to find a place to hole up. I start looking around and see a tree that looks like it is hollowed out. I move closer to it and see that it has a small opening where it looks like it cracked and hollowed out from the weather. It reminds me of the entrance to a teepee. I look inside and see that there is just enough room for me to squeeze my way in and stay with some shelter tonight. It is a tight fit to get in. I am just glad that I was able to find something. I was worried that I would have to sleep out in the open. Which would have more of a chance of me getting caught. I curl up as best as I can trying to get comfortable and start to drift off. I wake in the middle of the night to a loud boom and the sound of water. It is starting to pour down. I am glad I found this spot otherwise I would be soaking wet while trying to walk tomorrow. That would make this whole thing so much worse. I curl up more trying to get warm. The rain made it cool off and I am starting to shiver. I slowly start to drift off again it takes longer than before because I am so focused on how cold I am.

I wake up the next morning to see that it is still sprinkling. I peek out making sure that no one is around. Then I cup my hands and try to collect as much water as I can to drink so I can take a break from drinking from the stream. I am debating if I should start walking or if I should wait. I know that the delay could add time to making it to the town. But on the other hand, if I go out I could get sick from walking in the rain and having no way to dry out. Either way is not a winning situation. I decide to wait a little longer before I leave my shelter.

My arm is starting to feel stronger. What I thought

was broken was a giant gash that had tried to heal over, but it was not successful. I should rinse it off again at some point today. I know it is infected from the nasty white goo coming out of the wound. My leg looks like it is in the same shape. When I look at both of my wounds I think he stabbed them when I was unconscious. No matter how hard I try I can't remember what happened to me. Thinking back, the water did taste off when I was drinking it the first day. There was probably something in it. I think back trying to remember how I got into this mess.

The last thing I remember was smiling up at the sun and basking in the warmth like I would do when I was a kid. I had just arrived in the area and was walking down the main street. I had seen the cabin off in the distance near the treeline at the edge of the ghost town. The weird thing is I don't remember how I got to the town. I remember I planned to come out here for inspiration but I did not have my rental car yet. If that was the case why did no one come look for me? Next thing I knew someone was behind me and everything went black. He must have knocked me out as I have a giant lump on the back of my head. It takes everything in me to refrain from rubbing it as I don't want to open it up and make it worse. I have enough problems on my plate already. If I get out of this mess alive I need to take a real vacation. One where there are people and I am not alone.

I let out a sigh coming back to the present and decide that I need to start moving. I grab another drink and rinse out my arm wound. Then start the trek along the stream.

I hear rumbling in the distance. I can't tell if it is a train or someone running through the woods. As I keep walking it gets louder. Then I realize that it is a helicopter. I have no clue who the psycho is that kidnapped me so I am not taking a chance. I duck into the trees and watch as it flies over. It circles back so I move further into the tree line. Luckily the trees are thicker and I can hide out easily. Eventually, the helicopter sounds like it is getting farther away so I carefully make my way forward staying in the treeline instead of out in the open.

I hear someone yelling. I freeze listening to the person. They are still a ways off. I thought they were yelling my name but I was so wrong. The distance had to have distorted his voice, or I am starting to become delirious.

"Elle! Where are you? You had to have come this way. This is the way to the town. " he yells increasing in volume that is sounding more angry with every word. "I will find you if it is the last thing that I do!"

I hear a shot go off, it causes me to freeze. He is shooting at who knows what. I don't want to stick around and find out but I need to find a place to hide. I hear him getting closer. I know that if I try to run he will find me from all the sticks on the ground. I need to find a way to climb up into one of these trees. I see a pine tree that looks like something I could get up into and the branches would hide me. I make my way as quietly as possible. I hear his shouting getting closer. It makes my heart start to race even faster than it did when I heard the shot.

I start to climb the tree and feel my arm start to bleed from using it. I have to bite down on my lip to stop myself from screaming out in pain. My hands are getting scratched up from the bark of the tree. I can feel tears coming down my face. I have to get up this tree or I am going to die. I have so much I want to do. People I want to make amends with. I refuse to give up and make this easy on him. If he wants me he is going to have to find me and fight me. I make it up the tree at a slow pace. I find a branch that will hold my weight and stop. I hear him down below talking to himself. I pat my pocket and realize that I did not lose the flash drive. I try to control my breathing. I don't want to give my position away. I see him lift his pistol and point it at the sky.

I panic thinking he has found me. I almost scream out when it goes off. If I had not put my hand over my mouth I would have. I wrap my arms carefully around the trunk of the tree again and rest my head against it. I am starting to feel light headed and I don't want to fall out of this tree. If I do, there is no way that I am going to make it to help. I hear him talking to himself about how I must not have made it this far. He will need to circle back and try closer to the road. How maybe I got a ride from a car that was passing through the area? I decide based on his comments and the fact that he is talking to himself again that I will stay in this tree until dark. I can not chance running into him. He is becoming more unhinged and even more convinced that I am Elle and have evidence against him.

I try to think happy thoughts about what my plans will be once I get to college. How I will meet my goal of being a published author before I graduate? I plan to find someone that will help me with the process. Before I was kidnapped I had just sent off a pitch email to a well-known publishing company's CEO Amethyst. She is known for searching for young writers and giving them a chance with her publishing company that she built from the ground up. I notice that the sun is setting and I should slowly start to make my way down from the tree so I can find a better spot for the night.

I will fall out of this tree if I fall asleep. I slowly make my way down, only almost plunging to the ground twice. When I make it close to the bottom I stop to listen to see if I can hear anyone coming. I hear nothing but the animals so I finish my descent. I start to walk back to where the stream was. Using trees as cover I think of it like a game of hide and seek where you have to be moving at all times. I make it to the stream and grab a drink. My lips are so cracked from not drinking all day. I hiss as I put water on my reopened wound. It looks way worse than it did before. I know I should figure something out but I need to keep moving. Once I stop again for the night I decide that is when I will try to figure something out to cover my arm.

As I walk I start to get into my head and the anxiety starts to make me have questions. I wonder what day it is now. How long I have been gone? How long since I have escaped? Will anyone miss me? Will my ex-best friend show up if I die? That spirals me more into the thoughts of what I did to make him hate me.

I then start down the path of what if I am just such a horrible person that this is why this is happening to me. I trip over something and it brings me back from my internal downfall. I look and see I have been on autopilot and I tripped over a downed tree limb. I decide that I should stop soon as it is getting dark out. I grab a drink from the stream and sit on the tree limb. I look around to see if there is anything that I can use for shelter tonight. There is not much other than a few downed tree limbs. I head over to them and see that one is a giant tree that has fallen. It looks hollowed out. I peek inside hoping that an animal is not going to attack me. It is clear so I decide that I will climb in here. Hopefully, this will keep me out of the elements and hidden from anyone long enough for me to find an escape route. I close my eyes. I drift off to the sounds of the stream.

After the sun comes back up I start making my way through the trees. It feels like hours later, I do not have a concept of time anymore. I notice that just ahead the trees are not as dense. I slowly make my way to the edge of the tree line. As I make my way there I start to hear vehicles. I must be getting closer to a town.

As I look out from my hiding spot I see the sign to the town. I also hear a vehicle coming. It pulls over and I hear a male get out shouting directions that they are going to search the woods for me one mile at a time. As they start walking down the road I see it is some type of law enforcement or security company. I come out from hiding behind the trees. Walking to the road I yell out to the guy in charge. They don't look like typical law enforcement. They're wearing cargo pants and t-shirts, but they do have that commanding presence. Still, I decide to keep my distance. But that doesn't keep me from being pissed they didn't find me earlier.

"You're Late! I just had to hike for days after being kidnaped." I yell over. "I heard you call out my name"

He approaches me cautiously like someone would a feral animal. "My name is Roark," the guy who I thought was in charge based on him yelling out instructions to the others tells me. I stand my ground. They look like they're here to help, but after the last few days, I'm not taking any chances. I reply telling him "I am Astrid, though you probably already guessed that".

"We will give you a ride to the hospital to get checked over." Roark lets me know. I am not sure that I trust him yet. I need more assurance before I get into a vehicle with anyone of my own doing. If they are not who they say, they are going to have to force me into the vehicle.

"How do I know you are not with the pale-eyed psycho? " I ask since I never got his name.

" Your friend Stella warned us that you may ask that. You missed a meeting with Amethyst and she sent us, we work for her security team. We are all prior service. She went to your house to talk to you and your friend

Stella told her you were missing. Stella told us to tell you that and I quote, that Lilac the purple and blue wolf is real. I am not sure what that has to do with anything." He says in confusion.

I burst out in laughter with tears coming down my eyes. I tend to laugh in the worse situations, it comes out more when I am stressed. I feel a sense of relief wash over me. I know that this is not over but the only way he could know that joke is if Stella really sent him. Someone came for me. The joke is an ongoing argument that we have been having for a long time. I thought I saw one a few years ago when we were on a camping trip I affectionately named her Lilac. Stella never let me live it down. I still believe that she was real. I like to think of her as my spirit animal. I sometimes dream about her. I know I am not safe until he is caught but I feel safer being with a group.

The group starts moving towards the SUV. I hear yelling in the distance that I can not make out yet. It gets closer and I hear it more clearly. I wish I didn't.

"Elle I know you are close!" my nightmare screams.

Everyone in the group turns and looks at me. I feel frozen in place.

"Who is that?" Roark asks me with concern in his voice. "Do you know him?"

"That is the voice of the guy that kidnaped me," I whisper my voice shaking, and the panic of being found sets in. They could choose to leave me here to deal with him.

The group splits up and Roark directs me over to

the vehicles. He puts me in the back seat of one of the tinted SUVs. I wish the tint was darker so no one could see in, but that is not the case. I see the man that has been my nightmare since I started this trip being walked to near where I am. It looks like he is cuffed behind his back with zip ties. When they approach the vehicle parked next to the one I am in my heart feels like it is going to beat out of my chest. He is yelling and fighting the men holding him.

"I told you I was looking for Elle!" he yells at them. He looks over at the vehicle I am in and starts to struggle more. "It looks like you found her for me. Let me go and we can go on our way" he yells still struggling to break free.

I am frozen looking out the window at him. There is no reasoning with this monster he is too far gone in his delusion. I startle when Roark speaks.

"Are you okay?" he asks me.

I watch as they load him into another SUV while thinking about how I can answer that question. I decide to skip it and I ask Roark "What happens now? Will he go free?"

"No, he will be booked into the local jail and then moved. But first thing is first we need to get you to the hospital to be checked over. You will probably be staying a few days until you are cleared to travel. I called Stella and Amethyst so that they can meet us there." he lets me know. "Do you want to try to call Stella now?"

"I'm good let's just go home instead," I reply fast. Probably too fast as he raises an eyebrow at me.

"Not going to happen. We are going to the hospital to have you checked out." Roark says.

I know I need to go but I hate going to hospitals they are all the same and make me feel like I am crazy.

Roark lets me know "They will have to photograph your injuries once we arrive so that the case will hold up."

It does not surprise me. I want him to go away for a long time. I know if I try to call Stella it will make me panic even more. I want to explain everything in person. I don't want to relive it in the back of a vehicle alone. There is one thing that has been bothering me I decide to ask Roark and the guy next to him.

"First what is your name?" I ask the guy next to Roark to file it away for later.

"Z" he replies then says nothing else turning back to his phone. I decide to ask what I really want to know.

"I want to know his name. He never would answer me. He just demanded to know where Ashton and the flash drive were" I question.

Roark slams on the brakes. "What did you just say?"

I look at him confused. "About the flash drive or the name he used?"

"The name please." he looks at me with hope.

"He said the name was Ashton. Why is that important to you or something?"

"It is need-to-know information," Roark says to me

with a clenched jaw. He looks like he is barely holding it together

"Well if you want the information from me I need to know," I say. "I am not going to just give information over without information in return".

"Fine, yes! One of our people is named that and in a coma we have been trying to find the same flash drive that he hid. I did not realize that this guy was involved."

"What's on it?" I ask curious to see if he will be honest with me.

"Need to know information" Roark replies with a sigh.

"Well I guess you will never see it again, so what does it matter if I know," I ask

"Why are you being so difficult about this?" Roark asks frustrated with me.

"I was kidnapped over this, I want to know what I am up against," I say

"It shows all the evidence Ashton gathered on this guy's crimes. Elle was Ashton's girlfriend before he started with our team and she somehow ended up in trouble. No one knows what happened to her." he tells me.

"What if I said I could produce the flash drive to you with some conditions?" I ask "Also wait is Elle alive?"

"What type of conditions? It will take time to get the money together if it is a large amount," he says to me. " Also, we have no idea, no one can find her. If we had not met her before I would think she was just a ghost, someone Ashton made up".

"Money? I meant like protection from this person from the security company you are with, but I guess that will cost money." I reply "Can we continue driving and talking, please? I want to get cleaned up. I smell like a swamp." I ask with some exasperation in my tone. I am tired, hungry, and want to see Stella, she gives the best hugs.

He shakes his head and puts the vehicle in drive. I notice the other SUV is gone and that Z is texting someone, as I lean forward I catch a glimpse and it looks like updates.

"Where is the other SUV?" I ask

"Change of plans, we are getting you out of this town to a better hospital." Roark lets me know.

"Okay, can we grab my stuff from that bed and breakfast, please?" I point to it as we are driving up the street "My important things are in there, like my wallet and computer," I say.

"Yeah, but we will have to be quick and I will go grab it while you two stay in the car," he informs me.

That is fine with me. I just want to get out of here. I need to put this behind me and start my new life. That has been the goal all along. Get to college and follow my dreams. I see the bed and breakfast up ahead.

"Shit, the key was taken with my phone and notebook." I let them know

"Don't worry about it. I will be back in five minutes tops." Roark says

I watch out the window for him. Not much time passes before I see him coming out with my writing bag and suitcase. I sigh in relief that it is still there. He sets it all in the trunk. Then jumps in the driver's seat and takes off. I see someone coming out trying to stop the car.

"What did you do?" I ask

"Gave them no choice but to give me your stuff and then deleted your information from the computer that is why he is coming. We can't chance to leave information behind if there is someone else involved to have them find you."

"It's just the pale-eyed monster. What is his name anyway?" I ask "I am tired of referring to him as the pale-eyed monster."

"John is his name," he tells me

"Well, that is anticlimactic," I say with a sigh "I thought it would be something that a villain would have," I huff. I am at the point of not making any sense. Not sure what type of name a villain would have but I was not expecting something so common. "Does he have a cool last name? I ask after a little bit of time passes. I am way more invested in this than I should be.

" Last name is Green. So probably not what you were hoping for." Roark says to me.

We make the rest of the drive in silence. After about 2 hours we pull up to a gate. Once they punch in the code we head through. I see it looks like a mini town. I wonder if this is one of those secret law enforcement towns that people talk about in books. We stop in front of what must be the hospital.

"Let's get pictures done so that you can get cleaned up." Roark directs me into the building. "Stella should be here by the time you are done."

They have me change into a gown after documenting my clothing in photos. After that is done they give me a gown to change into putting my clothes into giant ziplock bags. Next, they have a female come in with the nurse and take pictures of me head to toe. They end up doing some swabs of me and a pelvic exam so they can have the results if something had happened. They also take a ton of blood. I hate it so much I feel more exposed than I did when I was in that basement. After that, they have me shower so that I can get seen by a doctor.

"When you get done showering, put this clean gown on and come to the station right outside the door. We will take you to be seen. Are you okay to shower? There is a bench in there to sit on and a help button if you need it." the nurse asks

"I want to try to do it on my own," I tell her, my words catching in my throat. I do not trust anyone to see me like this right now.

"I will be right outside the door if you need me," she tells me.

I take what feels like the longest shower of my life sitting on the bench in the shower stall. I am still processing things. The shower hides my tears in its stream. I hate that I'm crying but I can't help it. I can't tell if it's because everything in my body hurts or because the sight of it is so atrocious. There is so much dirt and blood coming off me. I start scrubbing my hair and body until it feels raw. I realize I opened the wound on my arm and thigh in the process but I don't care. I want the nasty feeling off me. I keep wondering who Elle is and why she was his obsession. What made me a target—even if it was by accident. Was it really just a wrong place at the wrong time situation? It isn't fair that I was kidnapped.

My hair is a tangled mess. I will have to have Stella help me get out later, but I just can't have her see me until I'm clean. Even though I've scrubbed so hard, my body is bleeding again, I'm still not clean. But I can't keep scrubbing.

After I brush my teeth I decide I need to head out to find the doctor. I am bleeding quite a bit by this point. I feel cleaner physically though and that is what matters to me. I am sure the nurse will have something to say about it. The only reason I was allowed to shower is because my wounds were not bleeding and they wanted them fresh for when I was stitched or bandaged up.

I see her before she sees me when I come from getting cleaned up. Stella is grilling Roark about where I am and what is taking so long. He smiles and points to me. Next thing I know she is running at me full force and hugging me. I hiss out in pain but do not stop her. I have been looking forward to this hug. I let the tears flow. I am so happy to see her. I never thought I would see her again after he almost found me. She notices that she is wet and pulls back. My blood got on her from the wounds. This makes me internally cringe.

"Sorry," I choke out.

"Let's get you cleaned up and seen" is all she says.

We follow Roark to where the doctor is. They start with cleaning then stitching and bandaging my two most significant wounds that I reopened in the shower. Now that I am not bleeding all over the place they say I need some scans. Along with starting an IV on me. They give me meds for the infection in both wounds. The IV is already starting to help me feel more human.

I turn to Stella. "Thank you for not giving up on me. I would have been so close to being caught if they had not shown up when they did," I tell her.

Roark cuts me off " You saved yourself, you are so strong." If you had not made your escape we may never have the evidence we needed to put him away."

"Bring me my laptop, please. I want a copy of the flash drives and then it is yours. I want to have all the information in case I need to run in the future."

Roark does not argue to my surprise and heads out to bring me my laptop. Thankfully this gown had a small inner pocket that I had slid it into when no one was watching me.

"Why do you need your laptop? What flash drive? Run where? What is going on?" Stella asks me all in one breath.

"I need it to copy the flash drive I found when I was kidnapped. It has evidence the guy that took me wants.

I don't know where I would run." I say trying to answer her rapid-fire questions

"They are just letting you copy it?" Stella asks.

"It was part of our agreement for me to hand it over. I have not shown it to them yet." I explain then stop talking when Roark walks in handing me my laptop.

I quickly pull the flash drive from my secret pocket and plug it in once my computer boots up. I back it up to my computer and then my secure writing cloud. Once that is done I email it for good measure and then hand it to him. He nods in thanks and sticks it in his pocket.

"What happens now?" I ask no one in particular

"Once you are released you will be able to head back to your life. They will most likely not have you come in person to the trial, you will be in a secure location via video to testify on your portion. That could always change though" Roark lets me know.

"Can I see Ashton before I leave here? I know it is a weird request and he does not know me but I have a gut feeling that I need to see him." I say to Roark.

"Of course. Let's get you better first." Roark says.

I settle into the bed and Stella crawls up next to me. I drift off to sleep. When I wake up I am alone and start to panic. Where did everyone go? Why would Stella leave without me? I hear her coming down the hall talking with someone.

"Hey! You're awake! I am so sorry I thought you would be sleeping longer." Stella says. I notice someone with her that I have never met before.

"Who is with you?" I ask confused

"This is Amethyst. These are her security friends that saved you, well picked you up." Stella tells me.

Roark cuts her off "I am Amethyst's best friend in the whole universe! You should introduce me properly."

I let out a little chuckle at his antics and say " It is so nice to meet you, Thank you for your help in getting me out of there. Sorry, I never got your meeting request and ended up missing it. It is an honor to meet you even under these circumstances."

"Don't you worry about that, we will have plenty of time to get to know each other. I feel like we are going to all become fast friends." Amethyst says with a genuine smile on her face. She is one of the most beautiful people I have ever seen. She has long brown hair pulled back in a bun with piercing blue eyes. Standing next to Roark she looks tiny. He is tall and muscular with short brown hair and hazel eyes.

I smile and notice the doctor standing in the doorway. "What's wrong?" I ask him.

"We just have some results to go over if everyone could clear the room, please." the doctor asks. As soon as everyone starts to move I shout. "No!" trying to control my panic. I take a deep breath.

"I want them all here with me I still have a long road ahead of me when this all hits me. I will need their support" I say a little calmer this time. I really do not want to be alone in this place.

Everyone takes a seat. He explains that there is an

infection in both my larger wounds so I will need to stay on antibiotics until it is gone. I will need to keep my bandages clean and change them regularly when I am discharged. I am also very dehydrated and need to eat. I am sure that I have lost weight from how long I was gone. Our best guess it was around a week. I also need to watch for depression and other mental health issues that may arise with the ordeal I have been through. I admit I already feel the anxiety but I want to try without medication to start. He says he will prescribe me a sleeping med and calming med so that if I need them I will have them on me and not have to wait. He recommends I find a therapist to help me process all of this once I get settled.

After the doctor finishes he asks me if I have any questions.

"Not right now, thank you," I say. He nods and walks out. I don't realize I am crying until Stella is wiping my face with a tissue.

"For how nice this place is that tissue is horrible" I state trying to avoid my feelings. I know that I will need to talk more about everything that happened, but right now I just want to avoid it for a little longer. Everyone smiles sadly at me. That turns into laughter when my stomach growls and startles me.

"I could really go for some soup to see if I can keep it down," I say

"We can make that happen, what does everyone else want? I will go grab it." Roark says.

Everyone puts their orders in and he heads off to

grab the food. I close my eyes and before I know it drift off into a light sleep. I wake to the smell of food. When I open my eyes I look around. My eyes widen at the amount of food that he brought back for everyone. It looks like he robbed a buffet. He brings me over a bowl of soup and some small oyster crackers. I take a bite closing my eyes. It's one of my favorite soups, vegetable soup. My room looks like a busy train station with people coming in for food. After everyone finishes eating he takes food to the nurses and doctors that had not made it into the room yet. Once the flow of people stops, everyone settles into their chairs again. I notice they are the kind that are made for people to sleep in.

"Are you all staying in here?" I ask

Everyone nods. That makes me feel a lot better. Stella turns the TV on to fill the silence. We are all exhausted from the day that we have had. I drift off to the TV. I wake with a start my breathing heavy and look around in a panic. I can see everyone is sleeping so I lay back down and try to calm my breathing. I was having a nightmare. It felt like I was back in the basement and all I could do was hear and smell what was around me.

I have to stay a few more days that are uneventful. Just bloodwork and bandage changes. They teach Stella how to help me change them so that I can have help once I go home.

On my last day, a few days after I got here, I remind Roark that I want to see Ashton. He lets me know he will come get me after lunch and take me there. I eat Lunch in my room with Stella. Amethyst had a business call to take and she will be back later when I am discharged. Right as I am finishing up Roark walks in.

"Are you ready to go?" Roark asks me.

"Ready as I will ever be" I reply.

Roark directs me down the hall to another room. "This is Ashton's room. Are you sure you want to do this? It is not a pretty sight." he lets me know outside the door.

"I don't know how to explain it I just have a feeling I need to meet him," I tell him.

"I will let you go in, I will check in with you in a little bit. I will stay close by in case you need me" Roark tells me.

I take a deep breath and enter the room. Meeting Ashton is a weird experience at first. I sit next to him and I can't help myself. I grab his hand. I look around and his room is like mine. Plain white walls a TV, dresser, and bathroom.

I don't know why, but I talk to him as if he was awake. I tell him about what happened to me.

"Did you know I found your flash drive? It is a funny story actually. I found it when I bashed my head on the board it was hidden under," I tell him. I wonder what he'd think of that. I wonder if I'm actually like his Elle. I am so lost in my own thoughts that it takes a minute to register that he is squeezing my hand.

I scream and try to pull my hand away. He still won't let go. Was it what I said about the flash drive? He's not moving other than holding onto my hand. His eyes are still closed, I watch expecting them to fly open.

Everyone comes running into the room in full panic.

Roark demands to know "What happened? Are you hurt?"

"Sorry, he squeezed my hand. I panicked. " I apologize to everyone.

Roark yells for the doctor and runs out of the room in a panic. Roark comes back with the doctor and I tell them what I just told everyone else. They decide that means it is time to slowly change his dosage and try to wake him up. I look down, noticing that I never let go of his hand. I decide that if it was me I would want someone to hold my hand so I keep holding it. Roark is pacing the room waiting to see what happens. They let us know it can take some time for him to wake up and that they will monitor it from the nurse's station. That if he wakes up we should grab someone. What feels like hours later I feel a squeeze again and look up. I look right into the greenest eyes I have ever seen. They remind me of the forest.

"Who are you?" he asks me, his voice cracking. "I thought you were Elle at first".

"I'm Astrid, I was the one talking to you when you squeezed my hand. You are not the first person recently who has confused me with Elle" I let him know.

"It's your eyes," he tells me softly.

"Who is Elle? Why does John Green, our kidnapper, want to find her so bad?" I ask.

"She's the key," Ashton says drifting off to sleep.

Courtney is an emerging writer that writes in a few

different genres. Courtney is based out of North Dakota, where she lives with her husband, daughter and 3 dogs. Courtney completed her M.B.A and is excited to start her Doctorate of Business Administration journey.

About The Author
Courtney Mae

Courtney contributed a chapter to the collaborative book Infertility Success, MORE Stories of Help and Hope For Your Journey that released April 2023. She spends some of her free time as the host of the Ripollsworkshop Reads Podcast where she has the exciting opportunity to interview Authors about their books and writing journey.

Follow Courtney and her Journey on Instagram or YouTube.

https://www.instagram.com/ripollswork shopreads/
https://www.youtube.com/@ripollsworkshopreads

The Evil Within

SALEEMA ISHQ

CHAPTER ONE
Now

What usually takes me seven paces only takes four today. I know because I've counted the steps from the lobby door to this elevator dozens of times. Every Monday and Wednesday at 9am.

One…. I am calm.

Two…. I am brave.

Three… I am strong.

Four… I am safe.

Five… I am in control of my mind.

Six… I am in control of my body.

Seven… I will get through today.

Each step and mantra is accompanied by an eye roll. I'm not entirely sure if the statements make an impact, but I'm willing to try anything. And I've tried *a lot*. Every trick, practice, or supplement that could help me with my "situation," as Dr. Finch describes it.

The mantras were her idea, of course. It's a technique she recommended so I could learn to feel more grounded in my body. But right now, there's no time to spare—no time for groundedness or intentions—so I leap across the linoleum in four enormous steps.

One… I

Two… Am

Three… So

Four… Close

My breath catches in my throat as I reach the elevator door. The pages clutched to my chest rise and fall with each heave. They're still warm from the printer, or maybe from my nervous body heat. Either way, I've got them. And without these testimonials, I have nothing.

On the days we meet, Dr. Finch always sends the elevator down to the lobby a few minutes before the hour, so it's waiting there for me as soon as I make that seventh step. But that's not the case today. Today is a Tuesday, so I'm forced to wait. And waiting feels especially excruciating right now, given the circumstances.

I jam the UP button repeatedly, jiggling my legs as I tear at my cuticles with my teeth. The soft tissue bleeds, but I barely feel the sharp sting. I'm too focused on the floor indicator light.

The sooner I get upstairs, the sooner I can have my life back.

***

As the elevator glides up to the sixth floor, I can feel my heart rate stabilize. The last year has felt like a whirl-wind—a nightmare that I'm going to wake up from at long last. Dr. Finch will finally understand that this is even bigger than either of us anticipated. Because it is *big*.

I can't wait to see the look on her face when she reads this, I grin and glance down at the stack of papers in my hands. Each floor I pass means I'm closer to freedom.

Three…

Four…

Five…

Just before I reach Dr. Finch's floor, the elevator lets out an enormous shudder. It rises slightly, then propels downward. My hand finds the metal handrail, my heart pounds against the inside of my chest. There's a loud thud as the metal box settles somewhere between the fourth and fifth floors. The lights flicker as I hold my breath, waiting for any sign that the elevator will start moving again. The lift stays illuminated but it remains completely still.

It's not unusual for the elevator in this building to bounce a little every now and then, but this is definitely strange. Still, I'm clear-headed and calm. *Jae would be so proud.* Not to mention, I've studied enough apartment and hotel preparedness manuals to know how to proceed. *That's one benefit of being the only one who worries about these things,* I reason with a shrug.

I press the DOOR OPEN button, then the DOOR CLOSE. Nothing. Next, I press the button for the sixth floor, then the fifth, and fourth until every single light on the control panel is illuminated. Finally, the call button. The elevator remains eerily still and silent. My fingers instinctively reach for the cell phone in my pocket as my Hail Mary, but I'm greeted with a "No Service" label at the top of the screen.

"It's OK, it's OK," I repeat to myself, not ready to admit what I already know. That I'm most certainly trapped.

As the panic sets in, my breath becomes fast and shallow. A tight lump of fear forms in my throat. I start to pace back and forth, trying to keep my mind occupied, yet all I can think about is how ridiculous it would be to die in an elevator. Suddenly I hear a soft metallic hum.

"Is someone there? I think the elevator is stuck!" I shout. But as the strange noise intensifies, it transforms into a wicked chuckle coming from within the elevator. My blood runs cold.

"Oh yes," it hisses. "Someone is definitely here."

CHAPTER TWO

6 Months Ago

My back aches from the position I've let my body fall into, precariously draped over my desk, but I'm too tired to move. Physically and emotionally. The alarm clock in the corner of my studio apartment reads

2:37am, yet time feels meaningless these days. I can't seem to get more than a few minutes of sleep no matter what I do.

I squeeze my eyes shut and will unconsciousness to take me, and for a mere moment, life doesn't feel quite so heavy. I'm floating through the clouds with Jae. We're holding hands and laughing, tossing M&M'S into each other's mouths just like we used to.

Yet the feeling doesn't last. We start to fall, faster and faster, out of the sky and toward the ground. I feel Jae's scream pierce my heart, and I want to shriek but can't. My mouth is wide, but I can't seem to draw any sound from my throat. Why can't I speak? Suddenly, two bright lights emerge from the darkness. They approach quickly, occupying my entire visual field until all I can see is light. It's too late.

I envelop my trembling body with my arms and shuffle across the room to the bed. There's a possibility I could fall asleep again, though it's unlikely after that nightmare. My thumbs find the meditation link Dr. Finch emailed me last week, and I doubtfully pop my earbuds in. Gentle oceanic waves fill my ears as tears fill my eyes.

"Jae," I whisper. "I'm so sorry."

***

My eyes blink open with a start. I hear the raspy whisper. "Wake up." I jolt upright and fumble for the light, but the voice stops me.

"No, don't. I don't want you to see me yet."

My entire body freezes. The warning makes me that much more desperate to turn on the light, but my limbs refuse to move. I'm shackled to the bedsheets by fear.

"Why did you hurt your friend?"

My breath comes out sharp and shallow as my heart starts to race. A downpour of panicked thoughts pushes sleep from my mind. *Who is in my home? Where are they? What do they want?*

My fingers inch toward the switch on the side of the lamp, my lips pursed tightly together as my mind swirls. *Wait, how do they know about Jae?*

"I know everything."

Light floods the room, and my eyes quickly search it. Nothing. I gingerly step out of bed, anticipating someone leaping out to grab me.

"Hello?" I peer around my studio apartment but am reminded there aren't many places someone could hide. I search under the bed, behind the curtains, in the shower, and in the furnace closet to locate the origin of the voice.

"Where are you?" I pant. Still, I see nothing. Until I reach out to push aside the clothes hanging in my closet and catch a glimpse of my left wrist. Rather, what was once my wrist.

The typically slender and knobby area has grown to a large bulge nearly the size of a softball. In the center of the writhing skin are two beady, red eyes and a leering grin. The sight forces my stomach to flip, bile rising up to my throat. I squeeze my eyes closed and shake my head before I reopen them, assuming the illusion is mere exhaustion—but the haunting face remains.

"What are you?" I whisper urgently.

"I'm you," it sneers. "The evil parts of you that you can't bear to look at."

My heart hammers against my ribs, and I stagger backward, catching myself on the edge of the bed. All I can muster is a weak "No" of sheer disbelief. The creature cackles and I can feel its amusement vibrate through my body.

"I'll leave you alone for now," it hisses, "but I'll be back. When you least expect it." It suddenly shrinks down before my eyes, leaving my wrist looking normal once again.

But the memory of the evil creature won't leave my mind. I fall back into bed, tears streaming down my cheeks. *This can't possibly be real.*

I spend the rest of the night tossing and turning, unable to shake the feeling I'm being watched. I feel like I'm suffocating in my own skin.

CHAPTER THREE

Now

The chill of the cold elevator wall quickly seeps into my back and down my spine. It's a natural instinct to want to escape a threat, but no matter how far I back up or how small I try to make myself, I know it's no use. I can't escape the creature. Not when it has already surfaced.

Believe me—I've tried many times with no success. Early on, I thought maybe I could smother it with a pillow. I held the pillow over my wrist with my other hand, stacking books on top of it for weight, but that failed miserably. The creature still taunted me, calling me pathetic, uncreative, and weak through its muffled voice. I even tried strangling it with a rubber band. That only led to an Urgent Care visit where they had to cut off the band before it cut off the circulation to my entire hand. But my most recent attempt was when I tried to suffocate it with a plastic bag. I was sure it would work because I'd isolated it, but just like every other attempt, it failed. And each time, the creature would continue to taunt me through the calculated event.

"You're a murderer!" it shrieked between wicked laughs. "First Jae," it sputtered. "And now me."

That's when I learned that it feeds off my fear. It grows stronger as I become weaker; a vicious cycle I am desperate to break.

And I was so close to breaking it— but now I'm stuck in this elevator.

"Help! Someone? Anyone? Help me, please!" I shout again, my face pressed against the cool elevator wall.

"No one cares about the poor little baby," the creature mocks.

I quickly rise to my feet and begin pacing the short length of the elevator. I know all the things you're not supposed to do while trapped in an elevator, like not jumping or trying to force the doors open. *But what else can I do?*

"What else can you do? You can wait. But it's not like anyone is going to look for you," it responds to my thought.

"Shut up!" I screech. "I'm trying to think!"

The creature is unfazed by my outburst, though I recognize a gleam of glee in its eyes. I need to compose myself and remain calm. I rifle through my purse, searching for any of the soothing tools Dr. Finch provided. I have my earbuds, a few pieces of sour candy, which can help distract the brain during a panic attack, and a variety of crystals I've been instructed to rub and hold as a way to soothe my nerves.

I pop a candy into my mouth and select a slender amethyst wand. As the tartness hits my taste buds, my jaw starts to tingle. *Just focus on the taste.* I close my eyes and force long, deep breaths. The fingers of my right hand twirl the crystal, and I feel my heart rate slow.

"Jae used to love those sour candies."

My eyes shoot open, and my momentary bubble of calm splatters to the floor. I feel the cloud of remorse and anxiety descend and settle in its place.

"Too bad she can't enjoy those anymore," the creature jeers through the dark cloud.

CHAPTER FOUR

1 Year Ago

Jae playfully slaps my hand away as I reach for the volume knob on the dashboard. "No, we need to blast this one!" she squeals at me, then doubles over with laughter as we prepare to sing the chorus of "Sweet Home Alabama." We belt it out together, our voices float out the open windows and through the air as we drive down Highway 414.

"OK, now we need to turn it down a bit," I caution.

"No one can hear us!" she responds, shouting over the vibrating bass. "Let loose for once, Addie."

Jae's always been the more gregarious one of our pair. The Phoebe Buffay to my Monica Geller, the Samantha Jones to my Charlotte York. But that's why I love her. She encourages me to do things I normally wouldn't, and I keep her grounded. And safe.

So it's no wonder it was her idea to steal my step-dad's car. "Borrow" was the way she put it. I knew he wouldn't mind, but it still felt weird doing it without permission. Yet here we were, cruising all the way to the next town over to meet up with some guys Jae met online.

"It's not that I'm worried about anyone hearing us, I just can't hear my own thoughts," I snap back, feeling the heat rise in my chest. My grip on the steering wheel tightens as headlights zoom past us. This strip wasn't nicknamed Death Highway for nothing.

"See!"

"Whatever," Jae mutters under her breath. "You always get like this. Sometimes I wish you were more fun."

The words sting more than they should. This was supposed to be a girl's night out, not an opportunity for Jae to remind me of my shortcomings. That's why I agreed to this little adventure anyhow. To break out of my shell.

"I'm sorry if my idea of having fun is staying alive." I mumble back.

"Are you serious? I'm not asking you to BASE jump! Just turn the radio up a bit." A crease forms between her perfect brows, and her chin juts out.

We both know this isn't about the radio. It's a culmination of every uncomfortable thing I've declined to do because I didn't think it was safe.

"Can we have a real conversation about this?" I glance over to the passenger's seat to make eye contact, but her gaze is fixed out the window at the final sliver of sunset peeking over the mountaintop, her arms firmly crossed.

"We just did. Turn the radio back up."

"This is not about the radio. Please talk to me."

"Well, you're just kind of..." Jae starts, then stops short. She bites her lip, as if considering for a minute if she really wants to say what is at the tip of her tongue.

"Kind of what?" I jab back.

"No, never mind."

"Tell me!"

"You won't like it."

"Oh, you don't think I can handle it? I'm not as strong as you?"

At that, Jae's small chest puffs up. She nervously twirls the tight curls at the nape of her neck.

"*Fine.* You're kind of pathetic," she finally blurts.

"That's not true," I whisper, hot tears blooming in

my eyes. Coming from anyone else, it would have just rolled off my back, but from Jae, it felt like a knife to my fragile heart.

"Well, it kind of is," Jae shrugs. "If you didn't have me, you wouldn't have anyone." Jae finally faces me, her eyebrows knotted with concern.

"You can't really rely on yourself, Adds. Even you have to admit you're really bad at making decisions. You don't trust yourself. Most people have gut instincts. You don't. Instead, you have me."

She's absolutely right. I swallow the statement like a bitter pill. *I don't have a gut; all I have is Jae.* It's all true. Bile threatens to rise up to my throat as I squeeze my eyes shut, tears cascading down my cheeks.

My moment of introspection is cut short by Jae's scream. I open my eyes to see two bright lights emerging from the darkness. They approach quickly, taking over my entire visual field until all I can see is light.

***

I know where I am before I even open my eyes. My clues are the beeping of the monitors assaulting my ears, the searing pain through my arm, and the smell of antiseptic that fills my nose. I jolt upright, but my head immediately feels like it weighs several tons, and I'm pulled back toward the hospital bed.

"Not so fast," a nurse chuckles as she gives my foot a squeeze. "Don't want you falling out of bed now, not after the tumble you took last night. Do you know where you are? Do you remember what happened?"

"Jae… Where's Jae?" I croak, eagerly accepting the cup of ice chips the nurse hands me.

"Oh, now, sweet pea, we should really focus on you at the moment." She smiles. "The doctor will be in shortly to let you know how surgery went and give you all the updates you need."

Surgery? As soon as she scoots out of the room, I slurp down the ice chips and try to assess my body through the brain fog. I can wiggle both feet. My legs are a little sore, but both appear to bend and move the way they did the last time I used them, which was evidently last night and not a few minutes ago, despite what my memory was telling me. I touch my torso and take a sharp inhale as my fingers graze over a very tender area. *OK, probably a few broken ribs.* And that's when I realize my left arm, the one I'd just used to poke at my chest, is encased in a rigid cast.

"Well, hello there!" The doctor strolls into my room and I try to sit up again, this time with a little more success.

"I'm Dr. Love. Do you know where you are, Addison?"

"Sure, the hospital." I look around. It's not hard to work out, so I'm not sure why everyone keeps asking me that.

"It's protocol." She playfully rolls her eyes and gives me a wink. "And you're absolutely right. We're in

Willow Meadow Hospital. Do you recall what happened?"

"I've kind of pieced everything together," I reply, rubbing my throbbing head. "But I don't remember much after the bright headlights coming right at me, then Jae's screa— Wait, where's Jae?" I'm finally able to wade through some of the fog in my brain and am reminded of my initial thought upon waking. But the physician carries on without so much as acknowledging my question.

"When your vehicle collided with the truck, Addison, your wrist bent in an unnatural direction and you sustained a Smith fracture to the distal aspect of your radius. Because you didn't experience any other major injuries and your vitals were stable, we took you to surgery right away to repair the traumatic wrist fracture."

Dr. Love barely glances up, or takes a breath for that matter, while relaying all the surgical details. It would be impossible to follow even if I weren't still sedated from the anesthesia drugs, but right now, it sounds like an entirely different language.

"—finally decided to place one large plate and nine small screws for optimal stability. They'll stay in unless they cause you pain or give you any other trouble, though they shouldn't. One of my colleagues recommended using an innovative surgical hardware, which we had your mom authorize befo—"

"Wait, my mom is here?" The mention of my mother wakes me again from my daze.

"Not yet." The doctor shakes her head. "She's on her way, but Jae's parents just arrived."

I nearly jump out of the hospital bed. "Can I see them?" I shout.

Dr. Love scans the monitor displaying my vital signs, then nods and steps out of the room to retrieve them. Jae's parents burst into the room and to my bedside, their faces tear-streaked and etched with worry. They don't have to say a word because I already know. Jae is gone.

Both of them wrap me up in a tight hug. We hold each other, sobbing and rocking back and forth until my mom arrives; then we do it all over again.

CHAPTER FIVE

Now

The usually small scar is now stretched to the size of a dollar bill across the side of the creature's face. If you can even call it that. Its entire body is essentially a large lump, which varies from the size of a lemon to the size of a basketball, depending on its mood. Or mine. The shiny pink skin of my scar looks as though it could deflate with a single touch.

Before I know it, my hand reaches for the scarred skin, but it's anything but delicate. It feels hard and tough under my fingertips. And searing hot.

"Whoa there," the creature croaks.

"Oh, sorry." I shake my head in an attempt to clear my mind. The air in this metal box feels heavy and stale, and I'm reminded that I haven't had anything to drink or eat since last night. My eagerness is to blame; I wanted to have everything printed then get to Dr. Finch's office as soon as her practice hours began.

"It's *my* wrist though," I say.

"What's yours is mine, doll."

I wince at the reminder and pop another sour candy into my mouth. *Calm, stay calm.* It has been nearly two hours of pacing, shouting, and repeatedly pressing the elevator's call button, yet absolutely no signs of movement or rescue. I punch each of the buttons again with my thumb.

"You're so stupid, you forgot about that one," the creature jeers.

"That's not a button, dummy, it's a keyhole."

"Yeah, but you still forgot it."

"I didn't forget it, I just don't have a key!"

"See? Stupid. You could try something else."

I examine the opening. It's not a traditional keyhole, but one that a barrel key might fit in. A small, vertical opening at the top, then a circular depression that the key fits right into. If I can find something sharp enough to pick the lock, I might have some luck in turning it.

It's right, I could try something else.

"Of course, I'm right," the creature rolls its eyes at me.

I raid my purse again, then rummage through my pockets. My stomach does a flip when I finally finger a bobby pin. I gently wiggle the pin into the top of the keyhole and hear a quiet click, then attempt to turn it, but the lock doesn't budge. *I need a second bobby pin to unlock the pins in the bottom part of the hole.*

I scour the elevator floor, searching for anything that might work. *A candy wrapper? Edge of my nail? There has to be something.* The only item that comes close to being pointy is the amethyst wand.

I grasp the faceted crystal with my right hand and carefully insert the sharper of the two sides into the hole. It doesn't fit. After adjusting my angle, I lean my weight into the wand, careful not to catch my shoulder on the opposite end. I hear a loud crack as fragments of the beautiful purple crystal fall away from the metal of the lock, but there's no click.

"This has to work," I huff, replacing my sweaty hands further up the wand.

"I don't know, it looks like you're failing miserably at this," the creature says, its terrifying face just inches away from my own.

I roar and throw my weight forward. The crystal crunches and I collapse into the control panel. I expect to find the wand next to me on the ground, but instead, it's protruding from the elevator wall at an abrupt angle. The area around the crystal is recessed; the keyhole is destroyed.

"No!" I scream, kicking upward toward the wand. My foot catches the edge and a piece of the amethyst hits the ceiling, creating a reverberating tinny sound. What remains is a sharp shard, too short to grasp and pull out.

"Welp, you've done it."

I crumple to the floor. *I've failed. Again. I am pathetic.*
CHAPTER SIX
6 Months Ago

"Based on what you've told me, I believe you're experiencing what are referred to as bereavement hallucinations."

A prickling sensation creeps up my neck at the term "hallucination." The relief of securing a last-minute appointment with Dr. Finch evaporates off my skin as it grows clammy and my pulse quickens. *I knew it. There's something terribly wrong with me.*

"No, no…" she starts, detecting my palpable unease. "They're incredibly common after the loss of a loved one," she explains, then adds, "It's just interesting that they didn't start until several months after the incident, but it's not uncommon to see delays in these things."

Dr. Finch scoots her stool closer to me as she tenderly inquires, "Are you still experiencing intense sorrow and rumination?"

"I mean, of course."

She simply nods curtly and continues, "Trouble sleeping?"

"Yes."

"Feelings of being detached from reality?"

"Mmhmmm."

She tilts her head to the side, puts her notebook aside, and folds her hands into her lap, as if she's made up her mind.

"Grief hallucinations can be visual in nature as well as auditory or tactical," she states. "You might see, hear, feel, or even smell things that remind you of Jae—"

"But this creature has nothing to do with Jae," I interrupt exasperatedly. "It seems almost evil." My voice quiets as I utter the last word, out of fear that it might hear me. Although I suspect it always can.

"Addison," Dr. Finch sighs, "you might not feel like these illusions are connected to your friend's passing, but I can assure you they are."

"How do you know?"

"How do I know?" she scoffs. "I've been practicing for longer than you've been alive."

A quick gasp escapes my lips, and her eyes bore into me.

"I've seen this scenario hundreds of times. Catching glimpses of a dead loved one, seeing visions of butterflies, cats, or, in your case, made-up creatures, which remind the sufferer of the person they lost. This is often the case when patients feel responsible for the death and hold onto a significant amount of guilt. Are you still doing your affirmations and meditations?"

I nod, then open my mouth to elaborate, but she continues.

"Good. Well, your symptoms don't align with any of the mental health conditions that are typically associated with hallucinations, so there's no need to initiate any medical treatment." Dr. Finch's tone is now filled with disdain, along with a whisper of frustration. "In my professional opinion, this is the best explanation. The *only* explanation."

"But—"

She holds up a hand. "Addison, I have been treating you since Jae died. I *know* you. Don't you trust me?"

I hang my head and muster a weak nod. But I'm not sure that I do trust her. How can I, when I know how real the creature looks, sounds, and feels? How real it *is*. But I'm also not sure if I can trust myself. Is my mind playing tricks on me and fabricating this fictitious creature out of guilt?

When I finally raise my head and open my eyes, I discover Dr. Finch has slipped out of the room. I'm alone. And I feel more alone than ever before.

CHAPTER SEVEN

Now

Despite stuffing my wrist between my thigh and the elevator floor, I can still hear the raspy voice.

"You are alone," it taunts. "No one believes you. No one cares about you."

I grind my molars and lean deeper into the floor until my entire arm throbs.

"Even your own doctor thinks you're making me up." Its voice is barely audible, but the poison behind it is crystal clear. "But deep down, I think you're glad she dismisses me."

"Excuse me?" I spit, glowering down at the creature.

"That's right, I think you're glad you have me." It grins back, bearing its grotesque teeth.

I quickly look away; I can't stare at the creature for too long because its appearance makes me physically ill. And I am not about to vomit in this tin can.

"You need me. Because without me, and without Jae, you have no one."

My nostrils flare, and I can taste the fury as it surfaces. Before, this ridicule would have forced me into a weepy pile of self-pity, but today the words ignite anger rather than shame.

"I need no one," I bellow. The statement flies out of my mouth so quickly it frightens me. Not the words, but the conviction behind them. And for the first time in my life, I truly believe it. *I don't need anyone, least of all the creature. Now that I know the truth.*

CHAPTER EIGHT

The Night Before

My fingers tremble as I type the words into the search bar. I'm less afraid of the creature catching me and more frightened of what I might find. Or worse, that I might not find anything at all.

Car accident + hallucinations. The computer screen illuminates against the dark room, and my eyes widen at the number of links listed. Over 6 million results. *So this is a thing.* I skim through the first several pages, but none of them are very helpful until I see a post that prompts me to change my search terms.

Recent surgery + hallucinations. Still nothing close to my experience. Evidently 40% of people experience some type of delirium following a surgery, which is usually secondary to the anesthesia drugs used during the procedure and more common in senior patients. But what's interesting is that the type of surgery can impact whether someone experiences postoperative delusions. *OK, so what about* my *type of surgery?*

Fracture repair surgery + hallucinations. Bingo. I see the words jump out at me even before the page entirely loads. *Anxiety. Delusions. Hallucinations.* I click on the top-ranking result: a medical forum with 743 entries. All from people who started experiencing hallucinations shortly after having orthopedic hardware placed in their body. All just like me.

The hallucinations vary in content, frequency, and location. Some people report they discovered a specific trigger for their hallucinations, like a specific song or place. Others wrote detailed accounts of what they saw — anything from zombies in the middle of the road every time they got behind the wheel of their vehicle to a mermaid tail that sprouted from their torso and replaced their lower limbs.

I pore over the stories like a hungry animal. My pen tears through the pages of my journal as I scribble down important details. These tales aren't just fascinating, but I feel as though I am finally getting close to discovering what exactly is wrong with me. What I am becoming. Or have already become.

But it's one entry from a user under the screen name

BionicBeAsT that turns my blood ice cold. BionicBeAsT has dozens of posts recounting their experience with a "monster," as they describe it, that erupts from their knee. It taunts them with words of shame, guilt, and fear. Just like my creature. And it always emerges from the same spot on their knee. A spot directly above an orthopedic plate surgically placed at Willow Meadows Hospital.

***

The last update from BionicBeAsT was written 2 years ago, and it seems they've gone completely silent since. Or maybe they were blocked by the forum moderators? Which, truthfully, wouldn't be a surprise considering their last few comments are pretty erratic. They're mostly gibberish, lots of all-caps shouting, and it looks as though they even tagged Willow Meadows Hospital in a post stating "these products   oopppwe[shouldN'T be on the market jur fdfa. thyshouldn't be put in ppls bodies. f sacred temples. DO yOU EVENT KNOW WHAttt THIS IS DOING TO PPL?/????a?."

Is this my future? Eventually succumbing to the creature? Going absolutely out of my mind? I shudder thinking about where BionicBeAsT might be now. If they're even alive still.

Their profile hasn't been removed, so it's worth a shot to see if they can give me any more insight into this demonic hardware.

SaddieAddie06 at 11:14pm: I found your stories on

the metal implant aftermath discussion board and I think the same thing is happening to me…

BionicBeAsT at 11:17pm: well howdy

SaddieAddie06 at 11:17pm: OMG!! I didn't know if you'd respond! It's such a relief to know you're OK. You're OK, right???!

BionicBeAsT at 11:18pm: oh yeah better than ok

SaddieAddie06 at 11:18pm: Ok, good.

SaddieAddie06 at 11:19pm: Wait, so can you tell me what happened after your last post? Is your monster still with you?

BionicBeAsT at 11:26pm: oh no i got rid of that sucker a while ago

SaddieAddie06 at 11:27pm: Ok… can you elaborate? What did you do??? How can I get rid of mine???

BionicBeAsT at 11:29pm: yeah so i cant really talk about it like legally i can't. wmh had me sign sumthing saying i wouldnt

BionicBeAsT at 11:29pm: they even scrubbed all that toxic metallosis stuff off the interwebs

SaddieAddie06 at 11:29pm: Wmh? Toxic metallosis??

BionicBeAsT at 11:33pm: yeah willow meadows where i had the surgery after i busted up my knee

SaddieAddie06 at 11:33pm: Oh! That's where I had mine done too! Well, not my knee, but my wrist.

BionicBeAsT at 11:34pm: oh snap you need to act fast that place is up to sumthing

SaddieAddie06 at 11:34pm: So it seems from your last forum posts. Is that why they had you sign an NDA or whatever?

SaddieAddie06 at 11:48pm: You still there?

SaddieAddie06 at 11:55pm: Hello???

BionicBeAsT at 11:57pm: all ill say is uv got to vanquish it if you want it gone for good

SaddieAddie06 at 11:58pm: Wait, vanquish? Like exorcize it?

BionicBeAsT at 11:58pm: well not exactly

BionicBeAsT at 11:58pm: the monster comes from the metal right

BionicBeAsT at 11:58pm: cuz the hardware they use releases sum kind of toxic chemicals into the body when they rub on each other

BionicBeAsT at 11:59pm: so no metal no monster

SaddieAddie06 at 11:59pm: Ok... how do I do that exactly?

"Oh, poor baby got a bad plate," the creature mocks as my wrist twists and grows.

My throat catches, and I frantically move the mouse to minimize my windows. I knew it would discover what I was doing, but I thought I would have more time.

"You wish. But you know your time is almost up."

Its eyes glow with an evil I hadn't yet seen— an evil that makes me hot all over. Fear oozes through my pores. The fear the creature loves to feed on.

"I'm bored with your games," I feign, attempting a yawn and stretching my arms above my head. Even though I know the creature is not real, I'm going to play along, at least until I can figure out how to resolve this.

In order to keep the creature at bay until tomorrow, I'll fake disinterest. Boredom.

"I'm going to bed."

At my neutral reaction, its eyes narrow. The glare behind its pupils transforms from irritation to pure hatred.

Something BionicBeAsT mentioned keeps trying to make its way to the forefront of my mind, but I don't dare let the words emerge. If I don't push them back, the creature will discover exactly what I'm thinking. It could guess my plan and try to stop me.

Yet, before I finally close my book and turn out the light, I steal a glance at the notes I'd taken earlier, which I have tucked inside my book jacket. One line leaps out: Want to vanquish your monster for good? You'll need to vanquish the metal hardware first.

CHAPTER NINE

Now

I'd grown used to being cautious and uncertain Addie, but something inside of me has changed. That woman has been replaced with someone with characteristics I've only ever admired in others. The transformation didn't occur the day the creature started appearing. No, it was long before that, the moment Jae was taken from me. Losing her and being forced to cope with life on my own— finally trusting myself— is the most significant transformation I've ever and likely will ever make.

Yet my experience with the creature has shown me that I've not only taken on a great deal of Jae's strength to cope with her death, but also a tremendous amount of guilt for causing it. And although I have felt whispers of this guilt slip away day by day, I'm ready to let it go entirely at long last. Free myself from its fetters.

"Oh, you think that, do you?" My hands tighten into fists, and I try to calm myself through long, deep breaths. When I don't respond, it tries again, "You know you'll never be rid of me."

"No, this is it. This is the end for you," I breathe.

My eyes scan the interior of the elevator and linger on the amethyst crystal stuck in the keyhole. The pointed end glistens invitingly. I'd wanted to touch it to see just how sharp it was, but pushed the thought out of my mind.

"One. I am brave."

But now, the creature's face falls as it sees the crystal.

"Two. I am strong."

"You wouldn't dar—" it wails, but I've already positioned my wrist above the sharp point.

"Three. I am free."

EPILOGUE

"We've got another one."

The maintenance technician lackadaisically grabs his radio and speaks into it.

"No response from the elevator, but we see someone initiated a call for help."

"Thanks, George. You know what to do," the staticy voice replies.

"Right..." he grumbles, wiggling his cell phone out

of his cargo pants and selecting number 4 on his speed dial. She picks up after only one ring.

"Hey, Doc. Pretty sure it's another one of yours. Want me to call 911 or do you have it under control?"

"No, George, I'll handle it. Thanks so much for letting me know. I'm sorry this keeps happening."

"I know, me too. These poor kids," his voice becomes momentarily grave as he ponders it, then brightens as he adds, "Oh, almost forgot to tell you—there's another gift basket down at the front from that Willy Meadow place, but this time it's addressed to Finch Orthopedic Supply. I'm guessing that's you?"

"Why yes, it is," Dr. Finch responds.

After she thanks George and hangs up the phone, her gaze returns to the live surveillance feed on her laptop showing George ambling through the building's lobby, the hallway directly in front of her office, and the interior of the elevator.

About the Author

Saleema Ishq

Saleema is an emerging thriller writer. By day she is an established content and copywriter and crafts pet-focused content for a digital publication as well as technical articles for various veterinary journals.

However, by night Saleema writes unsettling stories inspired by her own deep fears. Her medical background and passion for research allow her to create twisted thrillers based on truths that will make your pulse race.

Saleema also enjoys updating her blog, Fearless Phrases, along with journaling, running, reading, crocheting, and spending time with her pets.

Folllow Saleema on https://www.instagram.com/saleemaishq/for updates on her work.

Subscribe to her newsletter.Https://subscribepage.io/fearlessphrases

Or, check out her best-selling short story, Haunting Figures: A Psychological Thriller Story.

Dog Days

MICHELLE TENNANT NICHOLSON

INSPIRED BY A TRUE STORY.

I couldn't get Ruby's story out of my head. I was alone as I watched the fire flicker in my Smoky Mountain cabin fireplace. The nearest neighbor couldn't hear me scream, which was a departure from my other homes in Cincinnati and Chicago where neighbors couldn't only hear your whispers, they could hear you making dinner. This cabin was small with two bedrooms and a shower. Its living room featured a fireplace and the adjoining dining room was part of the charm.

The days were still hot and sultry, but the evenings were finally cold enough again for a fire. I loathed summer, and any hint of cool weather inspired me to turn on the gas fireplace in the evenings to cozy up. I sipped red wine I had purchased from the Biltmore

Estate, a local tourist attraction. Wine tasting ended the house tour and I was always a sucker for purchasing gift store items at tourist traps. The red liquid swirled around my tongue. I knew the sulfites would make my throat itch later, but I didn't care. I focused on the story I had just heard at dinner. Tiny prickly pins all over my throat were the cost of drinking wine, but the buzz always helped soothe the day. Especially a hot September day followed by a cool evening. Mountain weather fluctuations were the highlight of living in Saluda, North Carolina, a town made famous by its steep railroad track grade.

Saluda sits at the top of the Norfolk Southern Railway's Saluda Grade, made famous for being the steepest, mainline, standard-gauge railroad track in the United States of America. The Saluda Grade is not the only unique feature of the town, tt also boasts natural beauty, pleasing weather, and an ozone-rich healthy climate. Since moving to Saluda a few months ago, I felt I had arrived in Heaven on Earth.

The water flow was the reason I moved there. My business partner, Drew, bought a house there—a cabin in the mountains, this cabin. I was all-in moving there with him because I was a whitewater kayaker, and Saluda was famous for its notorious whitewater rapid called, "The Narrows" on the Green River. I would eventually call the Green River my home river and would protect it from development later in my life. That's another story for another time, though.

After settling into Drew's cabin as his housemate, I

learned the town of Saluda was first built in the 1870s to connect Spartanburg, South Carolina, with Asheville, North Carolina. To transport goods to growing communities via the train, a solution to building tracks along the Blue Ridge Escarpment was necessary. Many train conductors were fearful of the Saluda route because it dropped 600 feet in elevation for every mile and it included 50 curves. Hence the fame of railroad conductors among this small mountain town populated by just about 700 people. In the height of the Smoky Mountains leaf-turning season, the population might rise to 2,000, but the core locals knew who they were. And I was proud to be one of them.

Relaxing in front of the fire I felt alone and isolated. Ruby's words circulated in my head as the red liquid enveloped my taste buds. The fire crackled. The cabin felt larger and lonelier than usual. With no one in the house with me, I started to imagine hearing it moaning and aching. I sipped the red elixir to soothe the story swirling in my memory. Earlier that evening, Drew and I had met our mutual friend, Angie, for dinner at the Purple Onion restaurant on Main Street. We knew Angie from personal development seminars we had done in Cincinnati. Showing her the Purple Onion, the jewel of Saluda, was one way to introduce her to the town and to Western North Carolina.

Purple Onion was an upscale restaurant that featured live music a few times each week. Its food was organic and curated by a talented chef and her artistic husband. The town was small but it boasted tasty establishments, like the Purple Onion, to cater to tourists. The locals made the businesses succeed through long winters. One of its locals made quite an impression during our dinner. Oh, the dinner story. It just made my head hurt and my stomach stir.

I couldn't believe the nerve of Ruby, Saluda's local realtor. How dare she not tell Drew the history of the house before he'd purchased it? He was so upset with the story she'd spun at dinner, he'd driven to Asheville to seek comfort with the guy he was dating. Having designed the Grove Park Inn Spa, his boyfriend had a beautiful mountain house getaway. It was the perfect respite from having just learned the horrible history of our Saluda home.

Drew and I had met in Cincinnati, Ohio. Tonight, his stunning good looks would sway no one's behavior except his own. When he needed an escape from our house, he had one. I did not.

Everyone who knew Angie quickly learned from her storytelling she had a gift: She could intervene between two worlds, seen and unseen. Her ghost stories included first-hand experiences of expelling spirits. However, those stories took a back-seat to tonight's dinner story from Ruby.

Drew's realtor, Ruby, had come over to our quaint table and invited herself to sit down as we ate the Mediterranean plate appetizer. Drew rolled his eyes as her chair scratched the concrete floor, whining as it was dragged across the unforgiving surface. I assured Drew with my grin and let-it-be eyes it would be fine to indulge an old lady who obviously had too many drinks and didn't realize that she was crossing socially acceptable boundaries.

Ruby was a middle-aged woman who drank in excess almost nightly. With salt and pepper short hair, she was the town's gossip. Anything that mattered to town folk flowed through Ruby's lips. She repeated gossip faster than she heard it. The town never judged her for being a notorious drunk. In fact, none of the town's local alcoholics were. Instead, if the town witnessed someone plastered, they simply helped them to return safely home. Life is simple in a small mountain town. I had, so far, loved it. I never expected to learn what I learned.

After crashing our dinner, Ruby announced to the server she'd be having another cocktail at the table of her latest client, Drew, who had so generously bought a house that had been too long on the market. Ruby revealed she had been snooping at our cabin by congratulating me on the beautiful dog pen I'd put up in the backyard to house my sled dog, Lex. I looked at Drew. He shot me a glance, furious at Ruby. There was no way she could know about the dog pen unless she had parked in the driveway and walked around into the backyard. The dog fence was not visible from the street, and certainly, most people wouldn't have known about a new dog pen. The jig was up on Ruby's spying. Since the house was small and secluded in the forest, Ruby must have waited for all the cars in the driveway to be gone before embarking on her nosy neighbor routine.

Ruby continued her accolades on renovations made, only making Drew more furious as she unconsciously exposed her meddling.

I'd poured myself another glass of wine, well on my way to approaching Ruby's state of mind. Her son came to rescue his drunk mother, but not before she told us the town's secrets about the house we now called home. Her revelation was as clumsy as her walk toward our table, peppered with alcohol and the aggression of a homeless person down on their luck. We all choked on our food as she blurted the unspeakable.

"The dogs ate her face off!"

Drew instantly stopped eating the olives and hummus. I coughed on my beverage. Angie put down her fork and wiped her mouth with her napkin. A nearby table glanced our way and pretended to not notice the scene and shocking story.

"Can you believe that?" Ruby asked, slurring her words. "Ate her face off. I guess the dogs were hungry being cooped up in that house for almost a week. I guess she died of asthma or some kind of heart-related incident. Literally fell over dead at the dining room table. The neighbor found her days after. That neighbor was so traumatized she refused to step inside the house after that. They were very close friends. Well, as close as mountain people can get. I mean, she was so alone in that house. Just her, the dogs, and her guns. That's a bummer to die and then your dogs eat you, don't you think?" Ruby's words spat at us like an alcoholic rain shower.

I had also stopped eating as Ruby recounted the tragedy inside the house we had just bought and moved into. For weeks now we had been cleaning and remodeling the house, having had to wade through and dispose of the previous owners' hoarded belongings. We knew she had been a country woman who owned guns, antique stoves, and knick-knacks from the turn of the century. We had been told the lady lived alone and that her husband had died many years ago. However, we were not told she died in the house and that her dogs had eaten her flesh to stay alive.

As Ruby's son helped her up and out of her chair, he said he would take her home and apologized for her drunken state. The entire restaurant watched Ruby as her son helped her leave. Everyone was quiet and unwilling to speak about the alcoholism afflicting their town realtor. As soon as her son got her past the front door, chitter chatter among dinner diners returned and so did the happy energy of our meal. However, the ghost of the house's history lingered over our meal.

As I replayed Ruby's story, I watched the flames flicker as the wine comforted my tongue. I didn't let my eyes wander around the house. I was so creeped out by the story I didn't know where to look in the house to get comfortable. One frame only separated the dining room and living room, completely open to each other. I thought I had seen shadows as the flames glistened against the walls, so I turned on the kitchen lights, hoping to illuminate any bad energy in the house. I could see the kitchen's reflection off the living room windows. As the moon rose outside, darkness fell on the house's porch and the flames tickled the shadows on the glass.

Without Drew in the house, I felt alone. So alone my mind played tricks on me as I recounted Ruby's house of horrors told during dinner.

"What do you think human flesh tastes like?" Ruby was so drunk she had no filter.

Drew, disgusted with Ruby, lashed out, "How come you didn't tell me how the previous owner died when you sold me the house? I thought it was the law that a realtor needs to disclose such facts!"

Angie and I remained quiet as Ruby and Drew had words with each other.

"Oh, you're just forgetting the fact that I told you," said Ruby as she slurped her beverage. She continued with her he-said-she-said facts. "Why on earth did you think the house was so cheap? Anyone would know the house was that cheap because something unusual kept it on the market that long."

I hadn't accompanied Drew to the closing on the house. So I didn't know what was true.

The flames continued to fluctuate and reflect off the windows. I noticed my Siberian husky roaming about the living room. He moved over to my face, smelled my wine, and licked my cheek.

"Oh, hi big boy. Don't eat my face. I'll let you out to pee," I heard myself say as I stumbled to my feet. My two tabby cats, Ebb and Flow, ran to the door right behind Lex to meet the dead of night to prowl, pee, and prance with the creatures of the night. All three ran out of the front door. I almost fell as Lex's strawberry-blonde fur and seventy-five-pound body pushed me against the door on his way out. He rarely barked, but he let out a big sigh as he made his way outside. For him, the sigh was a reaction to the fire on a balmy evening. It was simply too hot and the cool mountain air outside was preferable to the increasingly hot oven the cabin was becoming.

I stood in the open doorway and looked across the living room to the dining room. I thought about Ruby's words at dinner and Drew's horrified reaction to the history of the house. The dining room is where she would have fallen face down on the table upon her death. That is where her dogs ate her face off. This door is where the neighbor walked in to find her. I imagined the horrific scene as I swayed between my toes and my heels. The liquor eased my fears. I listened to the crickets outside, and felt the wind gently swooshing the door an inch forward and an inch backward. Toward the toes, back on my heels. Back and forth. The door swaying side to side.

Suddenly, there was a loud thud and I jumped forward. The wind had closed the door hard and fast. My heart was racing. With my cats and dog outside, I was alone in the house. I walked over to the dining room. Lex was right; the fire in the living room was too hot.

I recalled the hoard in the corner we had just cleaned out and placed in the rental dumpster. Why was the previous owner a hoarder? Ruby had said her name was Judy. What happened to Judy when she died suddenly? Was it asthma? Was it her heart? Was her hoard toxic? Did it cause her asthma?

Ruby thought it had been Judy's heart, but others had felt it was her asthma, which was something that she really complained about toward the end of her life. Ruby described Judy's dogs as she recounted the horror that plagued the house. German shepherds: Two males and one female.

My heart was still beating quickly as I stood in the dining room, the likely spot where the unimaginable had taken place.

I shook my head as I tried to rationalize what had happened. So what if the dogs ate her face? They were hungry. No one was there to attend to them, and their beloved human companion had turned into rotting meat. Of course, dogs would eat decaying meat. It's just natural. The thought of the dogs eating rotten meat turned my stomach and I ran to the bathroom. My bulimic teenage years reared their violence. I threw up the wine and restaurant food. Throwing up made me feel in control of my body and circumstances ... at least for a little bit.

++++++

After washing up in the bathroom, I notice that my hairbrush is missing and so is my hair jewelry. I look in Drew's room to see if I had left it in there. I hadn't. I walk outside on the porch to check on the pets and to see if I had laid my things down out there, but I can't find them. I also can't find my favorite shoes. I always leave them by the door. Worn earlier, I couldn't figure out where they were now. So weird. The dog is lying on the grass, very content. I can hear the cats rustling in the woods behind the house. I decide to not call them in the house and instead let them roam free. I wish I could be free like them without the worry of the house's history. The evening air is cold, and I decide to go back into the living room to sit by the fire again.

I sit back down on the couch, about to pour myself another glass of wine, when I notice my wine glass is now missing. Bothered by the missing items, I search for them through the kitchen cabinets. My memory must be playing tricks on me. My things just seemed to be disheveled. I tell myself it's probably sleepiness and I walk back toward the living room—but the dining room calls to me.

I sit at the dining room table and lay my head down on it with my left cheek soaking up the cold energy of the varnished wood. "Did Judy have her head like this when she died?" I mutter to myself. "Or did her face fall forward?" I rest my forehead on the table. Its coolness turns to warmth as I imagine dying at the table like Judy. I roll my head to the other side and allow my right cheek to find a new cool spot to cast a body-heat spell upon.

Suddenly, a loud knock at the door wakes me up and propels me out of my chair. My heart races again.

Lex is at the door trying to get in quickly. His husky paws are rapidly striking the door. I walk over and let him in. He scampers past the living room and dining room and into the side room where I've made my office. It's cooler out there because it has a concrete floor. His quick entrance concerns me, so I walk outside to see if there is something to worry about.

I step off the porch and into the yard near the forest where the cable man had warned me to not heed the sound of babies crying. He claimed that mountain lions sound like babies crying and have jumped investigating humans, ending their lives instantly. Standing near the forest's edge, again I only hear crickets, the swoosh of the wind, and an occasional hoot from an owl preparing for the evening hunt. I walk around to the back of the house where Judy had installed a hot water faucet. The dog pen I had erected stood a few feet from the hot water hose.

The cool mountain air chills my skin, so I turn on the faucet to feel the warmth of the water. It flows out so hot; I imagine Judy bathing herself in the backyard, not just her dogs. I spray my mouth, washing away the bile from vomit, pretending my secret habit doesn't still plague my third decade of life. I let the hot water fill my mouth and gums. Water washes away all sins of the flesh and I wonder if it's the same for animals. Does God wash away the sins of animals the same as humans?

I ponder whether Judy was a religious soul. I had been raised in the South and reared in a very religious home. While I was growing up, my father read the Bible every day, so belief in Heaven and Hell was a strong element of my childhood. I wonder if a woman who died and had her corpse defiled by her pets would end up in Heaven or Hell. I wonder how her family came to be at peace about what happened. Did she have any surviving children or relatives? I imagine what my Catholic priest in Louisville would have said about the woman's unseemly funeral, and how the people would have discussed the woman's face at the post-funeral meal. I imagine the church congregation being full of gossip and disgust, and I wonder if Judy deserved such gossip. Had she been a good woman in her life? Full of service to others? Or had she lived alone because she wasn't friendly?

I started to imagine my own death and what would happen if my own pets turned to my flesh for meals.

As my imagination gets the best of me, an owl swoops low and past me. I become concerned for my cats and turn off the water as I whistle them in for the night. The ground is wet and soaks my socks as I stand and call for my cats. I hear bushes bustling, bugs burping, and predators preying. The night sounds spook me, so I run to the front of the house, yank open the door, and just as I'm about to shut the front door, my two tabbies run past my legs. I feel their wet fur brush my cool damp calves. They too head for the side room and concrete floor as the fireplace continues to heat the house.

I stand in the living room and watch the fire shadows dance over the glass. My drunken state plays tricks on my mind and I think I see a woman's image beside mine in the window. I jump back and run to the kitchen. There, I slowly drink a glass of water. I must sober up, I tell myself.

++++++

The phone rang. It was Angie.

"Hello," I said as I picked up the phone. My voice was raspy from having thrown up my meal and drink. I smelled like wine, bile, and dirt.

"Hi Michelle, I just wanted to check on you. That story at dinner was pretty gruesome and I know you're home alone. How are you doing?"

Angie was not only a friend and past lover, she had promised to perform a blessing on our new house. Since she had the sixth sense, she could see dead people and help them cross over. It thrilled me she was going to help with the horror of the house we had just moved into. After Ruby's story at the restaurant, Angie had promised Drew and me she would clear our cabin.

I was thankful to hear from a friend, thankful Angie cared for me. Being alone had weighed on my senses. My imagination was playing tricks on me, and I was feeling frightened by the smallest noise.

"Oh, Angie, thank you so much for calling. I am feeling weird in this house tonight. I mean, shit is missing and I've now drunk as much wine as Ruby did cocktails. I'm just trying to numb out from the story she told us. Just gruesome, wasn't it?" I asked.

"Indeed, it was, honey. Listen, it's natural though, right? The dogs were hungry. They didn't see the previous owner as their person. They were just hungry. It's just their nature to eat meat."

"Yes, I guess," I said weakly into the receiver. "I've just been here looking at the dining room, wondering about how it all happened, you know? Did I ever tell you about the first time I stepped foot into this house, Angie?"

"No, Michelle, I don't think you have. Tell me. I have time. Do you?" Angie invited the story, and I could hear her settling into a chair to listen.

"Sure. Of course, and it will help me bide the creepy time in this house tonight," I replied. "Well, I was driving back to Cincinnati from a job interview in Greensboro, North Carolina, and I called Drew, who suggested I should make a detour and look at this house. I told him it would be dark by the time I arrived but he said it would be easy to find, so I took him up on the offer. Well, I couldn't find the house. It was about 11 p.m. when I arrived and, since the house is in the country, there were no streetlights. I almost gave up, but I drove down to Main Street where I saw a storefront police station. You know, it's just like Mayberry in that television program *The Andy Griffith Show*. I remember driving down Main Street and feeling like I had entered another show, *The Twilight Zone*. Do you remember the surreal storylines of that show? I loved it but it always freaked me out. I felt that way when I arrived in Saluda for the first time."

Angie laughed through the phone receiver and her

cackling filled the house. The fire crackled and popped as Angie's laughter flew through the space like glitter.

"Yes, I remember those shows," Angie confirmed.

"Well, I was so lost," I replied. "So I stopped and asked the police. I could see one officer through the glass window on Main Street. It was like he was in the actual show. Imagine that hometown officer character, Barney Fife, with a bulletproof vest on. I mean, for real, a bulletproof vest he had on." I emphasized this with a laugh.

Angie laughed even louder. "What?! A bulletproof vest in a small town of 700 people? I can't believe it!" Angie's laughter intensified. The fire's pops and crackles intensified.

"It's true," I told Angie. "At first he was just like Officer Fife on that show and asked me questions about my identity and what I was doing in Saluda at 11 p.m. on a Friday night. I explained to him I was thinking of moving with my business partner to Saluda to start our own firm, but I hadn't decided yet, was coming from a job interview, and that looking at the house he was looking to buy would help me decide if I wanted to sell my apartment building in Ohio to move to North Carolina. Boy, I also poured on my Southern accent real thick."

"You did?! I bet you did," said Angie, who'd also grown up in Louisville, Kentucky, like I had, and could turn her accent on or off at will.

"I really did," I agreed. "He not only took me to the house, he gave me a police escort. It was great."

Angie giggled.

"I was shocked at how hoarded the house was," I told Angie.

"Really?" Angie asked. "What do you mean, hoarded?"

"Well, the house was full to its brim," I told Angie. "I mean, every room was full, especially the dining room where she died. Behind the dining room table, there was a bookcase and all kinds of knick-knacks were there. You couldn't really move without possibly tripping over all the shit in the house. I mean, the story of how her dogs ate her face off is gross, but if you've ever seen a house hoarded to its brim ... well, equally horrific. This house was like that. Drew and I have been working so hard to donate items to charity, throw away trash, and just clean up the house to live in. Thank you so much for offering to help with your energy blessing."

"Well, Michelle, you are so welcome. It's my pleasure. We'll do just what I told you to do to clear out the energy in your house in Ohio, remember?" asked Angie.

That was when Angie and I were dating. She and Drew visited my house one night, and Angie had walked through the house only to exclaim, "You have ghosts in this house!" I laughed at her and said, "I know."

It was right after 9/11. Angie explained that the reason ghosts cling to old homes is that the people left behind think about them and love them so intensely that their connection to the Earth is challenging to sever and they get stuck between the worlds. She said lost souls need our help to move on.

The night Angie told me I had spirits living in my west-side duplex, I went to the top apartment and set up a moving-on ritual on its back porch. I didn't really believe her, but had felt unexplained cold spots in the house and sensed someone was staring at me when I was alone. (Much like how I felt now, alone in the Saluda house.) On the night of the ritual to ask the ghosts in my Cincinnati house to move on, I could not feel any breeze or wind when standing outside. It felt like stagnant air. Half-hearted, I said a prayer out loud, laughing some too. I said, "Spirits in this house, you must move on and you are not welcome in this house any longer. Once I light this candle, I request you to leave." I lit a candle. A few seconds after lighting the candle, a forceful wind whipped past my body and blew out the candle. It also shut the porch door. After the gust of wind, the porch felt eerily peaceful, and I just sat in my chair in the darkness processing what had just happened.

I never felt the cold spots in the Cincinnati house again. I also never sensed people watching me when I was alone. I couldn't explain it, but after the ritual there was something different about my Ohio house. Curious about my house, I did research into who had lived there before me. It was registered as the *Covedale Share-A-Home,* which would explain the numerous bedrooms on each floor. Evidently, elderly people shared a home together and many of them had died in the house.

As I recounted the story to Angie and acknowledged her for teaching me how to help those who died to pass on peacefully, the fire in the cabin roared. I told her I was scared to be alone in the house and she talked to me with purpose, assuring me that my uneasiness was totally natural and that the woman who had died in the house had probably left energy behind.

"What are we going to do about it?" I asked with fear resonating in my voice.

Angie said, "I will help you. Don't worry."

I told Angie I wasn't feeling well and that I needed to take a bathroom break. Not wanting to leave me alone, Angie promised to call me back a bit later in the evening. I obliged her and agreed, even though the fire was spitting, the house was hot as Hell, and I just wanted to let her go.

Suddenly, I didn't want any help and certainly didn't want to talk to anyone.

After I hung up the phone, I went back into the living room to turn down the fireplace. It cracked and popped, and I saw out of the corner of my eye a shadow flickering in the window. Was it my reflection? Or was it the ghost of Judy looking for her dogs?

I turned quickly and snapped on the lights. I couldn't take the images any longer. Was it a ghost unwilling to leave, or was it my imagination playing tricks on me after a long night of drinking?

My socks were still wet, so I went into the side room where I'd made my office. It doubled as a bedroom, and all my pets were fast asleep. I changed into pajamas and put on dry socks. But they weren't my PJs and socks. Mine were missing, so I put on Drew's fresh laundry. Little by little, my things had gone inexplicably missing in the house.

Sitting on my bed, I woke up my dog to cuddle with me as I tried to sleep. Lex would normally cuddle for just a few minutes before he got too hot, but this night he indulged my requests for hugs and kisses longer than usual. I fell asleep and dreamed that I was the woman who had previously lived in the house.

In the dream, my hair was gray, and I owned the three German Shepherds Ruby had described. I finished bathing them in the backyard and fed them in the kitchen. They were energetic but played nicely together. After dinner, the two males lay down on the floor in the living room. The female curled up on the couch with me in front of the gas fireplace. The side room was closed; I used it only for storage. Near the couch was a shotgun I kept in case intruders came to the door. After all, the Jehovah's Witnesses had just been making the rounds, ringing doorbells. While they claimed to be Godly people, you never knew out here in the middle of the forest.

While I was petting my dogs, I heard a baby crying. It startled me at first, but I was no fool. I knew a mountain lion when I heard one. I stood up from the couch, carefully removing my dog's head from my lap. As I moved toward the door, I grabbed my shotgun then walked outside. The crying got louder and louder. Suddenly, down the tall mountain behind the house, I saw a shadow racing toward me. I fired the gun toward it but the shot didn't stop it.

I fell to the ground as I tried to turn and run back to the house. The lion pounced on my body, ripping my flesh, and I turned toward its face. As I met its eyes, it took a bite out of my face.

I woke up.

My dog, Lex, was licking my face, trying to get me to wake up. Evidently, I was crying in my sleep and Lex was worried. He's surrounded me, and so have my cats. They all seemed to be worried about me. They stared at me. Lex stopped licking me and simply stared at me.

"Are you all hungry?" I asked them as they watched me. The three didn't make a sound and simply watched me.

I felt different. I noticed they weren't begging for petting, nor were they responding to my suggestions for treats. They just blankly stared at me. My dog licked his lips. Then so did my cats. I felt self-conscious and worried for my safety.

The abrupt loud ring of the phone broke my gaze on the pets and had me jumping up and out of the side room back to the dining room table. It was Angie.

"Just calling you back. Is the night peaceful for you yet?" Angie asked.

"Peaceful? No, I just caught my pets staring at me like I was their dinner," I said in a breathy, worried voice.

"What? Are you imagining things now?" asked Angie.

"I don't know. I guess I was dreaming. I thought I saw a shadow of a woman reflected in the window," I informed Angie.

"A woman? Is there another person in the cabin now?" Angie asked.

"I'm sure it's just my imagination playing tricks on me. I fell asleep a little and dreamt a mountain lion was eating my face off, just like those dogs did the previous owner's face. Mountain lions cry like human babies. Did you know that?" I said, crying a bit myself.

"Calm down. I'm here to help you out. Don't worry so much," Angie said, reminding me to take deep breaths.

"I can't seem to calm down in this house, though. Did I tell you my stuff is disappearing? I don't understand why I can't find my stuff. It's like the shit is going into a deep dark hole," I reported to Angie.

"You're going to be okay," promised Angie.

"How do you know for sure, Angie? I mean, you're not here. You can't possibly understand what it feels like to be alone in a house where a person died and her pets ate her face off. I'm freaking out over here and you're casually on the phone stating platitudes like everything is going to be okay. Kiss my ass, Angie, okay? Just kiss my ass."

Angie started to laugh. "Well, bend over and I'll kiss your ass."

"What?" I said, wiping my tears. Anger turned into laughter.

"You're getting intense over nothing," stated Angie. "I'm calling to help you, remember?"

"I guess." I sheepishly apologized for raising my voice as the tears ran down my face. "I am just so upset over what happened. I don't want to be in this house by myself anymore. I just want to leave."

"You can leave, Judy," Angie said.

"What did you just call me?" I asked.

"Judy. I called you, Judy. Isn't that your name? Drew and Michelle told me your name is Judy."

I rushed over to the glass window and looked at my reflection. I saw an old woman whose face is half eaten off.

"Oh, I'm Judy."

Angie said, "I'm requesting you move on, Judy. I'm requesting you leave Michelle and Drew alone in this house. You are dead. You died of asthma. Your carpet liner aggravated your asthma, and you died suddenly in your house. After three days, your dogs fed themselves on your flesh. You may move on now. Your dogs are being cared for by other neighbors near you in Saluda. You don't have to stay at this house any longer. You are free to cross over. You don't have to be confused by haunting Michelle any more. She has a body. You do not and you are not welcome to use her body in this house."

I stared at myself in the glass window. The fire flickered and sparkles shone around me. I noticed the smell of sage burning in a dish. In an instant, I relinquished my hold on the house and my soul was free from its earthly tether.

. . .

About the Author
Michelle Tennant Nicholson

Good Morning America Producer Mable Chan calls Wasabi Publicity's Chief Creative Officer Michelle Tennant Nicholson a "five-star publicist," but Michelle calls herself a "storyteller to the media." An award-winning writer, Michelle peppers PR campaigns with insight from her master's degree in human development, BFA from a top 25 drama school, and expertise seeing PR transition from typewriters to Twitter.

She is the author of "The Dairy Princess Chronicles: My Journey to W.R.I.T.E. the Trauma," in which she shares how she at 17 years old incarcerated the neighborhood pedophile, healed her own mental injury, achieved a life filled with happiness, and shows others how to pursue the same. She writes a blog "Mental Injury is not Mental Illness: From Fight, Flight, Freeze to Flow" at http://www.writethetrauma.org/

Sign up for her email list https://mailchi.mp/7fd07c96fedb/michelle-tennant-author-newsletter

Find her short story, true crime thriller.

Isla del Coco

DEB COLLINS, SONJA DEWING, DITA DOW, AND
SALEEMA ISHQ

BELLA SINCLAIR (aka Denise Smith)

The clang of metal broke through the quiet, pulling my focus to the mail slot in the kitchen door. The brass surface, weathered by time and countless deliveries, bore the scars of its role. I watched as a cascade of envelopes streamed onto the floor. Among the stack of mundane bills and colorful advertisements, my eyes locked on a cream-colored envelope.

With a mix of anticipation and trepidation, I retrieved the envelope and stared at the calligraphed name above my address. I traced the delicate curves of the name, Bella Sinclair, with my fingertips. A rush of emotions flooded over me. It was not just a name, but my name. A name that was dead to the world.

Gently, I slid my finger under the flap of the envelope and pulled out a letter, unfolding it with care.

The words on the page swam before my eyes

momentarily, and an unexpected surge of tears clouded my vision. It was a letter from James Barlone, the son of Vera Barlone—a name that carried with it memories of laughter, camaraderie, and shared secrets from years gone by. As I read James's words, a heaviness settled over me, mourning not only the loss of Vera but also the passage of time that had eroded our once unbreakable bond.

The letter revealed Vera's final wish for me to attend her memorial service on Isla del Coco, a secluded and picturesque island off the coast of Costa Rica. Emotions swirled within me—grief, nostalgia, and a sense of duty to honor my cherished friend.

But there was a secret about Vera that I had guarded fiercely, one that had shaped the trajectory of my life in profound ways. As I stared out my window at the cityscape, I felt determination, anxiety, and a gnawing fear of what the memorial service might reveal.

I couldn't shake the memory of that fateful night, the night when everything changed. The echoes of that evening still reverberated through my mind, a constant reminder of the pact Vera and I had made. A pact I had sworn to keep hidden at all costs.

I carefully folded the letter and placed it back in its envelope. I pressed it against my chest, feeling the weight of the decision settle over me. My journey was not just to an island; it was a voyage to protect the truth and to shield myself from a past that threatened to resurface.

· · ·

Darcy Lloyd

Leave it to Vera to orchestrate her own memorial, but that was Vera for you—always the planner, the boss, the one to make you do something you didn't want to do. I hadn't interacted with Vera for three decades, and here I was at her beck and call once again. But little did Vera know that when she'd planned her end, it would benefit me perfectly.

What a huge ordeal it had been to get here. It had stormed from the moment I landed at the San Jose airport to the moment I stepped onto this God-forsaken island. The driver of the pontoon boat—the "private boat transportation" that was promised—had thrown my bag into the hold without a word and pointed to a cooler with "Complimentary Beverages" scrawled in marker on the top. Inside were lukewarm water bottles. For the entire thirty-minute ride, harsh rain pelted me sideways. I was soaked by the time we arrived at Isla del Coco.

A middle-aged man in a drab brown ranger outfit was waiting for me in an old Army-green Jeep parked on the slender beach. The air was a mixture of humidity and the scent of seaweed that had washed up from the storm. The ranger sat behind the wheel, staring at me, so I hoisted myself up and into the backseat. He started right in.

"So how do you know the recently deceased?"

"An old ex-friend," was all I knew to say, because that was pretty much the truth of it. As I squeezed water from my pant legs, I added, "Not even sure why I made the guest list, to be honest."

The beach disappeared behind us as we drove into a dense jungle, where a cacophony of bird calls and buzzing insects accosted my ears. I could barely hear him when he said, "Well, memorials are sometimes the best way to bring the truth to light."

I shivered—from his words or my wet clothes, I wasn't sure which.

About ten minutes later, we drove into a clearing with a massive two-story stone lodge and an outbuilding. He parked at the front door and again made no effort to grab my suitcase or help me out of the Jeep. "You're the first one here. Electricity's out from the storm," was all he said before he sped away.

The lodge was stately and looked out of place on this little outpost island. I walked inside and was instantly hit with the smell of moss and oak from candles that were burning on what seemed to be every possible surface. There was no natural light—despite the sun having broken through the clouds, all the window shutters were closed.

There was a piece of paper taped to the wall with a schedule of events for the weekend. I had to squint to read it in the dim candlelight. I could see I was going to have to suffer through a formal dinner tonight with a bunch of random people. Tomorrow looked to be just as painful with a group breakfast and a late-afternoon jungle excursion. It looked like the memorial service and reading of the will was tomorrow at noon in the… *Surely that doesn't say 'in the cemetery'?*

Maybe I wouldn't go to that. Lord knows I didn't need anything from Vera, or from anyone for that matter.

I walked around the room and ran my hands along the old furniture. Curious, I opened the doors to a dark wood console table. Inside were cream-colored envelopes—smaller versions of the envelope that had come in the mail a week ago. They were sitting inside a basket with names written on the front.

I looked through the pile and recognized the names: James Barlone, Vera's son; Lola Danvers, Vera's business associate; Terran Falco, Vera's latest conquest; Meghan Butler, Vera's lawyer; Calliope Hadsell, Vera's step-daughter; and my name, Darcy Lloyd. And on the last envelope—Bella Sinclair.

Sparks flew behind my eyes and my on-again, off-again vertigo kicked into high gear. I leaned onto the table to steady myself.

I was there with Vera and the others the night it happened, which was the last time I'd seen Vera. We were so young, but I remembered it like it was yesterday—Vera running toward me in the dark, screaming, the low branches of the trees slicing into her cheeks. "Run!" she yelled as she careened past me. I'd followed blindly, calling out her name for her to stop. We made it to the edge of the forest and back to her boyfriend, Dean's, cabin. Vera shook violently and sobbed in an old rocker by the still-warm fireplace as I stood above her, crying a bit in solidarity. "Vera?" I'd dared after many minutes.

I shuddered, remembering the look on Vera's face when she'd turned to me. "She's dead, Darcy. Bella is dead."

Lola Danvers

I took the boatman's hand and stepped carefully onto the beach. This was not my idea of "the perfect location for a memorial" as Vera's son had said in the letter. A memorial should be in a neat and tidy house or perhaps in a garden, but not on some tiny, unheard-of island on the edge of Costa Rica. But, I figured Vera had planned her own memorial in the middle of nowhere to keep away all of the marks. Not that they ever knew they were marks, but they would not be welcome to this party.

A man stood at the edge of the jungle wearing a wrinkled tan ranger uniform. His hat was low, his eyes hidden.

The boatman placed my four suitcases on the sand. I handed him his tip and, from his demeanor, assumed the ranger wasn't going to help me with my things.

I took off my shoes, useless in this deep sand anyway, then took off the skirt that I wore over my leggings. The wind on the boat had been cool, but here on the beach it was warm, and sheltered from the wind by the trees. My unnecessary clothing went into my suitcases, then I stacked them two and two.

I'd never regretted bringing too much on my trips, and I wasn't going to start now. I could feel the impatience from the ranger, but if he wanted to move faster he could damn well help.

I pulled the suitcases up the sand, over numerous broken branches and washed-up seaweed. Evidence of a previous storm was everywhere. I hefted the suitcases into the back of the jeep while the ranger got into the driver's seat.

"Do you get many storms here?" I didn't expect the enigmatic ranger to answer, so I was surprised to hear his gruff and very North American voice.

"Yes. It's the season for that sort of thing. Do you like the beach?" He nodded back at the way we had come as he sped up the Jeep.

I laughed. "I like beaches with umbrellas and drinks, not with driftwood. I'm Lola, by the way."

He grunted, then looked over at me—and continued staring. I could see the Jeep was heading for a pothole, and he still wasn't looking at what passed for a road, so I grabbed the door grab bar and tried to breathe. Only after he looked back at the road did I relax a little.

"Lola," he repeated under his breath. Louder he said, "I'm Jax, the ranger here. So you were a friend of Vera's? Her son told me about the memorial."

"More than a friend, I worked with her."

"Oh, what kind of work?"

"We were in the import/export business."

"Really? Will you still run the business then?"

So many answers ran through my head, like: *'None of your business.' 'Maybe, but I need the right partner.'* And,

'No. We made it big on our last job and I don't need to ever work again.'

"I don't know," I finally said. I didn't want to talk about any of it with a stranger. I changed the subject. "You don't have much of an accent."

He nodded. "I'm not originally from here."

No shit.

We arrived at the lodge, a two-story stone structure with big verandas. I was surprised when he pulled my biggest suitcase out of the Jeep.

"This way."

I grabbed my other bags and followed. We went upstairs to the farthest room down the hall. Small, but there was a bed, an armoire, and a desk. I assumed I'd find a shared bathroom somewhere.

"What terrible thing did you do to end up here?" I asked Jax.

He set down my bag inside the room and looked me in the eyes. An electric current ran straight to my toes from those green eyes. He finally said, "I love it here. It's quiet and stress-free. What terrible thing did you do to end up here?"

I stood, open mouthed, as he turned and walked out.

Bella/ (aka Denise)

As I stepped onto the sun-drenched shores of Isla del Coco, a sense of foreboding filled me. The distant shrieks of birds intermingled with the crashing waves. The island was breathtaking—the turquoise waters stretched to the horizon and teeming jungles rose from the shore.

I stumbled across the sandy beach towards a disheveled ranger. He leaned lazily against a rust-eaten Jeep, his hat pulled low over his eyes. I waved at him as I approached.

"Excuse me," I began tentatively, "I'm here for Vera Barlone's memorial service."

"Isn't everyone?" he replied with a yawn, a hint of nonchalance tainting his words.

"Everyone? How many others are here?" I inquired.

"Too many, if you ask me." The ranger hopped into the Jeep and started it, the engine sputtering. "Get in."

My backpack, a relic of countless journeys, found its place on the rotting floorboard as I took my seat next to the ranger.

He might prove useful.

"Do you have a name?" I asked as I gathered my unruly copper-colored hair into a makeshift bun. I couldn't help but steal a glance at his rugged features.

The ranger shifted his gaze and looked at me intently. His green eyes seemed to study every inch of my face, and a faint smile tugged at the corner of his lips.

"Jax," he said finally, revving the engine and taking off with a jolt. "And you?"

As we journeyed through the dense jungle, my heart raced with a mixture of excitement and fear. I had thought about how I would introduce myself to the others at the memorial. Vera had always called me by my old name, but no one here would know that I was once Bella. "I'm Denise Smith. Jax," I repeated softly, the word a tantalizing echo on my lips. "Unusual name for an unusual place, wouldn't you say?"

His gaze, as penetrating as a moonlit night, held mine in a shared understanding, a silent acknowledgment of the island's mysterious allure.

"I'd say unusual is the norm around here," he replied cryptically, the words threaded with a hint of amusement that danced upon the edges of his lips.

The Jeep's rumble along the untamed path provided a steady backdrop to our conversation. Each bump and turn seemed to mirror the unpredictability of the island itself, a living entity that played host to secrets both old and new.

As the jungle enveloped us, my curiosity surged. "So, Jax," I pressed on, my tone laced with intrigue, "you seem like someone who knows the ins and outs of this place. What else should I know about Vera Barlone's memorial?"

"Vera Barlone's memorial," he muttered, a scowl etching his features. He tightened his hands on the steering wheel, his knuckles turning white, and his jaw clenched. "Look," he growled, his voice laced with frustration, "Let's just say things aren't what they seem."

"I want to know what's going on," I retorted, my voice steady, refusing to back down.

The Jeep came to an abrupt stop, causing me to lunge forward in my seat. His hand shot out, his rough fingers grazing my cheek with an unexpected tenderness that contrasted sharply with his irritation. Jax's eyes bore into mine with an intensity that sent shivers down my spine.

"I'd hate to see such a pretty face get hurt," he remarked, his voice laced with an odd mix of concern and exasperation.

Lola

What terrible thing had I done?

Didn't he mean to say something about how terrible it was that my friend was dead? Okay, maybe 'friend' was the wrong word. Even 'partner' wasn't quite right. I had been Vera's pawn.

I closed my bedroom door, disappointed that it didn't have a lock. I scanned the room to find a hiding place for the things I didn't want anyone to find. The gun, the knife, my extra food, and the alcohol. Couldn't have someone getting into my favorite snacks. The gluten-free Oreos were all mine.

I got up on the bed, then used my luggage to step up and touch the rafters. Turns out someone else had once wanted to hide things. The top of one of the log rafters was hollowed out a little.

I smiled and sighed. I love a good hiding place.

Now, it was time to explore a little. I headed downstairs.

I was glad to see there was a caterer. On a table was a variety of food, fruit, cheese, salami, even gluten-free crackers. The caterer, in black shirt and black pants, sat in the corner of the room, reading a book.

"Good idea, bringing a book. Are you here for the weekend?" I asked him.

He looked up and smiled. His dark hair was swept to the side and his dark brown eyes seemed friendly. "Yeah, it's just me and five giant coolers of food. If you need anything, let me know. I can whip up everything from omelets to a Bloody Mary." He stood and held out his hand. "I'm Trent."

A friendly caterer was almost as wonderful as a good hiding place. "Lola," I said as I shook his hand. "I wouldn't mind a mojito, if that's possible?" I pulled out a hundred-dollar bill and set it on the counter near him.

He pocketed his tip and moved into the kitchen. "Absolutely. That was one of the things I was asked to have available."

The kitchen was crowded with coolers and every surface was organized into different spaces—pans for cooking, snacks, and of course, alcohol. Well, at least Vera's ill-gotten gains were paying for something worthwhile.

I had plans for our latest haul. Even after what I had to pay my other partner, I could finally buy that house I wanted with the dog kennels at the opposite end of the property. I'd quit this life of crime now that I was free from Vera and board dogs. And, who knows, maybe I was one of her beneficiaries. I salivated at the idea of getting back all the money I had made for her.

But what about James? Had she left him anything?

She and her son had never been on good terms, and I was surprised that he'd taken charge of her memorial.

Between hiding spots, mojitos, and a potential windfall, things were feeling less abysmal. But then Calliope walked in.

She clomped into the room on her high heels. "Hi ya, Lola! I'm so glad you're here. I have some things we need to talk about."

Trent handed me the glass and I drank down half my mojito before replying. "Calliope, unless you're dying of some horrible disease, I don't need to talk with you about anything."

I headed out of the room, but Calliope caught my arm with her cold hand.

"Lola, you're going to want to hear what I have to say."

Trent cleared his throat, maybe to remind her someone else besides us was here. Whatever the reason, Calliope let go.

"Later, Lola."

She turned and walked away. I hoped that she'd fall down the stairs in those heels and break her neck.

Darcy

I hid in my room until dinnertime. Everyone must be here—I'd heard the lodge's massive front door open and close several times.

My brain couldn't focus on any one thing, but I thought I was on top of everything. I thought I'd accounted for every possible scenario that could derail the weekend. But, Bella? Bella Sinclair? The walls of my room closed in as memories of those lost years exploded to the forefront. I had the urge to fling open every bedroom door until I found her. I wanted to pin her down and scream at her all of the things the investigators had accused me of. I wanted to know her biggest fear and exaggerate it until she fled, begging for safety. I wanted to expose all that she knew to be true in her life and tear it to shreds.

I laid there, sweating, part napping and part staring at the ceiling, until the sun had almost set. There was still no electricity, but the room had a few lanterns. Luckily, there was a battery-operated clock on the nightstand.

Thank God I'm in a bedroom with my own private bath. Since I was the first to arrive, all the bedroom doors were open and I was able to pick my room. A couple of the rooms shared baths, and that certainly wouldn't have been a pleasant experience.

The air in my room was stagnant and hot. Opening the window did no good. Despite the fact we were surrounded by water, there was no breeze tonight. In the yellowed lantern light, I pulled my cocktail dress down over my sticky stomach and legs and attempted to do my hair and makeup while sweating in front of the bathroom mirror.

The schedule of events said dinner was precisely at 7 PM. The clock said 6:58 PM. I procrastinated until I heard the footsteps of the others fade down the hallway.

I opened the door and there stood Terran Falco. Tall, rich, and stupid.

I pulled him inside before anyone could see him. "What the fuck are you doing outside my door?"

Terran shrugged. "I was looking for you. I wanted to say hello."

He leaned in to get a kiss, and I side-stepped his advance. "You've been smoking again. You're not getting a kiss from me. And we're not even supposed to know each other. Get out there and get downstairs."

He shrugged and walked out. I closed the door behind him and hoped to God no one connected us. I waited a moment and then walked out of my room.

The dining room table was lit with long white tapers that glinted off the crystals in the chandelier above, creating a flickering effect on everyone's faces.

I found my place card quickly and put it in my pocket. It was the first chair just to the left of the head of the table. We all sat in unison. Right away I recognized Bella Sinclair as she took her seat two chairs to my left. She hadn't looked my way. I didn't think she'd recognize me anyway, especially if she wasn't expecting to see me.

Jax was standing in the corner. I caught his eye and he winked at me.

A waiter set bowls of soup in front of each of us. Everyone held off eating, except for Lola who dug in immediately and continued slurping when James began to talk.

"Allow me to introduce myself. I'm James, Vera's son, and I'd like to welcome you all. While you enjoy your first course, I'd like to introduce our guests."

The sounds of clinking spoons pierced the air, as if we'd all gone days without food.

"Some of you may know each other already, but all of you are connected through being a part of my mother's life. She left specific instructions for you all to be here this weekend."

If Bella didn't recognize me, I wanted more time to think. Before James could begin, I raised my hand. "James, we don't need you to introduce us. Let's just get to know each other. I mean, we're here for a couple of days. Maybe instead, you could tell us how Vera died? All the news said was she died under mysterious circumstances. What does that mean?"

James glanced around the room nervously. "Vera Barlone was murdered."

I scanned the room. Almost everyone wasn't surprised.

Forrest Montgomery

"I knew it!"

I couldn't stay hidden any longer. Since my covert arrival on the island by fishing boat, I'd successfully avoided the guests and that pesky ranger—though it hadn't been too difficult, what with the electricity being out and all. That detail hadn't been part of my plan, but it was serendipitous, nonetheless.

I'd watched from the shadows as each of them made their way into the lodge. Several of them I didn't even know, but there was Lola, and James. My blood had boiled with each subsequent arrival.

"I'm more connected to Vera than any of these other people," I had murmured from my hiding place just outside of the dining room. There had to be a reason I hadn't been invited. And I was determined to find out why.

From the outside looking in, Vera's and my relationship may have appeared to be nothing more than an affair. Perhaps that's what it had been to her, but it had meant so much more to me. We'd shared everything all those years ago. Then, after a passionate afternoon of lovemaking in a Tuscan villa, she'd turned to me and said the two words I'd dreaded most: "I'm leaving."

I'd feigned indifference as Vera packed up her things and fled, but deep down, I was ripped to shreds. This magnificent woman had vanished from my life as quickly as she'd entered it. I wasn't ready to let go. That's why I'd been so thrilled to run into her a year later—but she wasn't alone. She had a newborn baby in tow: James.

"Forrest Montgomery!" James's voice boomed across the dining hall.

I felt my chest inflate and prepared myself for a confrontation. Possible rebuttals coursed through my mind: *'I loved Vera.' 'I deserve to be here.' 'You should have invited me.'* Yet his response shocked me as deeply as my presence shocked the guests.

"Forrest, I had a feeling you might be joining us."

"Y-you did?" I hadn't expected that.

"You had your suspicions about Vera being murdered, and I had my suspicions about you having me followed," James responded, settling into a chair at the head of the table.

"Take a seat, Forrest. Vera wrote letters for everyone. Yes, including you."

Lola

"Letters?" My hands waived in the air to accentuate the words that everyone else must be thinking. "James, who cares about letters? How did she die? Who killed her?"

And who deserves the medal?

James, who looked overdressed in his suit, glared around the room at each of us. "She was poisoned. The police don't know who yet. I do know they intend to question all of us when we return home."

Damn it. Even gone, Vera was creating trouble. The last thing I wanted was to be questioned by the police.

Meghan Butler, Vera's attorney, shook her head. "We can't solve a murder, but what we can do while we are here this weekend is mourn Vera."

Calliope laughed. "And see what Vera left me, right Meghan?"

James actually looked upset, poor guy. He was trying to do the right thing by Vera.

Forrest, dressed like a beach bum, which I had to say was quite a good look on him, looked like he was going to jump across the table and smack Calliope. At least, I hoped he would.

"Calliope, enough," Darcy, also looking overdressed in black cocktail attire, said, "I'm sure that Vera distributed her wealth to everyone who deserves it."

Wait. My brain did a double take. How did Darcy know who Calliope was? Sure, Darcy had connected me to Vera, but that had been a long time ago. Since then I had never seen nor heard of Vera or Darcy so much as emailing.

Trent came by with the next course, corn fritters with aioli, as per the menu I had scanned earlier. Gluten-free and they smelled delicious. Trent smiled and nodded at me as he put the plate down. I noticed that my plate had more fritters than anyone else's.

At least I had someone in my corner here. Maybe James needed someone in his corner. "I'm sorry, James. What's this about letters?"

James pulled a basket out from a piece of furniture in the room. "Vera wrote these letters for each of you."

"Surely she didn't know she was going to be murdered?" an unknown woman asked. I really wished James would have introduced everyone. And how was someone here that I didn't know?

Meghan shook her head as she put down her wine glass. "No. Vera had a monthly appointment to update these letters. She filled them out, signed and sealed them herself."

James walked around and handed the envelopes out. I took mine with my greasy fingers and set it on the table. Then I finished my fritters while everyone else opened their letters.

From the looks on everyone's faces, and especially Terran who looked like he had just received a knife in the heart, they were letters with poisoned words. I didn't need any more of that in my life. I took my letter to the fireplace and used a match to set it on fire.

There was a collective silence behind me until Darcy said, "Damn it, why didn't I think of that."

Bella (aka Denise)

I opened my envelope and read *"My dearest Bella, The past we've hidden is stirring, and the secrets we've held must now be unveiled. Brace yourself, for the truth awaits. With love, Vera."*

Unveiled? That was never what I wanted.

I recognized Darcy, although she wouldn't meet my eyes.

Whatever Vera had concealed, whatever secrets she had harbored, were now ours to bear. As I gazed at Darcy, I couldn't help but wonder if she was prepared to confront the specters of our shared history—even though I was not.

The room buzzed with tension as everyone

exchanged glances, each of us holding our own note from Vera, uncertain of its significance.

Even Lola getting up from the table and burning her note, and Darcy's response to that, didn't break the spell of quiet. Suspicion hung in the air, heavy and palpable, as if everyone were trying to decipher their messages.

After dinner, as we made our way to the living room, I cast sidelong glances at Darcy. Her face was hardened, her jaw clenched. I could almost hear her teeth grinding. I knew she must be wrestling with the same turmoil that had gripped me.

The living room was dimly lit, the overhead fans offering a welcome reprieve from the oppressive heat. James stood at the room's center, waiting for all of us to gather around. His once-confident demeanor had wavered since the start of dinner, as if he, too, was ensnared by the secrets his mother had left.

James began, his voice trembling ever so slightly. "I understand that this gathering, along with Vera's notes, has left you with a myriad of questions."

A murmur of agreement, tinged with skepticism, circulated through the room. Vera's message had been cryptic, and the circumstances surrounding our presence here were stranger than any of us had foreseen.

James continued. "My mother was a woman of profound complexity, and she must have had reasons for uniting all of us."

The implications were clear—we were all connected to Vera in ways we couldn't yet fathom, and that connection might be perilous.

. . .

Darcy

The living room was long and narrow, with enormous windows and thick, red velvet curtains that were pulled back, allowing us to look out into the heavy black nothingness. The room was lined on both sides with deep leather armchairs and plush couches long enough for two or three, yet each of us claimed one as our own.

James and Jax stood at the head of the room. Jax broke the silence and got right to it. "Vera left strict instructions for this weekend that all of you become acquainted, or… reacquainted in some cases."

"Tomorrow morning, we will meet back in this room at 10 AM for breakfast. At noon, the tide will be low enough to walk across the gap to the neighboring island for Vera's memorial service, when anyone who wishes to say words of remembrance is welcome to do so. After the memorial will be the reading of her will. After that, I will lead you on a jungle excursion."

Jax turned on his heels. As he walked through the French doors, the waiter brought in a silver tray with glasses of port. We each took a glass, and then the waiter left. The click of the lock on the French doors reverberated down the length of the room as an unspoken but firm signal to begin mingling.

Calliope made the first tentative move and walked toward Terran. It was obvious from their body language that they knew each other. Calliope put her hand on

Terran's arm and gave it a squeeze that looked to me like a silent "I'm sorry for your loss." I hated to admit it, but a quiver of jealousy ran through me.

To avoid any possibility of Bella approaching me, I went over to Lola and sat down next to her. I made a show of introducing myself to her. We'd never actually met in person. Our only communication had been talking on the phone—no emails or texts, no paper trail.

She acted the same toward me, even though we'd talked on the phone only days before.

I kept my voice to a hush. I was curious as to how much Lola knew. "I wonder who killed her. I'm surprised someone would do such a thing."

"I don't know," Lola responded. "A few days before she died, she told me she was going out for a lunch meeting. Next thing I know, she's dead."

And then I noticed that Vera's son, James, had been quiet since we left the dinner table. His hooded eyes made him appear downcast, even though his head was raised, and he was on a constant scan of the room. He had a bushy mound of dark hair on his head that belied his slight build. And... he looked *exactly* like Forrest Montgomery. That was very interesting, and maybe something I could use.

I drank rather than sipped my glass of port and refilled from the bottle the waiter had left on the side table. When the French doors opened again after an hour of thick tension, I was the first one out the door. I wobbled to my room.

When I came out of the bathroom, wanting only to slip under the cool sheets and sleep the night away, I saw Bella perched on my bed.

Forrest

Everyone slowly trickled out of the living room until it was just James and me. His brow was furrowed as he stared at the letter in his hand and nursed his whiskey.

"What's on your mind, bud?" My words pulled him out of his stupor, though it took him several minutes to respond.

"Just… Vera."

Vera and James shared an odd relationship. Not only did he refuse to call or refer to her as "Mom," but also she treated him more like a Pomeranian than a child—something cute to keep by her side, but annoying as hell when he started to speak. Poor James.

But then, James had everything to gain and absolutely nothing to lose by his mother's death.

As I studied his large brown eyes cloaked beneath a curtain of thick black lashes, I felt my heart break. Oh, how I wished I could have been there for him as he grew. There were so many times I wanted to reach out. But Vera had made it clear that there would be dire consequences if I did.

And I didn't dare mess with Vera. Not then, anyway.

"Do you want to talk about it?" I prodded.

"No," he quickly responded, though his eyes told a different story.

"Fair. Can I ask you a question?"

"Shoot," James invited.

"How did you know I'd show up here?"

At that, a smile crept onto James's lips. "The PI you hired?"

"Yes?" I said quizzically.

"He happens to be a buddy of mine." James chuckled. "He's also the same guy I hired to follow Bella after Vera told me about *that* evening."

"That evening? What evening?"

"Vera never told you?"

I shook my head.

James' words dripped with anger. "Vera was attacked by a guy named Dean, her boyfriend at the time. Her friend Bella intervened and killed him. Vera hid her secret away all these years. I think it was one of the things that Vera was proud of. She was protecting her friend."

I stood and put my hand on James' shoulder. "I'm sure she was proud of you too."

James laughed but the sadness was still in his eyes. "Nice try Forrest, but we all knew what kind of person Vera was."

James slumped down in his chair and I stepped back to mine.

So, maybe my son didn't kill Vera. This Bella might have killed her to keep her secret safe. If she was the one who killed Vera, might that put James at risk too?

· · ·

Lola

I had had enough of Terran and these others. I was disappointed that Meghan had retired early. Even though she was a lawyer, she was probably the most upstanding person on the island, apart from Trent. Two people who had nothing to do with Vera's life and crime.

I went into the kitchen and Trent handed me another mojito.

"Thanks. Hey, where are you sleeping?"

He turned and winked. "Why do you ask?"

I laughed and blushed. That wasn't my style. "No, that's not it. I was just curious. They're not making you sleep in some tent are they?"

He shook his head. "No. I'm sleeping upstairs too. Hey, this is some crazy situation here."

"Sure. Coming to the middle of nowhere for a memorial. Definitely crazy."

Trent stepped closer. "No. The ranger asked me to keep an eye on the food, in case someone wanted to put anything in it."

"What, like salt?"

Trent took another step closer and whispered, "No. I think he meant poison."

"Poison? That's how Vera died. And why would Jax think anyone would want to poison anyone here?"

Then I glanced behind me. Yeah, Calliope might want to poison me. She was mad that I wouldn't give her a piece of the action from Vera's marks. And Darcy might want to kill me if she knew I was ending our partnership. But she didn't know that yet.

Did anyone else here have reason to kill a member of the party?

I ruled out James, and Meghan. There was one woman who I didn't know, but the looks Darcy had given her during dinner suggested that she might be trouble.

Well, there was one way to see if anyone had brought poison to the island. Almost everyone was still in the living room.

"Trent, thanks for the info."

"Be careful, these people are nuts."

I laughed and raised my mojito to him. "So true."

Then I headed upstairs. I stopped at the first bedroom and listened at the door. Darcy and the other woman had left the living room before me. It was possible they were in their rooms already.

Then I heard the woman say hello to Darcy. I hung on every word.

Darcy

"Hello, Darcy." Bella's voice was sweet and upbeat, but it registered to me as a hiss, her tone dripping with venom.

"Bella." I felt the blood drain from my face, and I held onto the bathroom door frame to stabilize myself.

"It's actually Denise now. And how is my old

friend?" she taunted. "Come and sit. We must catch up." She patted the bed next to her.

I kept my mouth shut for a full minute, processing the fact that this bitch was sitting right in front of me and that I'd never call her Denise. I wanted the world to know that Bella was here and what she'd done.

Despite the fact that, until just hours ago, I'd thought she was dead, decades worth of hatred and hostility were preparing for battle in my head. And then all the ire that had been balling up since I first saw Bella's name on that envelope in the foyer came rushing out.

"Bella!" I seethed. "What in the hell happened that night? Vera came back to Dean's cabin and told me you were dead! My God! Did Vera think you were dead?" To my horror, angry tears streamed down my cheeks. I wouldn't have been surprised if I were foaming at the mouth.

"Oh heavens no," she laughed. "Vera and I enjoyed a long friendship after that night."

The room swirled. "I didn't even know that Dean was missing until the cops started hounding me. I was so in the dark. Bella, we were just kids!" My voice escalated to a pitch I didn't even know I was capable of. I didn't care if the others could hear me.

Her silence was infuriating. My fingernails pierced my palms in a desperate attempt to refrain from lunging toward her and choking the very life from her.

"Aren't you going to say anything? I was hounded for weeks. Only my belongings were found in the cabin when they came to investigate. I always assumed Vera had orchestrated that, but were you in on it too?"

Her smile got wider. She didn't care.

"For God's sake, WHY? Vera left town with her family for some European vacation, and I was left alone to deal with the mess. I wasn't allowed to leave town until the cops finally agreed that I had no idea of Dean's whereabouts. And where in the hell were you? My reputation was ruined. My parents had to move us to another town. I had to transfer schools. I had to reinvent myself."

Bella just sat there and stared at me with the callous grin I remembered all too well. She opened her arms and gestured to my clothes and jewelry on the dresser. "Well, from the looks of things, you've done well for yourself."

She had no idea… I ignored her comment and responded with an attempt at sarcasm. "I suppose this is why you never went to any of our high school reunions?"

"Oh Darcy. I always liked your sense of humor. But perhaps you've got a darker side too? Vera was alway a bit… nervous you'd find out the truth and come after her."

I teetered a bit. The port and this conversation was giving me a head rush. "My God, is… is Dean still alive too? Did he disappear with you? Was this some sort of joke?"

Bella took ten seconds to hoist herself off my bed,

walked right up to my face, and said with all the menace I was feeling toward her, "Darcy, you were a joke to all of us long before that night."

I could have killed her right then and there.

Bella (aka Denise)

After our little chat in her bedroom, I was convinced that Darcy didn't know the truth—that Dean was dead, or that I was the one who'd killed him. Vera had kept her promise. However, I was surprised to learn that Vera had hung Darcy out to dry.

I regained my composure and made my way back downstairs. The remainder of the group were still mingling. I scanned the room. James and Forrest appeared deep in conversation in a remote corner, Terran was smoking on the couch, and Calliope was stretched out on a couch half asleep or half drunk.

And, there, standing at the edge of the room, staring at the rest of the group, was Jax. His rugged demeanor and piercing gaze made him stand out from the rest. There was something about him that piqued my curiosity. I'd traveled to many places in my life, including Costa Rica. I never remember a ranger looking or acting like him.

As I approached him, I could feel my heart race with anticipation. There was a hidden layer to Jax, and I intended to unearth it.

"Jax," I said. I leaned in closer, my eyes searching his for any sign of vulnerability. "I have a feeling there's more to you than meets the eye. Something tells me you're not just here to guide us through the jungle."

A faint smile tugged at the corner of his lips, and he seemed to relax slightly. "You're perceptive, Denise. I'm here to ensure everyone's safety."

My curiosity deepened, and I pressed further. "Safety from what, Jax? What exactly is going on here?"

Jax hesitated for a moment as if weighing his words carefully. "Vera was a woman of many secrets, according to her son. Some of those secrets may have followed us here."

I couldn't contain my excitement. "Tell me more. What kind of secrets are we talking about?" I brushed my hand against Jax's tanned, muscular arm.

He leaned in closer, his voice warm against my cheek, barely a whisper. "I can't reveal everything now, Denise. But I can promise you this—there's more to this weekend than meets the eye."

Jax's eyes locked onto mine, and for a moment, the world seemed to fade away around us. "Denise, be careful," he cautioned, his tone laced with both warning and intrigue. "Some secrets are best left buried."

As Jax's warm breath grazed my cheek, a thrill surged through me. The closeness between us was electric, and I couldn't help but let my fingers linger against his arm a moment longer.

"Vera was a childhood friend, but I hadn't seen her in years. You can imagine my shock when I got an invitation to her memorial service," I confessed, my voice tinged with a mix of curiosity and concern. "I was hoping you could help me understand what is going on here exactly."

Jax's eyes bore into mine, and I could sense his internal struggle. He seemed torn between caution and an unspoken desire to confide in me.

"You're not the only one seeking answers, Denise," Jax admitted, his voice soft and laden with the weight of secrets.

"I need to know more," I urged. "Please, Jax."

"Denise," he said, his voice a sultry whisper that sent a thrill down my spine, "I've been watching you too. There's something about you that's... intriguing."

A teasing smile played on his lips, and his fingers brushed lightly against mine. It was a subtle gesture, but it left me breathless.

"Jax," I replied, my voice equally low and seductive, "you can't leave me hanging like this. Tell me why we're all here."

His gaze held mine, his eyes dark and intense. "Patience, Denise. All will be revealed in due time."

Jax's cryptic words hung in the air as he retreated, leaving me in a state of both bewilderment and irresistible intrigue.

Forrest

Everyone has secrets, but something this big? Why hadn't Vera told me? I sunk deeper into my chair at the harsh reminder that I was just another one of her flings. Still, that didn't change the way I'd felt about her, or the fact that we shared something so incredible. Someone so incredible.

I watched as James massaged his temples, a yawn escaping out his mouth.

"We have a big day ahead of us," I announced. "With that jungle excursion and all. Go upstairs and get some rest, James."

He simultaneously yawned and nodded in agreement. After a quick goodnight, we parted ways. James went to the kitchen, I assume for a drink.

My mind spun with questions, fears, and accusations. Who had murdered Vera? Why had they done it? And would they come after James next? It was too late for me to protect the love of my life, but I could still protect my son.

I ruminated and paced until a cloud of exhaustion settled over me. Only then did I realize I had no idea where my room was. Jax mentioned I could take the eastern-most bedroom, but which one was that? I'd find my way, I always did.

But as soon as I made my way up the stairs, I noticed someone crouched in the corner of the hallway, head pressed against one of the bedroom doors.

"Lola?" I whispered, to which she responded by simply raising a finger up to her mouth.

"What are you doing?" I silently mouthed.

She pointed to the door then her ear.

I heard muffled voices but couldn't make out what they were saying. Even though I hated to admit it, my hearing had been shot for several years. I refused to get hearing aids, but they would have come in handy for a situation like this one.

"What's going on?" I mouthed again.

Lola mouthed something back.

"Someone go run?" I asked silently.

She rolled her eyes and shook her head.

"Someone's after your son?" My heart dropped. I knew it. This had something to do with James. He *was* in danger. As I stood and puffed up my chest, ready to barrel into the room, I felt Lola's nails dig into my arm.

"No, you idiot," she hissed into my ear. "Someone here has poison."

Lola

I pointed Forrest to his bedroom then went into the next room that wasn't occupied, just before Bella walked out of Darcy's room.

So many secrets we all have to hide. But who had killed Vera?

I had always thought Darcy had put me in touch with Vera to help her out, but maybe it wasn't that at all. Did Darcy hate Vera? And this Bella woman, she had an enormous secret. Did she kill Vera to keep her secret safe? And what would she do now that Darcy knew she was alive?

This island was getting more dangerous by the second.

Focus. I was looking for poison. I knew by the open luggage filled with dresses that this was Calliope's room. As I carefully looked through her luggage, I wondered what exactly I should look for. It wasn't like there was going to be a bottle with a skull and crossbones.

I didn't find any bottles in her luggage. The lucky bitch had an attached bathroom with a tub. Why did I have to use a shared bathroom? Her toiletries were lined up on the sink. Next to them was a pink rolled-up canvas with something in it. I opened it with hope I'd find the poison and know who the killer was, but it was perfume bottles.

The door opened and I jumped. Jax was standing in the doorway.

He looked surprised. "Oh, I'm sorry. I must have got the wrong room." He closed the door, but now I was spooked.

I waited a moment then went to my own room. Searching everyone's room wasn't going to work. It wasn't like I knew what I was looking for, and I certainly couldn't taste test everything to see if it was poison. I had to go about this a different way.

Darcy

The next morning, I awoke to firm knocking on my bedroom door that lingered in the front of my head. Whoever it was had made their way down the hall to wake the other guests. Last night's port had left me with a whopper of a hangover and, combined with the visit from my chilling nighttime guest, I was in bad shape.

I rolled over to check my phone, only to see that it was completely out of battery. The electricity must not have come back on during the night to charge it. Now I understood why we all had to have a physical wake-up call.

Even though there'd been no air conditioning all night, my room felt crisp and fresh. Sunlight streamed into the windows, attacking my eyes. I made my way over to the windows for a breathtaking view of the jungle treetops in the distance, bright green and lush. I wasn't looking forward to the trip to the cemetery. I didn't need to see what was underneath the canopy of the trees. Same for the rest of the weekend's guests.

Beauty is only skin deep?

I joined the others in the living room precisely at ten. There wasn't a formal breakfast, just coffee and pastries laid out on a buffet table. We filled our plates and our coffee mugs in silence.

We resumed our same seats from the night before. James once again stood silent at the front of the room with Jax. Jax cleared his voice.

"There is a storm coming in later this afternoon, so we're not having the jungle excursion. We'll be walking out to the cemetery after breakfast for the memorial service and the reading of the will."

"Walk?" Bella asked. "Can't we ride in the Jeep?"

James shook his head. "The cemetery is an old family cemetery. No one in Vera's family has been buried there in a long time. There are no roads to get there, since this island is now a sanctuary for wildlife. It will be a walk to get there. So make sure to dress appropriately."

As I looked around the room, I realized that there was no one here I cared about. They could all die and I wouldn't bat an eyelash.

I'd make the walk to the cemetery, and maybe a few less would make it back.

I finished my croissant and coffee, then went upstairs to change.

Bella (aka Denise)

When James confirmed we'd have to walk to the cemetery, I knew what I had to do. It was the opportunity I had been waiting for.

While everyone else discussed what to wear for the walk through the jungle, I quietly slipped out of the back door of the lodge, my backpack in tow. The hidden path I had noticed the day before beckoned me forward. It was barely visible to the naked eye, but I had honed my skills at escaping during my painful years in foster homes, and spotting secret routes had become second nature to me.

After everyone had gone to bed the night before, I ventured out and explored the path, making sure it led to the North shore—a perfect rendezvous point for my escape. I knew I had to leave before Darcy reported to the authorities that I was alive and well, or even worse, that she suspected that I had killed Dean all those years ago. Murder had no statute of limitations, and I couldn't afford to let my past catch up with me.

Once I reached a secluded spot on the North shore, I carefully unzipped my backpack and pulled out a satellite phone. It had been my lifeline for years, enabling me to maintain connections while staying off the grid. I dialed a number I knew by heart.

As the phone rang, my heart pounded in my chest. This was my escape plan, my ticket to a fresh start under a new identity. The voice on the other end answered, and I spoke in hushed tones. "It's time," I said, my voice trembling with a mixture of fear and anticipation.

There was a pause on the other end, then a quiet acknowledgment. "I'll be there," my contact replied. "Stay hidden and be ready."

I felt a sense of relief and determination wash over me. I knew that leaving this island was the right choice. As I waited for the boat to arrive, I knew that this escape would be just another chapter in my life of survival and reinvention, and I was more than ready to begin anew, under a new name, in a world far away from the shadows of my past.

Darcy

Once everyone was gathered back downstairs, we were led to the portico on the side of the house where pairs of black rain boots stood in a row. I slipped on a pair of boots and stood next to Jax, the only person I trusted not to stab me in the back.

I, however, wanted to do my best to stir up trouble and shove my knife into the backs of a few of them.

"So, Calliope," I said, "how often did you see Vera after she and your father divorced?"

She jumped, clearly not expecting conversation, and fumbled for words. "Ummm. I mean… I saw her about once a month. We always had lunch. Even after my dad passed away, Vera and I stayed pretty close, I guess you could say."

"I see," I said. Calliope hadn't seemed particularly distraught over Vera's death. "How long was Vera married to your dad?"

"Only five years before he died." Then she mumbled, "But she certainly reaped the benefits of that."

Jax jumped in. "So then Calliope, you must know Lola well? Vera's assistant?"

Lola glanced over at Jax and then Calliope, but stayed quiet.

"We've met," Calliope said.

I exchanged glances with Lola. Of course, Calliope knew Lola. Calliope's father had been a mark for Vera, but Vera had gone too far and married the guy. Calliope had been onto Vera from the start, but she'd kept her mouth shut and demanded a cut. Lola, with insistence from me, made sure Vera didn't marry any of her marks after Calliope's father died. I had wanted Vera's life to be as lonely as mine.

I looked around, realizing Bella still hadn't shown up.

James came out carrying Vera's urn. "We're going to head out now, Bella will just have to catch up."

"All right, let's head out," Jax called out and started toward the jungle. Swinging at the plants with a machete, he led the group on to an indistinct trail. "I've made a bit of a path we can follow, but I'll widen it a bit as we go through."

The sunlight disappeared once we entered the jungle, and I concentrated on the sounds of shrieking and buzzing that pelted us through the wet air.

I had time to think as we walked, to think about that note Vera had left me.

Bravo. You finally found me, after all those years. I suppose I should thank you for bringing Lola to me—she made us both wealthy women, you and me. I'd watch over my shoulder if I were you, because she might also make us both dead women.

How little Vera had known the people in her life.

Lola

As we trudged along, Calliope came up alongside me. She whispered, "Listen. Vera's gone, but I can be the new Vera. I can find the targets, and you can do your work."

"The fuck you will," I said.

"No, look," Calliope insisted. "With Vera gone, I'll let you take more of the share."

I stopped and she stopped along with me. "How badly did you want into this scheme, Calliope? Did you kill Vera?"

Calliope looked off in the distance and shook her head. "I—No." Then she turned and walked away, passed Darcy, and continued walking fast to catch up with the rest of the group.

The trail was leading upwards and it momentarily left the jungle. We were on a cliff. I glanced out over the edge into that deep blue water. It was gorgeous. I could see why Vera would want her ashes to be here. She'd have the best view in the world from this place. I looked back and I could see the lodge. It looked like Trent was taking a smoke break.

I turned back around and focused on the hike.

Darcy was slowing down, making us lag far behind the others. I couldn't even see Calliope's back anymore. I didn't like that, not one bit. I moved to go around her and she held up her arm to block me.

"You're not the boss of me, Darcy. I'm catching up."

She turned and there was fire in her eyes.

"Darcy, you've spent your whole life manipulating people to get what you want. You got your revenge. Vera is dead. I'm not taking orders from you anymore."

"The hell you aren't."

She stepped forward, and I pulled out my gun.

She paused for a second, then laughed. "Oh, Lola."

She kept walking forward.

"Stop, or I'll shoot."

"Lola, if you were a killer I would have asked you to take care of Vera for me. But I knew I needed to go in a different direction for that."

She stepped forward again and I took a step back. I realized too late I was on the edge of the cliff.

She rushed forward, grabbed the gun away from me, and shoved me backwards.

I screamed, reaching out for anything to stop my fall.

Darcy

I ran to catch up with the group and when we emerged from the jungle, there was a tiny island about fifty yards away, just across a shallow pool of water. From our vantage point, all I could see was sand and more trees, and all I could think about was why in the world a cemetery would be over there.

Jax led everyone through the gap, navigating the slippery rocks, the cool water swirling around mid-calf level. Bright-colored fish darted in and out of our way.

As the arched gate to the cemetery came into view, I fingered the gun in my pocket. How many bullets did it have? Certainly not enough to take care of everyone.

Maybe later, back at the lodge, I could get Bella by herself and make it look like a suicide, like she had been so distraught over Vera's death and all. But I also needed to take out Calliope to keep her from telling anyone our secret.

I'd get the poison that Calliope had told me she brought with her and use it on the rest. Meghan, James, and Forrest. They would have to go. As for Jax and Terran, it would be a loss but not one I would worry about too much.

The view from the island was breathtaking. That bitch, Vera, would have a great view from here.

James led us into the cemetery. There were mausoleums with stone angels hovering, and head-stones with names and dates all the way back to 1703. Weird that I hadn't known about this part of Vera's life. This old family that went so far back.

James looked around. "Where's Lola?"

"She was getting tired. She said to start without her."

James nodded and said a few words and then poured the ashes into the sand along the beach. "This is what she wanted," he said.

Forrest moved to stand next to James. "Vera was my one great love of my life." He actually had tears in his eyes, the idiot. "She will be missed."

We all stood quietly, then James turned and walked away into the bit of jungle on the island. He was crying. A perfect cover for a suicide.

I followed him into the trees.

Lola

I hung on with one hand.

I flashed back to robbing a house where the owner had been walking around under me and had no idea I was there. But here, if I dropped, I wasn't going to jail, I was going to die on the rocks a hundred feet below.

I reached up with my free arm and finally found a hand hold in the rocks. I took a deep breath and searched around with my feet. A tiny shelf was all I found, but it was enough to grip with the side of my foot and push myself up. I clung to the cliff wall to get some strength back. I had at least one more foot to go.

I reached up with one hand and felt around for a hand hold. I couldn't find one.

"Fuck!" I screamed. I was not going to die on this fucking island by Darcy's hand.

I put that hand back on its original handhold and used the other hand to search. Still nothing, but then the touch of flesh surprised me.

"I've got you!"

Trent! It was Trent!

I could feel both of his hands touching my arms, and he handed me a rope.

"This rope is tied to a tree. You can use it to pull yourself up."

I blinked away the tears. Maybe I really wasn't going to die here. I gripped the rope and pulled with every-thing I had left. As I was able to pull my first leg over the top, Trent grabbed my hips and rolled me onto the cliff.

I lay there staring at the sky. "Dogs, I just want to take care of dogs for the rest of my life. No more climb-ing. No more stress."

Trent looked down at me. "Maybe we should start by getting off this island."

I sat up. "Shit. She has my gun. I can't let her kill anyone."

Trent helped me up from the ground. My legs shook but I took off running anyway. One foot after the other. That's all I had to do for now. I could hear Trent right behind me.

I followed the trail down to the gap and ran across the rocks as fast as I could. I found the group on the beach, reminiscing about Vera.

But James, Darcy, and Forrest were missing.

Forrest

James hadn't been out of my sight for even a minute since we'd started the trek, but seeing his eyes well up with tears was enough to convince me to give him a few moments alone to gather himself. But he'd been in that forest for quite a while.

He's a grown man, Forrest, I reminded myself, but something didn't feel quite right. Maybe it was James I couldn't trust. Whatever the case, I needed to find him, so I bolted into the forest as fast as my legs would take me.

"James!" My heart pounded against my chest as I called out for my only son. Each step took me closer to the heart of the jungle. The sun was barely visible, the deeper I went. I navigated over and under thick tree roots until one caught my leg, and I was pulled into the brush.

"Ugh!" I bellowed, clutching my throbbing foot. But as I attempted to pull myself back up, I caught a glimpse of James.

There, by his side, was Darcy. She appeared to be stroking his hair, which seemed odd, but I didn't give it much thought because I was just grateful to have found him. Before I could shout his name again, a gun came into view. Darcy was gliding it along James' back and across his shoulders.

That bitch.

They couldn't see me. I was perfectly hidden behind an enormous root, but I couldn't just sit there. I'd spent so much of my life remaining hidden in the shadows. I hadn't been able to save Vera, but I could save our son. Even if it put me in danger.

With a surge of determination, I leapt from the ground and collided with Darcy. The gun discharged with a roar, though the sound was immediately swallowed by the immense forest. We wrestled. A frenzy of survival and hatred along the jungle floor. Though Darcy put up quite a fight, I managed to wrench the gun out of her hands.

With the gun in my hand pointed directly at Darcy on the ground, I rushed to James's side. "Are you OK, bud?" I urgently asked. He simply stared, still shaken from the ordeal.

Finally, James spoke. "Yeah, I am," he whispered. "Thanks, Dad."

. . .

Lola

It was good to see Jax slap cuffs on Darcy and Calliope. Although, I wasn't too happy to know that he was actually a police detective.

Darcy spat on the ground. "You need to take Lola in too. She's a thief!"

Jax looked over at me and my chest tightened.

"I'm just here to solve Vera's murder. Since you told me Calliope poisoned her, well, that's done. And since you tried to kill Lola and James, I'm taking you in. Other than that, everyone is free to go their own way."

Darcy continued and tried to stand up, but Forrest grabbed her shoulder to keep her down. "Bella or Denise, that woman back at the lodge, I was practically accused of killing her. She's alive and someone needs to question her too."

Jax nodded. "She was caught leaving the island by our Costa Rican police. She'll be questioned."

Darcy stopped struggling.

I smiled and started walking back toward the lodge. I needed a stiff drink. Before heading back home I was going to find a cute beach town with a beautiful restaurant.

Trent walked alongside me. "So what's the plan? Where are we going?"

I laughed. This was going to be a good next chapter to my life.

. . .

About the Authors:

Deb Collins, Best-Selling Author

Deb Collins is a thriller writer from Austin, TX. She is an active member of the Women's Thrillers Writers Association and the Writers League of Texas.

She is a life-long copyeditor and self-professed grammar nerd. If she's not at home, you can find her on the tennis court, the soccer field, or at a Tex-Mex restaurant. Or maybe in Mexico.

Stay tuned for her thriller works-in-progress, and you can find her latest thriller, Blood Line.

Saleema Ishq, emerging author

Saleema is an emerging thriller writer. By day she is an established content and copywriter and crafts pet-focused content for a digital publication as well as technical articles for various veterinary journals.

However, by night Saleema writes unsettling stories inspired by her own deep fears. Her medical background and passion for research allow her to create twisted thrillers based on truths that will make your pulse race.

Saleema also enjoys updating her blog, Fearless Phrases, along with journaling, running, reading, crocheting, and spending time with her pets.

Folllow Saleema on https://www.instagram.com/saleemaishq/for updates on her work.

Subscribe to her newsletter.https://view.flodesk.com/pages/62f06da6aeb3ce8812ee2595

Or, check out her best-selling short story, Haunting Figures: A Psychological Thriller Story.

Dita Dow, Best-Selling Author

Dita Dow is a Best-Selling Author who enjoys crafting stories that sweep you into thrilling adventures. With over three decades of experience in law enforcement, private investigations, and consulting, she possesses a deep understanding of the human psyche, which she skillfully weaves into her narratives.

Her passion lies in all things: mystery, thriller, and the supernatural, where she takes readers on mesmerizing journeys into the unknown.

Beyond her writing, Dita's adventurous spirit propels her along rugged hiking trails, discovering archaeological wonders, and on globetrotting adventures. She calls New Mexico home, which she shares with her family, a plump feline, a pampered horse, and a tortoise.

To uncover more about Dita and her enthralling storytelling, visit www.ditadow.com. Immerse yourself in her gripping psychological thrillers, including "Cave of Terror" and "The Deceiver's Casket."

Visit her website at: www.ditadow.com

· · ·

Sonja Dewing, Award-Winning Author

Sonja Dewing is an award-winning author for her adventure/thrillers, loves travel, drinking too much coffee, and lives with her giant puppy, Bo. An agent told her no one would ever read an adventure book with a main female character. She proved him wrong.

Keep an eye out because Lola may be returning to a new story in the future!

You can sign up for her email and receive two free short stories http://eepurl.com/cAzV5v

Find her books at sonjadewing.com.

The Final Chapter

AS INDIE AUTHORS, we rely on your honest reviews to help others find and pick up our books. Please take five minutes to share how this book made you feel.

Thank you!

And, if you enjoyed this anthology, check out Weapons of Choice - find your copy by going to the Women's Thriller Writers Association website: https://women sthrillerwriters.com/weapons-of-choice-thrillhers-short-story-anthology/